THE
DARK
TIDE

THE
DARK
TIDE

ALICIA
JASINSKA

sourcebooks
fire

Published by Sourcebooks Fire, an imprint of Sourcebooks
P.O. Box 4410, Naperville, Illinois 60567-4410
(630) 961-3900
sourcebooks.com

Library of Congress Cataloging-in-Publication Data
Names: Jasinska, Alicia, author.
Title: Dark tide / Alicia Jasinska.
Description: Naperville, IL : Sourcebooks Fire, [2020] | Audience: Ages
  14-18. | Audience: Grades 10-12. | Summary: After offering herself to
  save her brother Finley and secret crush Tomas from capture by
  Caldella's Witch Queen, Lina Kirk and the witch soon face a terrible
  choice.
Identifiers: LCCN 2019059017 | (hardcover)
Subjects: CYAC: Witchcraft--Fiction. | Sacrifice--Fiction. | Love--Fiction.
  | Fantasy.
Classification: LCC PZ7.1.J3315 Dar 2020 | DDC [Fic]--dc23
LC record available at https://lccn.loc.gov/2019059017

Printed and bound in the United States of America.
MA 10 9 8 7 6 5 4 3 2 1

For my grandmother.
I wish you were here to read this.

The Witch Queen comes on wings of night.
The Witch Queen has your heart's delight.
Hold him, hold him, hold on tight.
Hide him, hide him, out of sight.

1

LINA

"IT'LL BE FINE. SHE WON'T pick me."

"Of course not." Lina pressed a fingertip into the door frame. "She only takes the pretty ones."

"And we both know that I am anything but pretty." Finley grinned at his reflection in the mirror, a lock of licorice-black hair falling forward into eyes as gray as the winter sea. Lina had the same hair, but dyed it. The same eyes, but they were set too far apart. The same sand-gold skin, but she'd been cursed with Ma's unfortunate nose. One day, she'd figure out how her brother had managed to steal all the good genes.

"It'll be fine," Finley repeated for the thousandth time, smoothing down his suit, grin fading into seriousness. "We'll stick together, be in and out of it all before you can worry. Ready?"

Lina looped the string of blood-coral beads he'd gifted her for her seventeenth birthday twice around her neck. Glossy red and round as marbles, they clicked as they fell to rest against her chest. "We can just go to Uncle's. I'll go with you. He'll skin us alive if he finds out you—"

"A lock of hair," Finley cut in. "Seven strands of a witch's hair to tie into a charm to heal your ankle. That's what you're hoping to get tonight?"

Lina hesitated. It wasn't to *heal* her ankle, which was healing fine on its own. It was to tie into a charm to curse the brother who'd broken it.

Finley's gaze locked on her leg. The plaster was off now, the bare skin still sickly pale and slightly swollen. Because she'd danced on it. She knew she shouldn't have. She wasn't allowed to, not yet. But she'd been laid up for weeks and weeks. The urge to move was like an itch. And she'd needed to know she *could* still dance.

Guilt crossed her brother's features, a passing shadow, quickly masked by a jaw-clenching determination. "I'll get the strands for you."

Why did he insist on playing the villain *and* the hero? Either way it piled the blame on her shoulders. Everything he did was somehow because of her.

She could imagine what the rest of the family would say if anything happened tonight.

Why didn't you stop him? He only took the risk for you. Because you weren't well enough to dance.

Finley's violin gleamed at the foot of his bed. She'd heard him rehearsing "The Witch's Reel" and "Seven Ravens." The same songs Marek had played at the revel last year to win a spell to enter someone's dreams. The same songs Lina had danced to in order to win a charm of protection for their mothers' ship.

She shifted, biting back her frustration, letting her strong leg take her weight. "I'll meet you downstairs. Your tie's crooked."

Finley's brow creased in alarm. He squinted at his reflection, tugging his tie, swatting at his cowlick, which immediately sprang up again just to spite him. "Make sure the doors are locked."

Lina nodded, a tiny grim smile pulling at the corners of her mouth. "Oh, I will." There was no use in arguing. She'd just waste more breath. She was finished pleading, done with listing the endless reasons why what he was planning to do wasn't safe. He was just as stubborn as she was.

She pulled the door closed as she left his bedroom, and then she locked it. A loud click echoed like a gunshot through the house.

There was an immediate pounding of footsteps, followed by fists smacking against wood. The frantic rattle of the door handle. "Lina!"

Lina dragged a chair away from the landing wall and shoved it underneath the handle. Just in case. She didn't think he had another key. She'd nicked the original from his desk and the spare from the kitchen cupboard. Lovely little things. Silver and skeletal. She smiled fondly at the one in her hand. "You'll thank me later."

"Like hell I—" A long, lethal string of curses filtered through the door. Lina filed a few away for her own use.

"Be a good boy, and I'll bring you back something nice." She crossed the landing, limping slightly, heart beating an uneasy stutter at what she'd done. But he'd be safe now. No witches would spirit him away. He didn't need to risk himself for her sake.

A salt breeze blew through her open bedroom window, the green shutters pinned to the yellow walls like butterfly wings. Outside in the flooded street three stories below, people were laughing, singing, and swaying as they sailed past in the little flat-bottomed skiffs Caldella's locals called their brooms. Everybody half-drunk already. Lina could taste the smoke from the witches' bonfires. Great plumes of it peeked through the gaps between rooftops, drifting up to cloud the star-dusted sky. And beneath all the noise and chaos she could hear it, a susurration like the drumming of waves beating against the shore.

She's coming.

She's coming.

The queen is coming.

Lina shivered. She usually loved St. Walpurga's Eve. The last night of winter. The one night of the year when the witches who ruled the island city came and danced with the common folk. The one night of the year when magic—which was so damn *expensive*—was given away for free. Or could be won, at least. A night of fireworks and shadow games, enchantments and music.

Honey for flies, she realized.

They lured you in with prizes—a string of pearls, each one

extending your life another year—and promises—if you kiss the person you love by the light of the thirteen bonfires, they'll be yours forever. But if the Witch Queen kissed you…

You were this year's sacrifice. To be drowned in St. Casimir's Square on the next full moon, fed to the dark tide to keep the city from sinking.

Lina dug though her drawers, unearthing neatly folded scarves and stockings that only this morning had littered the floor. Auntie Van, or maybe Auntie Iris—one of Ma's sisters, anyway—must've snuck into the house to tidy and snoop, because clearly Lina and Finley couldn't be trusted to keep the place clean while their mothers were away at sea.

She flexed her foot, pointed it, and flexed it again, grimacing. She'd been doing all her strength-building exercises, and she really had tried to rest like she'd been ordered, but it was so hard to stay still when she knew what her body could do. So hard not to just push through the pain like she'd been trained to after years and years of being yelled at by dance teachers. *"Again. Again. Yes, Lina! Like that. Breathe through it. You have to push hard. Harder."*

She plucked a pair of gauntlet-length gloves off the bed. Pale blue to match her dress. One more dance wouldn't hurt. And luckily, tonight's revel was safe for girls. The Witch Queen always picked a boy. As the women of the island said to their husbands, brothers, and sons: *It's different for us. It's not safe for you.* Which was why she'd had to lock Finley away.

Lina hummed. Music. Free magic. Maybe even a kiss?

Outside a firework exploded, a crimson flower blooming bright, its falling petals scattering red light through the window.

The revel had begun.

Her stocking feet slipped on the wrought iron steps as she hurried downstairs, her hip throbbing as it caught the curled edge of the banister. Caldella's locals made their homes on the second and third floors of their colorful townhouses due to frequent flooding; eerie ink-black water lapped darkly at the bottom three steps.

A shout rang out as Lina delved into the sea of rubber boots and umbrellas crammed onto a shelf set in the wall. A faint cry. And not a curse this time. Finley's voice. Sounding pained. Panicked.

Followed by a deafening bang.

Lina jumped, swallowed. "Finley?"

A second loud bang. Lina glanced over her shoulder at the ceiling, edging back upstairs, setting one foot on the creaking third-story landing. "Finley?"

The banging came again, growing louder as she neared his door.

Lina cursed and dragged the chair away, cursed again and hurried back to her room for the key she'd left there. She jammed it into the lock, heart pounding, hesitating before she turned it. "Finley?"

What if it was a trick? Some ploy so she'd let him out?

"Finley, are you okay? This isn't a joke. Tonight isn't a joke." Lina pressed her forehead against the wood and bit her cheek. She'd seen the boys the queen had picked as sacrifices. She'd known them. Finley had known them. Handsome Eli with his crooked grin. Aarav, who'd danced duets like a dream. Niko with his million freckles. Thomas Lin.

She banished their faces from her thoughts. Did Finley think she wanted this, that she'd be *happy* if he risked himself? Did he think she cared more for some charm than she did for his life? Did he think that if he magicked away her injury it would make up for his part in causing it?

Or maybe this wasn't even about her. Hadn't he been fretting about the flooding? Muttering about doing anything he could to make it stop? Studying crumpled tide charts and lunar calendars, faded, dust-coated histories of the island and the magic that kept it safe.

Maybe it had been different in the old days. When the dark tide had risen and threatened to sink the city, the islanders had had no choice but to strike a deal with the witch who would become their first queen. They'd fled war on the mainland, fled because of what they believed or didn't, because of who they loved or didn't. This was their new home, their haven, and they'd had no time to escape and nowhere to run as the black water rushed in. The first boys had gone to their deaths willingly.

But now…well, now they still had nowhere to go, and yes, the flooding was getting worse, and yes, there was something terribly romantic and brave about saving your home and the people you loved at the cost of your own life, but that didn't mean the sacrifice had to be her brother. It didn't mean it had to be Finley.

"Finley, please, please don't do this."

Another bang. Wood striking wood. The quaver of glass shivering in the wake of a violent blow.

Lina unlocked the door and peeked inside.

The room was empty. Finley's bed was shoved up against the wall. His desk chair was stranded atop the mattress, a pile of books and an old scuffed trunk stacked on top of its seat. His violin and bow were gone.

An icy breeze whispered in Lina's ears. The feather in her headband rustled against her bobbed blond hair.

The tiny window near the ceiling was open, its blue shutters battered back and forth with terrific bangs as the wind picked up. She had forgotten about that window. It was such a tiny thing, never opened, barely wider than her shoulders. How had he even fit through? He was a giant. Two heads taller than her and broad.

Lina climbed the teetering makeshift ladder, white-knuckled fingers gripping the window frame for dear life. She leaned out into the night, peering up, then down, red-hot fury fast replacing her fear. "I hope she does take you!"

The only response was laughter, bubbling up from the flooded street below. Amber lantern light sparked off black water, off shimmering dresses and faces painted with silver and gold.

"You lost someone, love?" a bearded figure called up. "Better find them before somebody else does."

2

LINA

WHEN LINA WAS FIFTEEN, SHE'D watched a queen drown. Watched as dusky water rose through the cracks between cobblestones, as the dark tide sloshed over the side of St. Casimir's Square that led into the sea. Black waves crowned with sharp white teeth. Stretching, reaching for the tiny, fragile figure chained to the stone pillar in the center. The queen hadn't flinched, hadn't broken as the boys before her had done. There were no cries, no whispered prayers. Only the deafening roar of the waves and a witch's face set as stone.

Lina liked to imagine she would be like that: fearless when it mattered most, unbreakable when it came to protecting the person she loved. She stole courage from the memory often, for small things, like the moment before she stepped out onstage, and big things, like the hours spent waiting while her mothers raced home through a shipwrecking storm. She stole some now as she sailed down the water roads alone in the dark. But it was hard not to picture her brother as that tiny, fragile figure chained in the center of the square.

The wind whipped her hair. Salt spray kissed her lips. She'd stolen her neighbor's broom boat, and she rapped the hull with her knuckles, sending the magicked skiff surging through the veins of the city, heading for higher ground. These roads were only supposed to flood when High Water hit, but that was most days now. The flooding really was worse than it had ever been.

Lina ducked beneath a line of laundry strung between two townhouses, fingers dusting the brick wall to her left, drumming an anxious staccato on a darkened windowpane.

Once. Twice. Three times. Three was a good number.

Another boat snaked past, an amber lantern swinging sideways from its stern. The islanders collected the amber the sea washed ashore after storms, and the witches made it glow. The boys the boat carried were bickering, taunting one another, taking bets as to who would be brave enough to enter the revel first. Wine sloshed in a bottle tossed between them. One loudly declared that it would be an honor to be chosen tonight, that his family would be proud…

Their voices faded. Lina turned her boat down a narrow alley, wincing as the hull scraped brick. She wanted to get as far as she could by boat, because on foot she would be slow. Too slow. She needed to catch up to Finley and…then what, what was she going to do? Carry him back? Drag him? Hold on to his arm and scream until he was so embarrassed he turned tail and fled?

Murder him herself? That sounded like a decent plan.

The boat's keel scraped stone. Lina jolted forward on the bench seat. A few blocks later she was forced to abandon the boat entirely, securing it to a red-and-white-striped mooring post. She continued on foot, limping slightly, frustration rising with every step.

More amber lanterns lit the way, swinging from terraces overhanging the street. They had electricity on the mainland, but Caldella's locals preferred magic. It was more expensive, more lavish. The witches only used magic, and the witches ruled the island. "What's good enough for them at the palace is good enough for the likes of us folk down here," Uncle always said. It was about status. The more magic you could afford, the closer you were to society's peak.

Lina caught the strum of soft music, paused, and looked back.

A group of islanders elbowed past, jostling and joking loudly. "And if the queen kisses you and takes you off to the palace, you remember to take a knife to bed with you. They say she has teeth down there!"

Lina bit her cheek and changed direction. There was the slightest chance Finley might have stopped, and even if he hadn't—

She rounded the bend, took a path she'd rushed by minutes before. Though she knew what was coming, she still caught her breath. Caldella's labyrinthine streets wound around hundreds of boxed-in squares, some hiding gardens and orchards ripe with juicy fruit. Others were stone plazas paved for assemblies and open-air markets. St. Casimir's was the largest. Lover's Square was much smaller but easily more beautiful, with a marble fountain made for catching moonlight, lush trees and blooming rosebushes, and a wide and twisting staircase leading up to streets and houses built on higher ground.

At the bottom of those stairs, a boy could be found singing for spare coins.

Fireworks burst overhead, explosions ringing in Lina's ears in time with the pounding of her heart. She was already blushing, cheeks red as the fire streaking across the sky. There he was. Sea-tanned skin and sun-kissed hair, brown eyes that held a hundred untold secrets. Only one boy had ever been chosen as sacrifice and lived to tell the tale.

No one dared ask Thomas Lin how he'd done it, how he'd made the wicked queen care for someone more than herself. How he'd made her sacrifice *herself* instead of him two years ago. Certainly not Lina, who could barely look him in the eye without turning red as a lobster. Even when she'd turned her ankle and he'd piggybacked her home, she hadn't managed to string together more than a stuttered thank-you.

He'd come back to them all as someone not quite real. A character escaped from a story. The boy who had seduced a queen. The boy who had won his freedom from a witch.

Another firework sparked, this one trailing pixie-green stars. Lina stood at the edge of Lover's Square, palms going clammy. There were also people, like Finley, who said Thomas Lin was dangerous, who claimed he had broken the magic that kept Caldella safe, that no matter how many sacrifices their new queen made now, the island was doomed to sink.

He had traded his life for all of theirs.

Lina shook the thought away. She wasn't here for the rumors or her hopeless crush. Tonight wasn't *about* her. She crossed the square; Thomas Lin lowered his guitar.

Lina took a deep breath. "I need you to tell me how you made a witch fall in love."

The words stretched in the silence between fireworks, like a plucked string ringing with the first note of a song. Lina sank onto the stone step beside Thomas, repressing a shiver as the cold seeped through her dress. The night was crisp enough to make her wish she'd worn a coat.

Glowing baubles and beads hung from the garden trees' branches, but Thomas's face was masked in shadow. His knuckles shone white where he gripped his guitar.

"Please. It's for Finley." Thomas knew her brother, even if they didn't *like* each other. There were no strangers in Caldella—save for the witches, who kept mostly to the Water Palace save for nights like this one. Lina knew every islander's face even if she didn't always remember every name. The island was closed to outsiders. And

Finley and Thomas had both studied music at the Conservatoire, the same school where she studied dance. "You could talk to him, tell him. He's fixed on joining the revel tonight, and I—"

"You think the queen will choose him."

Lina tugged her necklace, pulling the red beads so tight they bit into her neck. "We all know she takes the handsome ones. There's no one left to compete with Finley. No one who's going," she amended.

Thomas's mouth twitched. "Is that why you shaved one of his eyebrows off?"

"That was an accident. I meant to shave them both off, but he woke up."

Thomas's laugh filled the garden. People passing by stopped and stared. Warmth rushed through Lina despite the chill night air. It wasn't as if other boys didn't try to make themselves look unappealing. Finley should have thanked her.

"I don't think I've ever seen him so mad," said Thomas. "And that's saying something. We all thought you did it because he wore your pink gown to Josef's party."

"He what?"

"Oh. Shit. You didn't know?"

Her brand-new pink dress that shimmered like the inside of seashell. With its zipper that had mysteriously, inexplicably, broken. Lina's teeth came together with a click.

"He looked quite fetching," said Thomas.

Lina punched him in the arm, then jerked her fist back as if she'd been scalded. She'd just *touched* Thomas Lin. She'd just *punched* Thomas Lin.

And he was smiling.

He put his guitar aside and shuffled closer. Lina couldn't resist doing the same, angling her legs so their knees might accidentally brush. "You have to help. You can tell him how you survived, how you tricked the queen, how you…"

A faint crease formed between Thomas's brows. He pressed a thumb to his bottom lip, then smoothed his hands over his slacks. "He came through here a bit ago, with Istvan and Josef. I told Josef they shouldn't go, but he wasn't having it. They're already gone."

"Gone," Lina repeated. Wind whipped through the garden, ruffling her hair. There was something so gut-wrenchingly *final* about the word.

"Lina," Thomas said gently. "I did try to stop them."

"Did you? You didn't do a very good job. Did you tell them what to do if they were picked? Did you tell them what *you* did to save yourself?" Lina stood. He'd never told anyone, and from the look on his face now, she knew he hadn't told Finley. He'd kept the secret for himself.

"You can't keep him locked up," said Thomas. "He's a grown man. I don't think the queen will take him."

"Oh, and you can swear to that, can you? No one thought she'd take Niko."

Niko with his raven-black hair and dusting of freckles. Niko with his wild grin. Niko dead at the bottom of the sea.

Thomas reached for her. "Lina."

Why had she even bothered? Why had she even come here? She'd just wasted *more* time. She shrugged him off and lost her balance as she climbed the first step. Her heart slammed against her rib cage as she teetered backward.

She caught herself, walked more slowly, taking the steps one at a time, cheeks burning. She should have shaved Finley's whole head, should have knocked him out or tied him up somehow. Tears stung her eyes. She only ever cried when she was frustrated or furious. So furious she wanted to break something. Someone.

She pressed through the crowded streets, elbowing past people partying, people too smart or too scared to set foot inside the revel. The scent of whiskey blended with the scents of smoke and sweat. Column-lined arcades of shops enclosed St. Casimir's Square on all sides but one. The last opened straight onto the sea.

Lina paused in an archway beside a column in front of the closed ice-creamery. Its windows were shivering with the wail of pipes and strings. Fireworks crowned the scene before her, but she could barely see anything past the haze of heat from the bonfires. Shapes and shadows dancing. The great stone pillar in the center shot up to pierce the night.

Drums beat thunder into the ground, and the sound of it pulled, calling to that sinuous little voice inside of her, the one that urged her to jump when she stood at the top of a flight of stairs, the one that told her to leap from the deck of her mothers' ship even though she couldn't swim. Want filled her. She wanted badly to step into the square in spite of the danger. She wanted to dance, to leap and spin and snap her fingers.

She wanted to catch a glimpse of the wicked Witch Queen as she wove in and out of the revelers in disguise, changing faces, appearing one second as the person you loved, transforming next into the person the boy beside you loved, tricking you into taking her hand, tricking you into kissing her.

The dull ache in her ankle enabled her to shake free of the magic's pull. Her whole body trembled, and she wasn't sure if it was from fear or desire. A bead of sweat dripped from her temple. Truth be told, she wasn't supposed to be here tonight either. She was supposed to be resting, supposed to be celebrating St. Walpurga's Eve with the rest of the family at Ma's brother's house, where she and Finley should be now. Would anyone come looking for them? She'd caught snatches of the usual clamor as she sailed past the house: the familiar hiss of hot oil, the clatter of pots and pans drowning beneath the voices of five of her six aunts. Gossip and laughter so loud you could hear it halfway down the street.

Lina's nails dug crescents into her palms. She even would have stayed there with Finley like she'd told him. For a little while, at least. She would've snuck out on her own later on, just for a bit. While everyone was stuffing themselves silly with butter crab, while Nina and Ivy played piano or Finley played violin or cousin number fifteen played cello. All the aunties busy throwing smug looks back and forth like knives, each confident she had the most talented child, everyone too distracted to notice she was missing.

Her brother always had to make everything about him, even when he was *supposedly* doing something for her.

Lina started forward. A rough hand caught her wrist. Thomas kept a wide space between himself and the edge of the square, the border of the revel. His eyes danced with reflected flames, and she saw fear and hesitation lurking in their depths. Annoyance spiked.

"It's not like they'll pick you twice." Even witches respected dead queens' wishes. Lina shook her arm free and stepped backward through the arch. "And it's not like she'll pick me."

3

LINA

THE WORLD DIDN'T CHANGE SO much as it sharpened.

Edges cut like knives, colors flashed like the glimmer off a blade. Lina could see the revelers clearly now, spinning in wild circles. Linked hands. Linked elbows. Driven by the relentless pounding of drums. The shriek and wail of pipe and violin. Round and round the dancers went, clockwise and counterclockwise, forward and back. People she knew and people she didn't. Blurred silhouettes. Black-clad sirens with sharks' smiles and jingling bangles of amber and shells. Bare-chested figures with eyes as cold as sea glass.

Some said the witches were dreams and nightmares escaped from mortal minds. Children born after sundown. They still looked human, though, or chose to, and their black attire blended with the shadows, making it seem as if they blinked in and out of the night itself.

Lina's heart thrummed, pulse quickening at the thought of

being surrounded by so much magic. The music struck a chord deep within her bones. She moved forward, humming unconsciously beneath her breath, searching the crowd for a familiar black cowlick and eyes as gray as the winter sea. Those not dancing were gathered around the bonfires, trying to charm the witches with their talents. Just because magic was given out for free tonight didn't mean it was given out for nothing; you had to impress a witch. Others still were trying to catch orange sparks crackling off the smoldering wood. A burn from one of the thirteen bonfires brought luck to the wearer for the rest of the year.

One of the witches, a brown-skinned girl with silver hoops swinging from her ears, caught a spark and, waving it once like a sparkler, tucked it behind Lina's ear.

Blushing, Lina reached up to touch it, marvelling at the soft warmth that met her fingers. The witch winked, and a flustered Lina backed up, shoulders knocking into the firm chest behind her. She spun, apologizing.

Thomas stared down at her, expression so intent that guilt immediately pricked her conscience. She didn't know what dark memories she was asking him to relive by being here. Although technically she *hadn't* asked him to be here—he'd come after her. Followed her.

A strange tightness squeezed Lina's chest. Her anger from earlier vanished. When his arms swept around her, she didn't protest, just let him draw her close. So close their chests brushed.

He led her into the ebb and flow of dancers, hands leaving little spots of heat at the small of her back, on her arm, her hip.

Lina's throat ran dry. "I thought…"

I thought you didn't care.

"I can't lose him." It came out as a whisper. It sounded like an apology.

Thomas's eyes were so dark they looked almost black. He pulled her even closer, and when they moved together it was as if they'd danced these steps a hundred thousand times before. His body responded to her slightest movement. His gaze never once left hers. She could feel his hip bones as they turned together through the tide of bodies. Heated words tickled the tip of her ear. Lina couldn't breathe.

"You'll have to hold on to him tightly, then." His smile was knife-sharp as he pulled back. Sudden cold rushed between them as he let go.

Lina's mouth opened, but he was already spinning away, taking another boy's arm.

Someone grabbed her wrist. Lina jumped. It was Thomas. "Don't! Thomas?" She twisted, glancing one way and then the other, from the sea of dancers Thomas had melted into to the Thomas clasping her wrist. Her heart stuttered. Who…

But she knew who. There was only one witch who wore other people's faces on St. Walpurga's Eve. One witch who appeared to you as the person you loved.

A tiny, involuntary thrill shot through Lina. "Did you see—"

"Finley?" Thomas, the *real* Thomas, stood with all the tension of someone about to bolt, dread coiled in every muscle. "No, not yet."

Lina swallowed hard and didn't correct him. There was so much fear in his face already. She let out a breath. But the blood in her veins was still singing, humming.

"I'll help you find him. I heard you injured your ankle again."

A hot flare of indignation helped Lina regain her composure. "I'm not helpless."

"But you're slow. And small. Someone could knock you over. You could get trampled. Hurt. Look, it doesn't matter if she's not going to pick you. You can't trust anyone here. The quicker you find him, the better." Thomas flinched as a messenger spell—a small spiral of wind, a teacup-sized waterspout—whistled past his temple with a wind-chime tinkle.

Lina's heart ached. How could he fear magic when it was this beautiful? "We'll be quick then, I promise." And maybe it was a response to the taunt from a minute before, but she reached out and took his hand. "I'll hold on to you." She was blushing again, cheeks glowing brighter even than the bonfires, brighter even than the crimson fireworks blooming above their heads. "I mean—I mean," she stammered. "Like—like the song." She couldn't meet his eyes. She suddenly wanted to find whoever was currently playing and strangle them. The faint lilting strains of a single violin.

Hide him, hide him, out of sight.

Hold him, hold him, hold on tight.

Understanding dawned on Thomas's face. Lina was ready to dig a hole and bury herself in it. She may as well have screamed, "I love you!" in front of the whole damn square. Because it was a song all the islanders knew and a song the *queen* obviously knew. A song about a girl who had refused to hand her lover over as sacrifice, who hadn't let him go even when the queen used magic to try and steal him away. The witch had turned the boy into a sea serpent, a bear, and finally, a raging wall of fire, but the girl hadn't let go, and in the end, the queen had been forced to let the lovers be.

A passing dancer picked up the tune, singing the words loud and clear. Then another. And another. Voices raised in unison, in defiance. The whole island sang, waves of sound sweeping through the square.

The Witch Queen comes on wings of night.
The Witch Queen has your heart's delight.
Hold him, hold him, hold on tight.
Hide him, hide him, out of sight.

There wasn't a person here who didn't know the tune, who hadn't heard the words sung above their cradle, who hadn't been lulled to sleep by the tale of the girl who'd stolen love from the Witch Queen.

Lina sang, too, because screw it, there wasn't any way she could embarrass herself more. There was no going back now.

Thomas didn't take his eyes off her as he joined in, voice soft but carrying because of its haunting quality. His was a siren's song, luring in all who listened.

The circle of dancers swept them up. The current tossed them round the square, and Lina fiercely ignored the worsening ache in her ankle, the sharp bursts of shooting pain. She would pay for it later, but for now Thomas was with her, steadying her. He spun her stiffly, self-consciously, holding her at an awkward distance. It was Lina who had to steer their steps now, and she quickly shoved down the tiniest pang of disappointment. So he wasn't a very good dancer; what of it? She linked arms with him, guiding him through the other revelers.

"Have you seen Finley?" she asked Gita when she spied her. Her classmate was giggling, one arm wrapped around a bearded musician. Her painted lips parted in an O when she spied Thomas.

"Have you seen my brother?" Lina asked a witch draped in sealskin. "Black hair? Massively tall? He plays violin."

Gita shook her head. The witch kissed Lina's cheeks. Lina spied Finley's friend Istvan and grabbed his wrist. "Where the hell is Finley, knobhead?"

Istvan cursed and waved a hand in the direction from which they'd come. The great circle of dancers broke into lines, witches on the outside, islanders on the inside, everyone weaving in and out, skirts spinning like upturned tornadoes.

Sweat stuck Lina's dress to her back. "I'm going to murder him."

"Wouldn't that defeat the purpose?" Thomas's boot crackled and crunched on a broken bottle.

He moved in time with her as they headed for the far side of the square, finally finding the beat, and Lina let herself imagine, just for a tiny, tiny second, that she wasn't here searching for her brother. That she was here for the magic, for the witches' bold promise: she would kiss the boy she loved by the light of the thirteen bonfires, and he would be hers forever. She'd daydreamed about it, what Thomas would taste like, what his mouth would feel like moving against her own.

Hot. Insistent. Dark daydreams that twisted her stomach into knots and left her feeling flushed and a little ashamed. There was a deep and ravenous hunger inside of her. Sometimes she wasn't sure if she wanted to kiss him or eat him whole.

His hand closed over hers. Warmth seeped through her glove, and she wished she hadn't worn it, wished she could feel his skin pressed against hers. "Finley's lucky. When I...I didn't have anyone who cared enough to come after me. Who would've held on to me."

Lina swallowed.

Thomas smiled, the action undoing her like it always did, every bone in her body melting to mush. Because Thomas was the boy from her daydreams, the only boy the Witch Queen had ever let go, the boy at the center of Caldella's most famous love story, which was a feat in a city brimming with love stories. From the

girl who'd held on to her lover through enchantment and fire, to Laolao and Grandpa, who'd sailed from opposite sides of the globe so they could be together, to Ma, who had smuggled Mama onto the island just before its borders were closed.

Stories filled the witches' island until it overflowed.

But to Lina, it often felt like everything exciting, everything that *meant* anything, had happened before she was old enough to take part. The stories were over, the books closed, and she was stuck living in somebody else's happily ever after. A boring background character. She wanted more. She wanted to *be* something more. She wanted to change someone or save someone. She wanted a love people told stories about.

Thomas's smile promised she could have it.

The song changed, and he withdrew his hand from hers to carefully copy the boy beside him, pressing a fist to his heart and dipping at the waist as the steps of the next dance demanded. A lithe figure with ash-colored hair elbowed Lina aside, shoving her suddenly into the arms of another reveler, stealing her place as Thomas's partner.

She cried out in protest at the same time as Thomas did. She stumbled and lost her balance. Her new partner picked her up by the waist and twirled her through the air, the world smearing into a dizzying blur.

"Wait, wait!" Lina looked back but only caught the flash of Thomas's blond hair vanishing into the dark.

4

E V A

THE DAY HER SISTER DIED, Eva sealed her heart inside a bottle and cast it out to sea.

But sometimes, when she put an ear to the cold stone walls of her palace, when she tossed and turned at night instead of sleeping, she swore she could still hear it: a faint and steady beat. A drumming as she crossed an empty corridor, pounding up through the balls of her feet. She could hear it now in the rhythmic crash of the black waves at her back, a rushing in her ears as she trailed a hand through the fire.

Flames licked at her fingers, tickled the elegant curve of her palm. The air bent and rippled, smoke snaking up to meld with the star-studded sky. The thirteenth bonfire stood at a distance from the others, at the edge of the square leading into the tide, in the shadow of the great stone pillar where, a month from now, Eva would chain the boy she loved and leave him to be swallowed by the sea.

She liked it here, where it was not so crowded, away from the endless rush of revelers and dancers, away from the people she instinctively disliked for no other reason than that they were people and Eva did not like people. Here she could wait and watch her reflection change in the puddles at her feet. Could watch herself grow tall and thin or short and fat, young and old, in turn.

Her hair twisted into thick mermaid curls, tumbled sleek and straight down her spine. Skin paling and darkening in turn. She wore a thousand faces, but never her own.

And when the dancers stumbled near to catch their breath and warm their hands, she could listen, listen to what the city had to say about her.

"They say she has no heart."

"They say the witch is cursed."

"Frigid."

"*I* hear she's made of stone."

"She'll fail again this year, you'll see. Soon."

The last speaker smacked his lips as if the prospect pleased him. He stood on the opposite side of the bonfire from Eva, half-hidden by the flames. Thinning hair fading to gray. Leathery skin tanned by sun and sea. The end of his cigarette glowed red as he dragged in a ragged breath.

The men on either side of him echoed the action, each as timeworn and salt-flecked as the sunken ruins that filled Caldella's harbor. Smoke rose like ghosts between their gnarled fingers.

"The island will sink, and all of us with it." His voice was gravel grinding. The tide lapped at the city's edge, spilling over and pooling at the pointed tips of Eva's shoes. "It's not a sacrifice if she doesn't care. She has no love for us. No love for the boys she takes."

"If it's loving she needs..." The shortest of the three had a blue anchor tattooed on the side of his neck.

"You going to bed a monster, then?" The last man dug elbows into his companions' ribs.

"Better a monster than your wife." Snickers burst above the scuffle that broke out. "The witch'll look like whoever I wish. Good thing, too, if she's as hideous as they say."

"Still, bit hard to bed a girl made of *stone.*"

Eva unwound one of several bracelets tied around her wrist. Threadbare twists of her black hair and bloodred string. Every charm required a little piece of the witch who cast it. Every curse took a little bite out of you until you had no magic left. She looped the strings around her thumbs and the tips of her fingers, as if she were playing cat's cradle, what the islanders called the Witches' Game.

"Oh, I'm sure I can get her going. A couple of pokes and she'll be begging for more."

Eva shaped a net and then a fish. A wave struck the edge of the square, and spray burst through the air. Ice-cold needles sank into her skin where her dress dipped low to show her back. The rest of the droplets seemed to freeze, sparkling. She'd formed a second shape, a third, strings glowing hot, before the world came rushing back.

Water soaked the cobblestones. Cigarettes dropped from gnarled fingers, sizzling as they hit stone.

Eva stepped out from behind the bonfire. Three seagulls stood where three men had once been, peering up at her with the gaping, slack-jawed expressions common to old men confronted by girls who stood up for themselves.

One coughed, a sound that morphed into a caw. The second flapped its wings in a panicked sort of way. The third took off, screeching, turning angry circles above her head.

"You look like you're having fun." Boots scuffed as Marcin seeped out of the shadows to Eva's left. His hair as deep a red as the bonfire flames, a smile tugging at his generous mouth. "But if you keep turning every islander who irritates you into a seagull, we'll soon have no one left." He leaned his shoulder into Eva's, tugging playfully at the braids crowning her head. "I found a good one for you. Brown curls. Tall. A real charmer. You'll like him."

Eva relooped her bracelets, pulled the sleeves of her black dress down over her fingers.

"Unless you'd prefer to let the city sink." Marcin's tone was mild. It held no judgment, no accusation. It was almost...a suggestion.

A second wave broke against the city's edge.

It's not a sacrifice if she doesn't care.

No magic in sacrificing someone you cared nothing about.

No sacrifice if it didn't hurt you to give that person up. No power without a price.

Eva could feel the dark tide's rage in every lash it made against the stone, a hunger that hadn't been sated for almost two years. It gave her a kind of savage satisfaction. It was a petty sort of revenge.

You took my sister. Why should I give you anything?

"All great cities fall eventually." Marcin twisted the thick silver ring on his thumb. "It's the way of things. You can't always fight fate."

"But not this city. Our city won't fall." The words cut through the dark, but they quavered with a note of uncertainty. Yara had a way of speaking that made everything sound like a question. With dainty steps, pinching her long, glittery skirt so it wouldn't drag on the ground, she slipped into her usual spot on Eva's right. Firelight played off her soft brown skin, glinting where it caught the coral and pearls twining affectionately around her arms and wrists.

"It would only be temporary," said Marcin. "We could rebuild someplace else."

"Where?" said Yara.

"Somewhere across the sea." Marcin shrugged. "The mainland. One of the coastal cities. Things are different there now."

"You can't know that." Eva cut Marcin off before he could outline the entirety of his plan. She'd heard it a thousand times before. And she didn't take it seriously; Marcin liked to pretend he didn't care about the island, about anything or anyone, when in reality he cared more than most. "I won't abandon Caldella. I won't abandon Natalia's city."

Because it still felt like Natalia's city. Not hers. The misty water roads and slick cobbled streets, the pastel-painted town houses pressed too tightly together, the hidden gardens tucked into darkened squares, lit by amber lantern light and smelling of roses after the rain. They all belonged to her sister. There wasn't a place on the island that didn't make the hollow in Eva's chest ache.

She caught a flicker of emotion in Marcin's hazel eyes. He had been her sister's closest friend, had helped her flee the mainland when Natalia was a child and Eva even younger, no more than a witchling, barely old enough to walk. Long before they'd all been adopted by Caldella's then-queen.

Yara placed a gentle hand on Eva's arm. "The sacrifice will work this year. You just need to let go, let yourself care."

Let yourself care. But what she meant was: *Let yourself* hurt.

Natalia's ghost settled over Eva's shoulders like a shawl. The first rule of magic was never to give away too much of yourself. Never to trade away more power than you could stand to lose. Never to love a person more than you loved yourself.

Eva would not make the same mistake her sister had.

Safer never to care at all.

"For two witches so desperate to save this city," drawled Marcin, "*I* seem to be the one doing all the work. The one finding boys for Eva to pick as her sacrifice. What have you been doing?"

He looked from one girl to the other. "Turning men into seagulls? Stuffing your face?"

There was a dash of sugar below Yara's lush lips; she'd always had a sweet tooth.

She scrubbed at her chin, frowning, as Marcin's smile turned malicious. "There was a boy who baked pastries in the hope of winning some magic."

"So kind how they do that," said Marcin. "Show off their talents so we can pick the most appealing ones."

"A redhead," Yara continued, ignoring him. "You can pretend he's Marcin when you chain him to the pillar. But the most handsome one of all is playing violin by the third bonfire. I told Omar to keep an eye on him."

"Mine has curls," said Marcin. "The brunette I told you about."

"Mine has dimples," said Yara. "And winter-gray eyes and bed hair. Black."

"No blonds?" said Eva dryly. The words slipped out before she could think better of them.

Marcin and Yara exchanged a look.

Eva quickly decided she preferred it when they were squabbling. "I danced earlier. With many boys." *And found not a single one appealing.* She smoothed her dress down. "I can choose for myself."

Another look. Another wordless exchange that cut her out

completely. Not so much distrust as a lack of faith in her. Climbing anger crept into Eva's voice. "I let you choose the last one. And look how that turned out."

"Because you put absolutely no effort into it," said Yara. "You didn't even try to fall a little in love with him, E. You didn't even try to *try*. I always choose the handsomest ones. For Natalia, too. There's not an endless supply."

"Kiss the boy with brown curls. Or the one with the violin. You like music," said Marcin, as if that settled it.

Eva had liked music and musicians, once.

"I can choose my own sacrifice," she repeated, and started forward, falling once more into the rush of the crowd. It wasn't hard to lose the others amidst the revelers. Eva wrapped the shadows around herself, and when she moved it was as if she dragged the night behind her. Her reflection flashed by in puddles, in the lovelorn eyes of twirling dancers. Ever-changing.

She was a witch. An islander. A boy.

Young. Old. Middle-aged.

Long hair. Short hair. Black hair. Brown.

Blond.

Eva paused with one foot frozen in the air. The puddle at her feet shattered as a reveler swept by, but the second before...the second before, it had shown a ghost.

Dancers streamed by in an endless chain.

Eva stared at the rippling water, at her trembling reflection, holding on to her current form. She raised a hand and traced the familiar jawline, shuddering at the roughness she found there. The faintest stubble. The soft mouth. The dark brown eyes. She stared at her hands, sun-tanned and calloused from repeated plucking at guitar strings. Earlier she'd caught a glimpse and she'd thought she was seeing things. She'd been changing so quickly, switching from one set of arms to another, spinning, spinning, spinning.

She spun now, searching for whoever had caused her to change, caused her to take this form of all forms.

She shut her eyes and listened, sorting through the sounds, filtering out the music, the loud crackle of bonfire flames, the laughter. She'd thought she'd heard his singing too. That voice like a lilting whisper, like a lullaby as it coaxed you into sleep. A song that tucked you in before it slit your throat. She'd ignored it, dismissed it as fancy because Thomas Lin wouldn't dare join the revel in St. Casimir's Square. Not tonight. Not while she was here.

The nearest bonfire spat, red hot sparks summoning cries of pain from those they scalded.

Eva snaked through the crowd in search of a voice, in search of a ghost, two questions in mind: Whose face would she wear when she found him? And, would the dark tide still accept her sacrifice, if she drowned the boy with her own two hands?

5

LINA

"IT'S WRONG, THAT SONG."

Lina glanced sideways, startled. She'd backed away from the bonfires and the revelers, retreated into a dark arch between the columns of the surrounding arcade to catch her breath. The air was cooler in front of the line of closed shops. She hadn't realized her dance partner had followed her. A tickle of unease raced down her spine.

"The one you were humming just now? 'Hide him, hide him, out of sight. Hold him, hold him, hold on tight'?" There was a soft *scritch-scritch* as the witch scratched his stubbled cheek. He looked about Ma's age, but you could never tell. Did dreams and nightmares even age?

He used a sleeve to wipe the gleam of sweat off his pale brow. "Personally, I prefer a song where the heroine doesn't burn to death at the end."

"She doesn't burn to death," Lina protested.

"Oh, she does. Did. The lass who held on to her lover and never let go? She let go. When Queen Jurata turned the lad into fire, her heart failed her. It wasn't spite, you see, but a test. Love can break a spell, but in the end, the lass didn't love him enough to keep him. She lost herself to fear and forgot what she was holding. She and the lad burned alive. Burned until there was nothing left." The witch's teeth cut a crooked crescent. "But none of you lot sings that part."

He shuffled closer, smile growing when Lina tensed and took the tiniest step back. Witches only smiled when they wanted something, because they knew they were going to get it.

Lina's heart was pounding, but she raised her chin in defiance. "Even if that's true, the queen still lost. The girl still won."

"Is death winning, then?"

"The queen didn't get what she wanted. She couldn't steal the boy away."

"And now you know why none of *us* likes the song." The witch dipped his head. "You should tell the lad that, the one who played it just now." His eyes flicked past her. Lina followed his gaze, looking out at the crowd, eyes widening. "It won't win him any magic. Thought I'd mention it in return for the dance. You look alike, the two of you. Same eyes and—"

Lina didn't catch the rest, because she was already moving, charging toward the nearest bonfire and the figure silhouetted by its curling flames. Had that been a threat? Was the witch trying to warn her? A warning in exchange for a dance instead of a charmed trinket or lock of hair?

Someone had painted a gleaming band of gold across her brother's eyes like a mask. Dimples appeared in Finley's flushed cheeks as soon as he spotted her. Drinking always turned him red as a tomato. "And this here angry-looking bird's my wee sis," he informed the girl at his side. An extremely pretty girl in glittery black whose long chestnut hair rippled like waves.

Finley waved his violin bow. "Come and dance with your brother, Lina. We'll soon put a smile on that face."

Lina did smile, at the girl in glittery black. "He has a girlfriend. I know it's hard to tell, because he flirts with anything that moves and can't keep his hands to himself, but—"

Finley let out a choked sound. The girl's expression soured like she'd sucked on a sea plum. "Now, hold on!" said Finley as she turned to walk away. "She's making that up. Don't listen!"

Lina grabbed his sleeve. "We're going to Uncle's. Right now."

Finley swayed and lumped a sweaty arm over Lina's shoulders. "Don't be like this. Here. Look." He struggled to dig a hand inside the inner pocket of his suit jacket and hold on to his bow and violin at the same time. "Look what I got."

Lina turned her head away. "You reek." She started backward.

Finley tottered after her, one arm still heavy around her shoulders. His breath was hot on her cheek, rank with the stench of strong alcohol. "Here. See. *See.*" He waved something, and the end whipped her neck. A length of braided hair and twine, knotted and threaded through with mother-of-pearl and shards of bone. A witch's ladder, for hanging in a ship's cabin, to calm the waves and ward off storms. A talisman to protect against the monsters that roamed the Eastern Sea.

Magic worth more than her mothers made in a year.

Lina stared, speechless.

Finley tucked the witch's ladder back into his jacket. "For the parentals, so they can come home quick and safe." He tapped his chest proudly and winked, or tried to, face scrunching with the effort. "You didn't think I came here just for a laugh, did you? And here, for you—"

"You shouldn't have come at *all*." Lina headed for the edge of the square, something like envy twisting inside her stomach. She'd won magic before, impressing the witches with her dancing on St. Walpurga's Eve. They'd said she danced so beautifully she could stop a person's heart with her steps. But she'd never won anything so valuable as this. Glass glinted as Finley drew more magic from his pockets. A bottled spell this time, clouded glass, cork-stoppered.

A round-bottomed bottle filled with tears and wishes, bone and breath and sand. Anchors for powerful magic. You could use a witch's hair to weave charms, their teeth to cast curses. Mainlanders were said to boil witch bodies down to the bone. The only way to have magic if you hadn't been born with it in your veins.

Unless you paid for it, of course. But not everyone was willing to pay.

"Is that—" Lina paused, biting her lip, as a flood of dancers swept by. This wasn't the time. Bodies swelled around them on all sides, a living tide. She scanned the crush for Thomas. "Let's just go."

"Don't worry," said Finley, misinterpreting her look. "I'll protect you from the wicked queen."

"I'm not looking for the queen. I'm looking for Thomas."

"Of course you are." Finley's expression darkened. He shoved the bottled spell into his pocket. "That coward won't come here."

"He *was* here. He was helping me look for *you.*"

This was too much for Finley's ale-addled brain. He blinked, lips parting, closing, parting again. He scrubbed a hand over his face and smudged his left eyebrow.

"Did you *draw* your eyebrow on?"

"I may have borrowed a bit of your paint."

"You used my makeup? I swear—" The weight on Lina's shoulders lessened as Finley teetered sideways to smash fists with his friend Josef. *Another* idiot risking his life for free magic. For ropes and wreaths of sailor's knots tied with strands of hair. For bottles filled with spit and saltwater. Why were boys so utterly stupid?

"Mate!" The clash of their shouts almost burst her eardrums.

The three of them skirted a group of passing musicians, Lina peering anxiously through the fray. "We've been looking for you for *ages*, Finley," she complained. "Everywhere. And Thomas doesn't *like* being here."

"Lin's here?" Josef's eyes were wide in his tanned face. His hand scraped through his tight-cropped black curls, and his hip knocked Lina's, surprise fading quickly into the sly, crafty look worn only by the drunk. "Oh, he'd only risk that for you, hen. Only you. 'What is it with Lina? Why won't she talk to me? Why does her brother hate me so?'" Josef mimicked in a high-pitched version of Thomas's lilting accent.

Finley looked murderous.

Lina blinked. "Wait, what are you—what do you—did he really say that?"

"He's too old for you," said Finley before Josef could answer.

"He's only twenty, same as you, and I'm practically eighteen," said Lina.

"He's dangerous. I told you," said Finley. "It's his fault the sacrifices have stopped working."

They crossed into the shadow cast by the pillar in the center of the square. Words carved deep into the dark stone shone silver, twining over its surface:

Our love keeps us from drowning.

A shiver ran through Finley and found Lina. Josef looked suddenly very serious and sober, almost sad. A mournful note crept into his voice. "Didn't I point him out to you that first time? Didn't I introduce you? Why don't you bring your friends round to meet me, Lina?"

"You're disgusting."

"Finley, tell your sister. That brunette girl, now, with the big...you know." Josef gestured at his chest.

Lina aimed her next step to crush his toes, but Josef dodged and stole Finley's violin and bow, wringing a sour wail from the strings.

Finley cursed. "Give me that!"

Josef darted out of reach. Blond hair flashed at the corner of Lina's vision. She spun quickly. "Fin—" The word died on her lips. Finley's back was turned, arms gesturing madly. Lina swallowed, staring straight ahead, throat dry as sand. "Finley." Then more urgently. "*Finley.*"

Her brother didn't respond. She didn't dare look away. The roar of the bonfires, the pipes, the cheers and chants as another firework exploded—everything faded into the background, leaving only a ringing, a strange and soundless thunder, the pounding of blood through her veins.

Lina moved forward as if in a trance. Revelers, dancers, reeled and whirled out of her way. Spat insults and threw dirty looks. Liquid lashed her arm. A flask clattered to the ground. Lina stumbled on with more urgency, fear cresting like a wave as she chased after the girl in the pale blue dress. The girl with beads looped around her neck. The girl with bobbed blond hair and a peacock feather in her headband.

She chased after herself. Elbowing people, knocking them aside.

The girl glanced over her shoulder once, then kept going. Panic reached out a hand to choke Lina. Dread came thundering back a hundredfold. The crackle of the bonfire flames sounded like laughter.

The Witch Queen comes on wings of night.

The Witch Queen has your heart's delight.

Who had she danced with to look like that? Who?

Lina—*False* Lina, *Not*-Lina—called out a name. A figure turned, separating from the crowd, a second blond head catching bonfire light. Hands reached out, caught Not-Lina as she ran forward.

A body smashed into real Lina's side, knocking her sideways. She snatched at their shirt to steady herself. Shoved someone else out of the way.

The crowd parted. Lina opened her mouth, but no sound escaped. For a single disorienting instant, her mind refused to comprehend what she was seeing; she couldn't grasp the image. It shimmered before her like heat.

Not-Lina's arms were wrapped around Thomas's neck, her hands tangled up in his hair. His hands were on her waist, drawing her body flush against his. And he was kissing her, hungrily, desperately, as if it were the last thing he would ever do.

It was every dark daydream come true.

Except it wasn't with her.

"Thomas." The word escaped this time—a soft, inaudible whisper. The scene swam, rippled. Changed.

The girl kissing Thomas looked up, her hands still tangled in his hair, her lips swollen. She wore her black hair in braids that circled her head like a crown. Her gaze locked with Lina's, and her eyes glinted like moonlight on dark water. She smiled. A flash of sharply pointed teeth.

Every bonfire in St. Casimir's Square guttered and went out. A great gust of black smoke swallowed the revelers whole.

6

LINA

THERE WAS A MOMENT OF complete and utter blackness.

Darkness settled like silt at the bottom of the sea. A heavy, choking darkness. One Lina dared not disturb with sound or movement, because it was not an *empty* dark.

She did not wish to wake whatever else was in it.

The wind was a breath and a howl in one. Great twists of bitter smoke filled Lina's nose and throat and lungs. Clawing its way inside of her, clawing its way back out. And still she did not move. She was frozen as a statue.

A body slammed into her back. Someone else tripped over her as she staggered forward, a splintering crunch sounding somewhere behind. An elbow caught her jaw and her vision exploded in a burst of blinding light. She spun, trapped in a dance of terror, shoulders smacking hers, turning her first one way and then the other. Shrieks rang out. Boots pounded.

She thought she heard someone shout her name.

Just as quickly, the press of bodies thinned. The smoke was lifting, light creeping through the haze, seeping back into the scene. The embers of thirteen bonfires flickered.

"Lina!"

Her eyes took a moment to focus. She was still seeing Thomas. And that girl.

Finley's hand was shockingly hot on her arm. His mouth tight with worry.

Around them, people shared shaky smiles. A few started to laugh sheepishly. "Did you see it? Did you see her? That was the queen leaving. Did you see who she took? Did you see who she chose?"

Lina's throat closed. The words came out in a whisper, but they cut through all the other sounds. "She took him."

Finley's fingers clenched around her forearm. "Who?"

"Thomas."

"Oh. Well. That's…" A medley of emotions warred for control of her brother's face. Shock. Relief. Glee, and a hint of guilt.

Lina didn't wait to hear him lecture her on why this was a good thing, the right thing to happen, didn't wait for him to offer her comfort whilst hiding his grin. Her body filled with sudden furious energy.

"Hey, now, just hold on!" Finley chased after her, putting himself between her and the crowd, acting as a shield and clearing a path. "Hold—"

Lina sped through a shadowed arch, past the empty shops, pushing out of the arcade and into the misty, moonlit streets, cutting down the first alley to the left. A startled water rat streaked across Finley's boots.

"Lina, calm down! Stop!"

She couldn't. Urgency had its hooks in her. She'd never been able to sit still whilst a person she loved was in danger. When Lina got an idea in her head, she was physically incapable of doing anything but acting. "I have to get him back."

The words drew Finley up short.

Lina kept moving, rushing through a mist that left wet kisses on her clothes. The kind of mist you wandered into knowing you might fall through it and into a completely different world, never able to return to this one. She turned down another narrow alley. The walls on either side shimmered and swirled with enchanted murals that made you lick the bricks if you stared at them too long. Caldella's builders had a strange sense of humor. It was a side effect of living with witches.

Lina's heart stuttered. Witches. Murderers. Queens who chained boys to stone pillars and drowned them on full-moon nights.

Thomas had come after *her*. Thomas had tried to *help* her. He wouldn't have set foot in St. Casimir's Square or joined the revel if not for her. She'd dragged him into this. She'd asked him to help her brother and lost him instead, lost the boy she loved. Lost the boy who loved *her*.

Lina bit the inside of her cheek until she tasted copper. She wanted to cry. She wanted to scream. She'd ignored his fears, had thrown them in his face. Every inch of her was on fire with shame.

Finley overtook her, broad shoulders scraping the brick as he squeezed past, blocking her path. The alley sloped and ended at the city's edge, crumbling and opening out onto slippery black rocks and glowing green moss.

Behind her brother rose the gray spires of the Witch Queen's home, jagged teeth jutting out of the ink-black sea. You could see the half-sunken palace no matter where you stood on the island. Lina didn't know if it was magic or clever architecture. She'd never paid the place much attention. The Water Palace lost its wow factor when you passed it every day on the way to class. The wicked towers and turrets seemed unimportant when your cousin's bike was jolting from side to side and you were trying desperately to fill in the answers to last night's homework while leaning against their back. Now neither she nor Finley could stop their eyes from darting toward it.

"Lina, if she's chosen him, there's nothing you can do." Finley was trying to keep his voice even, his tone gentle. "You need to let him go. For the city's sake, for everyone's sake. It was always going to end like this, I told you. Look around." He gestured toward the water puddled by their feet, at the ugly stains on the walls from flooding at high tide. "The last sacrifice didn't work. He broke the magic. The new queen must have realized. She's trying to save the island."

"That's not why she took him." Lina's eyes had gone glassy. "I saw her. That, that *thing*, that girl, that witch, she looked like me. She wore my face. Finley, she wore my *face*."

"Why would she be wearing your—" Finley's expression darkened.

Lina tried to edge past him.

He blocked her with his body, palms up and out but very deliberately not touching her, not grabbing for her. "*Think* about this." He delved into his jacket pocket and held up a cork-stoppered bottle. The clouded green glass glowed with soft golden heat. He inched closer, carefully, as if she were something wild that might startle. "Here, for your ankle. This'll help it heal up, good as new. Stop the pain, that throbbing you complained about." He forced the bottled spell into her gloved hand. "Let's go home now, and you can try it."

"I don't *want* your stupid bottle, Finley!"

Glass shattered against the cobbles. Gold liquid left a splatter on the wall.

An awful sinking dread pulled Lina's stomach toward the ground. She shouldn't have done that.

Finley blinked once, then slammed a fist into the wall, knuckles bursting red against the brick.

Lina flinched.

"I risked my life for that bloody spell! I've been out here risking my life for *you*."

"I didn't ask you to!"

"I'm trying to make things right, here. I'm trying to *fix* things."

"For who? To make yourself feel better? None of this is for me. You don't need to fix me. I told you I didn't want you to go."

"You said your ankle was hurting! I heard you talking to Ula about those strands of hair you wanted for a charm. How else am I supposed to—" Finley's voice was almost a roar.

Lina cowered, curling in on herself, shoulders hunching, and Finley's words cut off abruptly. His temper was a quick thing. Fast to flare and fade. A brief righteous high followed by the deepest of self-loathing lows. A look of utter devastation crumpled his features. He sucked on a bloody knuckle, breathed out through his nose. A long breath, forcing down the anger that came so easily. His voice cracked. "I just want to make things right with us."

Lina shut her eyes, willing her heart to stop pounding, pounding, pounding. "If you want that, if you truly want that, and you want me to ever forgive you for everything, you'll help me get him back." Guilt churned inside her stomach. A part of her knew she shouldn't throw her forgiveness around like a bribe when, deep down, she also knew he'd never truly meant to hurt her. She knew how he struggled to control his temper, knew how much he hated himself when he lost that fight. She knew that *their* fight and her broken ankle had been half her fault.

But the rest of her was still furious with him and felt that he owed her. If she hadn't been injured, Thomas wouldn't have felt the need to join the revel to help her. And if Finley hadn't been so thickheaded and run off tonight in the first place.

"He was helping me to find you. And if you try and stop me, I'll never speak to you again." Lina soldiered past him, aiming for the line of boats bobbing beside the mossy rocks. Fancy crescent-shaped broom boats with red velvet seats and blankets to guard against the cold. Their curving hulls painted to a shine with black lacquer.

Her heel skidded in the moss and she staggered.

Finley rushed to steady her. "Let's talk about this."

"Oh, like we talked about it when *you* ran off?"

"Most of them are still partying in the square."

"That's why we need to go now. Fewer witches to worry about."

"There's the *queen* to worry about."

Lina reached into Finley's suit pocket, pinching the little sailor's knife he always kept on his person.

"Aye, you're going to fight her with a toothpick."

"You don't have to come." Lina shoved the knife down the front of her dress and into her brassiere, staggering again as she reached the first boat. The wind picked up, and gooseflesh rose on her arms. She clambered aboard, landing hard on a red velvet bench seat amidst a nest of woolen blankets.

Finley cursed, glancing back at the alley, at the city, at safety.

He half fell across her lap as he hauled himself after her. Lina's elbow nearly took out his eye. He let out a yelp as the boat pitched and bobbed out into the current.

7

LINA

THE BROOM BOAT CLEAVED THROUGH black water roiling like a witch's brew. Salt spray stung Lina's cheeks and soaked her dress. She squeezed her gloved hands tight between her thighs. The night was a blanket of cold, growing colder as they sailed farther and farther from the bonfires, from the light and warmth of the city. The Witch Queen's palace loomed ahead, glowing with the flickering light of a flame in the dark. Its wavery reflection stretched out over the waves, which bled white where they broke against the hull.

Finley dropped his chin to his chest. "It might not have been the queen who took him."

"Who else disappears in a puff of smoke? Who else kisses someone on St. Walpurga's Eve wearing someone else's face?"

"He made it out the last time on his own."

"Because he made the last queen fall in love with him," said Lina. "She's dead."

"Maybe he'll make this new one love him too."

In the dark, her brother's wintry gray eyes looked almost black, making Lina think of the queen in the square, reminding her of the false version of Thomas she'd thrilled to dance with and the beautiful girl with eyes like midnight-lit waters and smile sharper than a blade. The image of Thomas kissing her was burned into Lina's vision. She could no longer see the illusion, see the false version of herself kissing him, only the other girl, and Thomas kissing back.

"Hey, now," said Finley, reading her expression. "I didn't mean it."

Lina hugged her arms around herself. "It's not his fault the sacrifices aren't working. You're wrong."

Finley sighed but didn't respond, just leaned heavily into her side. Some of her guilt and fear melted under the familiar weight of his shoulder. He might be a weaseling traitor with an unfair height advantage, but he was still her best friend, still her brother. She wasn't alone out here. He hadn't let her go alone. She wished she could make herself hate him. There was something terribly wrong with her that she couldn't.

"It's my fault Thomas was there." Her voice sounded shaky and small, and she hated that, too. "And yours."

Taut silence stretched over the boat, broken only by the slap and slosh of the waves. They sailed past the rusted spire of a clock tower, over sunken rooftops and the submerged copper-green dome of a bygone cathedral, over the swathes of the old city that had been lost to the dark tide when it had first risen two hundred years ago.

Lina moved to sit at the stern, looking back as they glided by the old bell tower, its crumbling cupola and pointed gray hat spearing up out of the waves. When the witches froze parts of the sea in winter, you could skate out to it, if you were brave enough. Lina had ripped the top layer off her tongue when she'd tried licking the ice-crusted bell.

Sea mist whispered and wound around her body, circling her neck like a noose. She found herself making small bargains. If she blinked three times each time they passed a spire, Thomas would be saved. If she held her breath for a count of eight, if she crossed and recrossed her fingers and toes—

The Water Palace rose before them, but they never seemed to draw any closer. Lina ground her teeth together. She crawled to the prow, rapping her knuckles impatiently on the black lacquered wood at the front of the boat, urging it to keep going, to move faster. The tide was fighting their approach now, as if some part of it knew they had come to steal its prize.

The boat bucked, the curved prow shooting almost vertical as a great wave rushed head-on to meet them.

Finley yelped and cursed. Lina gripped the bench seat for dear life, heart shooting into her throat. Neither of them could swim. To learn was to tempt fate. It was just asking the tide to take you, Ma would say.

The boat slammed back down in a great wash of spray.

Finley spat into the water for luck. Lina spat too. Once. Twice. Three times, just to make sure. She wished she had some saint-blessed salt to feed the waves; the kind the fishermen swore helped calm them. "Why is it taking so long? Why aren't we getting any closer?"

Another wave smashed against the prow. The boat rocked and swerved off course. Lina rapped her knuckles on the starboard edge of the hull. If they approached from a different route, maybe…

"Lina," said Finley.

"Shut up."

The mist writhed as if someone were stirring it with a wooden spoon, thickening until it was almost impossible to see. It stuck to their skin, trailing like damp gray cobwebs. The boat skimmed over more sunken houses, shot past an orange buoy where someone had dropped a crab pot, through a crumbling arch crusted with barnacles. The witches had sunk magic like anchors at the edges of the shallows to keep outsiders from reaching the island, to keep storms and sea monsters at bay, save the single sea serpent the queen kept as a pet. Of course they'd have placed a barrier around the palace, too, but there had to be a weak spot somewhere.

It couldn't end like this.

Hadn't Lina promised to hold on to him? Hadn't she just discovered he liked her? Hadn't she finally worked up the courage to show him she liked him, too?

Violent shivers wracked Lina's body. Her teeth started to chatter as the adrenaline wore off and doubt crept in. Minutes ticked by, maybe hours. She couldn't see the night sky through the mist to know if it was lightening, to know how much time had already been lost.

"Well, we tried," said Finley. "Now let's go back."

Lina didn't even bother to turn and glare at him.

Finley joined her at the prow, a woolen blanket slung over his shoulders. He wrapped another around her gently. Closed her half-frozen fingers around a small rectangular bottle of cobalt-blue glass.

The bottle was hot, even through the fabric of her gloves. Her scalp prickled as her thumb brushed the cork stopper. "Where did you get this?" And then she felt like a fool, because of course he'd gotten it at the revel, another piece of free magic won while playing his violin. "What does it do?"

"It's a squall, I think. A thunderstorm."

Hair pricked on Lina's arms. She felt the phantom patter of raindrops on her skin. Spell bottles weren't labeled, but each gave off an idea, a sense of what magic lurked inside. An electric crackle settled into her bones. There was something dark and destructive about the bottled storm. Anger sealed behind glass.

Finley's voice was soft. "Let's go home, Lina. Please."

"I can't."

"Uncle and everyone will be fretting. This isn't working. You

can see that. They don't want us here. The queen's not going to let us reach her palace. We'll try again tomorrow, maybe. Or the next day. They won't sacrifice him until the full moon. It's part of the magic, part of the ritual. There's the regatta, too, where they'll bring him out so people can say goodbye." Finley's eyes were pleading.

Lina felt herself wavering. Another violent shiver wracked her body. But if she gave up now…

She might lose her nerve. Finley gave her grief sometimes for always rushing into things, but the advantage was that she never had time for second thoughts. Never had a chance to second-guess herself. If you hesitated, if you gave yourself time to think, that was when the fear crept in.

And there *was* fear, a niggling, all-consuming panic that ate at her courage more and more the longer they were out here, the harder the tide fought the boat, the more times they failed to reach the palace. She wasn't the first person to chase after a loved one, and it rarely ended as well as it had for the girl in the song.

It *never* ended as well as it had for the girl in the song.

"You said she took him to make things right. That means they think he broke the magic too, that they blame him too. It was her sister, wasn't it? The last queen, the one who died for him. Even if they wait to sacrifice him on the full moon, what do you think they'll do to him until then?" Lina twisted away from Finley, rapping the prow, urging the boat to change direction, attempting another approach.

Finley didn't reply, but she could feel the anger burning off of him. His body going as stiff and unyielding as brick.

They continued on in the quiet, in the cold, huddled together under the woolen blankets, hearts hammering each time the boat heaved and shuddered, water crashing over the prow, sloshing over the sides. The Witch Queen's palace loomed out of the mist, a dark crown upon the sea, taunting them with its presence. Wicked gray spires and turrets. Slick stone walls rising from the deep, the lowermost levels completely swallowed by the tide. White foam gushed from a row of gaping arches that might once have contained windows, though the glass that had resided there was gone.

No visible entrance. So close and yet so far. They could swim to it, maybe, *if* they could swim.

The sky was growing noticeably lighter, the mist blushing with soft streaks of ballet pink and fiery copper. The crescent-shaped broom boat bobbed in place as if its magic was dissolving with the dark, as if it too was giving up.

A lone fish broke the surface of the water, splashing back down into the depths.

Lina jerked when the first bell tolled. A distant, echoing clang from the city they'd left behind. Caldella's church bells ringing in the rising sun.

Finley scrubbed a hand down his face. "Thomas Lin is not worth this."

Lina's chin shot up. "He *is* worth it." Her voice was crackly

with cold, hoarse from lack of sleep. "I've liked him forever, Finley. I love him." It was a truth that came from somewhere deep inside her. A truth she'd known from the moment she first saw him. It was like Ma and Mama, like Laolao and Grandpa, like all the stories. There were other people sometimes—sure, she wasn't completely naive. But you only had one true love. One love that counted more than all the rest. "He's the only one I feel this way about, the only one I'll *ever* feel this way about."

Finley started to roll his eyes.

Lina waved the bottled storm at him. "Do you remember that time we sailed into a squall because you thought Jeanne's boat was caught in it? If this were you, and you were going after some girl, you'd say this was romantic. *Everyone* would. So don't you dare roll your eyes like it's different because it's me." She put a hand on top of his head for support, clutching the blue bottle in the other. Shrugging the blanket off and ignoring Finley's protests, she rose to her feet.

She faced the palace. She could see the Witch Queen smiling at her over Thomas's shoulder, mocking her, daring her to do something. She could hear those taunting whispered words: *You'll have to hold on to him tightly, then.* The guilty memory of that dance, of hips, of another body pulled flush against her own surfacing all too easily.

Anger and embarrassment hissed and seethed inside Lina.

"I got Thomas into this. I'll get him out. And if she won't let me into her damn palace"—Lina's voice rose, her jaw setting with grim determination—"then I will tear it down." She pulled her arm back and hurled the bottled storm at those hateful gray walls, at that invisible barrier, with all her might.

8

EVA

"WHAT IN HELL WAS *THAT?*"

Eva jolted awake to the shock of Yara's voice, a sharp ringing in her ears, a choked tightness in her throat. The feel of sand and saltwater scraping her lungs, as if she'd spent the last hour drowning instead of dreaming.

"How..." said Yara. There was a sharp crash of porcelain shattering.

Eva sat up, squinting, the scarlet chaise lounge dipping beneath her.

Early-morning sunbeams poured through the Amber Salon's arched windows, light painting falling dust motes in a thousand shimmery specks, glinting off the coral bangles climbing Yara's brown arms.

The other girl was still at the sideboard, where she'd been when Eva had dozed off, mixing enchanted cocktails in fat-bellied teapots and sulking because Eva hadn't kissed the boy Yara had picked for her. Marcin was on the other side of the room, a flame of red hair lolling in an armchair, a long thin cigarette holder dangling from his pale fingers, crackly old maps spilling off his lap and onto the carpet as he planned imaginary mainland conquests.

There were other witches crowding the room, too, in various states of consciousness, still dressed in all their glittery black finery from the revel. Bodies slumped over coffee tables and low chaise lounges or twined together like rope. Other witches were still dancing, hips swaying gently to a record someone had smuggled over from the mainland.

Last night, upon their return, a sense of giddy euphoria had seized the Water Palace. Its amber walls had lit up with a bright honey-gold glow. The air itself was syrup-sweet, scented with jasmine and rose.

It irritated Eva that she hadn't noticed how damp and gloomy her palace had become in the days since her sister had died, in the time since her first sacrifice—a boy with raven-black hair and a dusting of freckles—had failed. A witch's house reflected those who dwelled within it. It was a mirror held up to their souls.

Eva decided her soul must be a very black and twisted thing, because she missed the cold silence, the dark and its merciful shadows.

She stood, head pounding, one stocking foot catching on a discarded feather boa. Her ears wouldn't stop ringing, and the carpet seemed to have come alive and was currently trying to slither out from under her. She stumbled sideways, reaching a hand to the gold wall for support. She hadn't drunk *that* much, only one teapot.

And then she realized it wasn't her. The Water Palace itself was quaking.

"What in—"

A forked tongue of blue lightning struck the tower outside the Amber Salon's windows, burning her vision white. Stone cracked. Sparked. Split, flying through the air. Glass shattered, and someone shrieked. There was a great earsplitting boom of thunder.

A second fork of lightning struck the tower they were in. Eva staggered as the walls shook, dust raining from the ceiling. The chandelier swung perilously from side to side. A candlestick flew off the marble mantel by the record player, bouncing, rolling. Vases splintered, spilling water and moon blossoms over the carpet.

Marcin sprang to his feet, maps and cigarette abandoned. Eva ran to the windows. Wind rattled what glass remained unsplintered, howling, screaming to be let in.

"An attack?" said someone, shrill and high pitched.

"They made it past the anchors! A fleet from Skani?"

"Whoever they are, they won't make it far." Marcin's voice was lethal, a blade scraping bone as it thrust through flesh to pierce the heart. Everyone's heads snapped toward him, eyes aglitter with fear. "And if they've come for our magic they won't get it."

His face was the pale heart of a fire. The Amber Salon darkened at the edges, folding into shadow. Other faces flashed with relief, then hardened into resolve. Witches around the room turned to Marcin for orders, for reassurance.

Not to Eva.

She had the sudden pressing urge to hurt something, someone. "Don't be ridiculous. Skani has no reason to attack us. If it's anyone, it's mainlanders." She kept her voice low. She didn't need to raise it in order to be heard; a queen's voice made its own silence, Natalia had taught her that. A queen never panicked. Even when she had no damn idea what was happening or who was attacking her home.

The hollow in her chest expanded.

She raised a hand, gave a rapid series of orders. No prisoners. No mercy for mainlanders.

Mainlanders who boiled witch bodies down to the bone.

Her sisters dissolved into smoke, twisted into chill salt winds, grasped each other's anxious hands dashing out of the room to gather and hide the witchlings. There were still those who hesitated, too many who whispered and cut glances at Marcin for permission first. Eva pinned each whisper to a face and each face to a name, filing them away to be dealt with later.

If there was a later.

Stay calm. Keep your head.

A boy with silver-dyed hair tumbled out of the press of bodies at her back, blinking and rubbing crusty sleep from his eyes. Jun had a witch's ladder already in hand: skeins of his hair tied around a length of cord, ratty gray gull's feathers and shards of shell and bird bone tethered to seven large knots.

Like Eva, he worked magic the island's way, mixing small pieces of himself with sand and salt and seashells, tying sailor's knots and playing string games like those who had taught them. Although he, like Eva, also mixed in old, half-remembered charms from the places where they'd been born, like Eva's red string, a nod to the red ribbon Natalia had tied to her wrist as a child to ward off wicked spells. Caldella's magic was a tangle of traditions carried here by people who had fled from all across the world.

Jun's arm brushed hers. Eva waited the briefest second, watching his tanned fingers thread a loop, his furrowed forehead press to a pane of window glass in concentration. More witches joined him, ready to banish the storm, ready to bend its wrath to serve their own purposes. Eva forced herself to return to the scarlet chaise lounge. To sit with ankles crossed. A queen took command of the battlefield, devised a strategy; there was no point in lashing out blindly, not knowing where to aim or where to sink your knife. What was her enemy's weakness? Was the city under attack, too? Should she release the sea serpent? Had the attackers already breached the Water Palace's walls?

"Yara."

Yara rushed forward with a tray, a teapot, and three delicate teacups rimmed with sugar. She set the tray on the oval table in front of the chaise lounge. Rain was thrashing the windows, and the Amber Salon grew murky and glacial as unnatural roiling clouds rolled in to engulf the palace. It took every ounce of Eva's self-control not to snap at Jun and the others to hurry, not to rip another red string bracelet from her wrist and seize control of the storm herself.

The walls shivered with each fresh crash of thunder. Wind battered the tower with angry fists.

Yara sat on her right. Marcin on her left. Yara filled the trembling teacups, handing them out on pastel-painted saucers. "Sour cherry liqueur. For clarity. I already added a few of my tears, so you don't have to"—Yara grimaced as Marcin spat into his cup—"do that."

People claimed witches were nightmares, dreams, but Eva felt they were closer to plants; wild magic grew inside of each of them, waiting to be harvested in the strands of their hair, their salt tears, their spit and blood.

She stirred the concoction with the tip of her finger and watched the cherry liquid ripple.

Yara licked a dash of sugar from her teacup's rim.

The rain and wind cut off abruptly, leaving behind a quiet so deafening it seemed to sing.

"That was fast," said Marcin.

"I am just that good," called Jun from the window.

"Shh," shushed Yara.

Clouds continued to shade the salon. Eva shut her eyes and concentrated. Yara and Marcin did the same, all three going perfectly still. When the liquid in all three cups was also still, mirror still, Eva opened her eyes. Three teacups reflected three different skies. Night, day, and dusk. Starry, stormy, clear.

Yara let out an irritated huff. Eva leaned in next to her to peer at Marcin's stormy-skied cup. He had always been able to conjure the clearest visions—Eva told herself it was only because he was older. Thirty-two to her nineteen years. Ancient, practically.

Jun shuffled across the room, peering over their bent heads. "*Children?*"

"Oh." Yara clapped a hand to her mouth. "Oh, that's him."

"You *know* them?" demanded Marcin.

"The boy was my pick at the revel. The one I told you about, that I found for E."

"What's he doing here? How did they *get* here? How did they conjure a storm?" Marcin looked at Eva, a lock of red hair falling across his brow.

But Eva didn't respond. She was too busy watching the *girl* from the revel. The blond whose face she'd worn when she'd stolen Thomas away.

She leaned closer to the image in the teacup. The girl and boy were in another tower, far below the Amber Salon, in one of the lowest levels of the Water Palace, one half swallowed by the sea. Their battered broom boat knocked against the bottom of a wide stone staircase flanked by faceless statues, steep gray steps climbing up and up and up.

They were drenched. And they were arguing. The girl's lips were white and pinched, her shoulders hunched defensively, making her body small. The boy was shouting and waving his fists.

"Islanders," said Jun with so much relief it sounded like a sigh. "Ordinary islanders." A beat passed in silence. "Do you think they've come after Thomas? It's been a long time since anyone tried to save a sacrifice. At the spring regatta, wasn't it? That mother who begged for her son's return. No one's ever breached the palace before though."

"They can't have him." The acid, the *anger* in Marcin's tone startled Eva so much that she almost dropped her teacup. Its contents sloshed from side to side, and the dusky sky it had shown vanished in a flurry of ripples.

"How I am going to enjoy watching that boy drown."

That was what Marcin had said when he'd learned who Eva had chosen as this year's sacrifice, gifting her a genuine smile of his rare and treasured approval.

And it was strange how that enthusiasm, that savage eagerness, had put a damper on her own. Before that moment, all she'd felt was triumph. This was revenge. This was justice. This was what Thomas Lin deserved. This was the boy who had taken Natalia from them.

This was also the boy Natalia had given everything to save.

Eva set her cup on its saucer, memories and unease surging through her veins.

"I want him to live. I want him to be happy. I'm so tired, Eva. They all leave while I remain. I don't know if I can be the one left behind again."

And yet Natalia had been content to leave *her* behind.

Tiny pinpricks of fury danced across Eva's skin. Thomas *was* happy, happy enough with someone else. With this girl stealing through the palace like a rat. How dare he disrespect her sister's memory like that? Was Natalia so easily forgotten? Was she merely a thing to be used and discarded?

And how dare this girl disrespect *her* by coming here? How dare she attack Eva's home?

"You can have the boy," she told Yara.

Yara let out a breath she might have been holding, breaking into a catlike smile that would send any sane creature scurrying fast and far in the opposite direction.

"Mar—"

"I'll check the damage and calm the others. See if anyone was injured. Jun, take Omar and check what state the East Tower is in."

Eva's lips pressed together. *She'd* been about to give that order. There were times when Marcin still treated her like a witchling, acted as if Natalia had made *him* queen.

"And then I'm going to have some fun with our visitors."

Marcin drank the tempest from his teacup and smiled with storm-stained teeth. "If you don't find them first."

Yara immediately pushed off the lounge, hips swishing to a beat only she could hear. She downed the contents of her cup in a single quick gulp. "And you? What are you going to do, E?"

Eva's gaze strayed to the ceiling, where a giant mural in gold leaf depicted figures from two hundred years ago. The very first Witch Queen kneeling on a rock-strewn shore, her long hair streaming out behind her, her face hidden as she tied stones to the ankles of the boy she loved, as the great ravenous waves of the dark tide bore down on them both.

It's a bit morbid, isn't it? Natalia had whispered to her once when they were younger. *Macabre.*

Which was exactly why Eva liked it. She placed her cup and saucer on the table in front of the chaise lounge with a soft clink. "I'll take the girl."

9

L I N A

"WE'RE DEAD. WE ARE *SO* dead. We are *beyond* dead." Finley's voice spiked into hysteria. "They're going to kill us. The queen'll feed us to her sea serpent. She'll sew our lips shut and fill our lungs with saltwater like she does to criminals. Turn our hearts and eyes to stone. Peel our skin off like we're grapes and carve our bones to make bone whistles and—"

"That's mainlanders," said Lina. "The bone whistles."

"I don't care!"

"I told you not to shout!"

Finley stalked ahead, fuming. Even his panic managed to twist itself into fury; his every emotion did. His hands, clenched into white-knuckled fists, swung at his sides.

Lina struggled to keep up, following the ripples her brother left behind, his black boots splashing through puddles that made mirrors on the floor. They'd scaled an endless spiral of stairs to find themselves in an equally endless corridor, its walls and ceiling gilded gold with amber. There were closed doors to their left— dark polished wood, shimmering with shifting glyphs and changing symbols—and to their right soaring windows and a series of balconies stretching out over the sea. Gossamer drapes billowed and snapped in the doorless archways leading onto each one. A bitter breeze carried in the scent of salt and the raucous cry of seagulls.

Guilt knotted Lina's insides.

Why, *why* was every choice she made the wrong one? Why couldn't she ever do anything right? Everything she did only made things worse. She'd been so focused on Finley. She'd tried to protect him and damned Thomas, tried to save Thomas and nearly capsized the crescent boat, almost dooming Finley and herself.

Tears pricked at her eyes, furious and burning.

Don't think. Don't think. Keep moving. Keep going. Find Thomas. Get out of here.

Somehow.

She was limping badly now. Her nose and fingers were numb with cold.

But she was used to pushing herself, used to forcing her body past its limit. She plastered on her dancer face, a determined mask that didn't crack even when an ankle turned, when blisters burst and toenails broke. She might look small and slight, but underneath it all her body and will were iron, shaped by thirteen years of punishing daily practice.

A single drop of water fell from the high vaulted ceiling and struck the crown of her head. It was from the rain, from the storm she'd unleashed, like the puddles speckling the floor.

Or maybe it was always like this. This *was* the Water Palace, after all, a palace the witches had dredged up from the depths of the sea. Damp and cold.

Like she was. The storm had soaked her to the bone. Lina rubbed her hands up and down her arms in vain. She'd stripped her gloves off, left them behind in the crescent-shaped broom boat. The tips of her fingers were pale frozen prunes.

Finley paused, wringing out the hem of his shirt for the hundredth time, unkempt black hair plastered flat to his skull. Save for his cowlick, which stuck up with an air of stubborn defiance. It, too, would not be beaten.

Lina hurried to catch up, free hand digging into her brassiere for the little sailor's knife she'd stolen from him, unsheathing it. They hadn't glimpsed a soul so far. But it was barely past dawn, so maybe everyone in the palace was still in bed, too exhausted and hungover after the revel to have been woken by the thunder.

She hoped. Prayed. Though for that matter…

Did dreams and nightmares sleep?

Music was playing somewhere. A tune she knew. *Hide him, hide him, out of sight. Hold him, hold him, hold on tight.* The melody teasing, lilting and low, muffled and indistinct, like a sailor's chantey heard from underwater.

Lina's heart pounded as she ran through all the battle dances she knew, traditional flings and jigs where you flourished a blade, imitating the use of the weapon in fighting. It wasn't as good as knowing how to fight, but it was certainly better than nothing.

Finley's eyes flicked to her and away as she drew even with him. He opened his mouth, then shut it abruptly.

Footsteps. Percussive. Heels clipping stone.

Lina grasped for the handle of the nearest door, nearly collapsing with relief when it opened. Finley shoved her inside ahead of him. Lina drew the door closed with excruciating slowness so it wouldn't slam and give them away.

They held their breath as the footsteps grew louder and louder. Closer and closer.

Pausing.

Before starting up again, a little faster this time. Fading, finally.

The breath Lina let out blew the bangs off her forehead. Finley cracked an uneasy, relieved grin.

They were in somebody's bedroom. Their tiptoeing, waterlogged steps left damp prints on creamy carpet. Their anxious faces flashed like ghosts in mirrored wall panels, in the glowing amber sunburst stamped on the ceiling and the silver filigree screen standing guard over a merrily crackling hearth.

Lina and Finley rushed past the massive canopy bed to hover around the flames, hands outstretched toward the glorious, glorious heat.

They both kept looking over their shoulders.

The room had an eerie, just-vacated feel, like a still-warm chair. The bedsheets were flung back in a tangle. The air was heady, as if someone spritzed in sweet perfume had just moved through it. Smoke curled from a long, ebony cigarette holder left idling on an ashtray.

A record was spinning on the player in the corner—silently now, save a barely audible crackle.

Lina set the knife down and picked up a half-empty teacup from a tray on the dressing table. Crimson lipstick stained its porcelain rim.

She gulped the contents down. Choked and pounded her chest.

Cherry liqueur?

Oh, thank God.

She reached for the teapot, refilling the cup to the brim, drowning fear and worry with liquid courage. As she often did before a performance, a classmate's secret hip flask passed from dancer to dancer, anxious mouth to anxious mouth. She hadn't had anything to drink since before the revel. Her throat was desert parched.

Finley struggled to keep his voice down. "Hey, don't drink it all." He spied the plate of egg tarts at the same time as she did and lunged.

"Halves!" hissed Lina.

"I think the hell not," said Finley, and crammed one into his mouth. "It's punishment."

Lina cursed, and when he darted close and stole the teapot, too, she kicked him in the shin.

Finley skipped back out of reach, sculling straight from the teapot's spout. But then he relented and gave her the remaining two egg tarts.

Lina ate them, sipping from her cup, savoring the burn in her throat, the warmth starting to curl in her belly. Her eyes skimmed their surroundings. Even in disarray, this bedroom was much tidier than hers. No clothes were spilling out of the wardrobe. The shelves were dusted, strung prettily with bundles of dried seagrass, stacked neat with rows of bottled spells and old jam jars containing tiny, luminous jellyfish.

So this was a witch's bedroom? A little part of her couldn't help thrilling at the thought. The same part that had thrilled when she'd danced with the Witch Queen in disguise at the revel.

Though the islanders lived in peace with the witches, they still lived somewhat separately. The queen and the rest secluded themselves in the palace, coming to shore only for festivals and to sell their magic at the city's markets. And though the islanders might bow and be grateful to the queen for keeping Caldella from sinking, they were not *overly* grateful. There was still dislike and superstition.

There was something so deliciously forbidden about being here.

"It's not like how I imagined," said Finley quietly. His expression was calmer now, pinched by something that might have been wistfulness. Or longing. It brought back memories of when they were little and had played at being witches, watching for pictures in plumes of candle smoke, climbing the slick, crumbling ruins in the sunken harbor and pretending the old bell tower was their Water Palace.

"Why?" said Lina. "Because the room's not full of decapitated heads and all the different faces the queen wears?"

She trailed her fingers over the rouge and mascara pots on the dressing table, over vials of strange perfume and a gold compact shaped like a seashell, eyes lighting up when she spied a blush-pink sugar bowl labeled "Sweet."

It was overflowing with fat black pearls. Each one flawless and shiny as a promise.

Lina couldn't help herself. She shot a glance at Finley in the dressing table mirror—he was frowning at the door they'd come in—then plucked a pearl from the bowl and dropped it into her teacup, snatching a spoon from the tray and stirring as the pearl dissolved. Red cherry liqueur turned an oily midnight black, tiny rainbows dancing across the liquid's surface.

She licked the spoon and downed the entire cup. It tasted like seaweed and licorice, like enchantment. "Finley," she whispered afterward.

His head snapped toward her.

Her voice was not her own. It was warm honey, hypnotic. "Fetch me a coat?" She batted her lashes.

Finley's eyes glazed over.

"A nice one! And some house slippers?"

He'd taken a sumptuous fur coat down from the witch's ash-wood wardrobe and was obediently helping a gleeful Lina into it before the charm's effects faded and his face turned suddenly to thunder.

"It's harmless," she said quickly, the words tripping over one another in their hurry to leave her mouth. "A spell to make your voice sweet. Irresistible. The sopranos at the Conservatoire are always accusing each other of buying them." Usually when they were vying for a solo. Lina grasped a handful of the black pearls, letting them fall through her fingers and clink back into the sugar bowl. "You take one too. If we meet anyone, we can charm them, compel them. It'll help. Don't be mad."

Anger and uncertainty warred on Finley's features, fighting the cloying sweetness of her voice. "Don't be mad," she stressed. "Please." Every muscle in her body had braced instinctively at the first sign of his temper rising. She wondered if it would always be this way between them now. As if it wasn't just her ankle that had broken, but something else, something irreparable.

"I'm not angry," said Finley, sounding slightly dazed, words sticking to his tongue like thick molasses.

Lina pulled the fur coat tight around her shoulders, pushing away the question of whether things would ever go back to normal, growing angry at *herself* now for getting distracted. Thomas was here somewhere, alone and in danger.

"Did you hear that?" Finley cocked his head. "It's that music again, that song."

"It's been playing for ages." And the witch she'd danced with at the revel had claimed they didn't like it. What a liar. "You should borrow a coat, too." Lina shoved her feet into a pair of house slippers and cast about the room for anything else they could take. Like the black pearls, some small charm that might help.

She grabbed Finley's knife from the dressing table, gaze lingering on a handheld fan with a tortoiseshell handle and great plumes of peacock feathers. The kind of fan that not only cooled and veiled your face but could fan away bad luck.

"I swear it's like—" Finley paused, drifting away from her. "It sounds like my playing, doesn't it?"

Lina held back a shiver. Did it? That faint, thin, high, and unearthly wail. For a second, she swore she could feel the vibrato of the strings in her teeth. Feel each note curling around her wrists and ankles, tugging at her, attempting to steer her body like a ship.

Sock-soft footsteps padded behind her. The door creaked open. Clicked shut.

Lina whirled around. "Finley?"

10

LINA

LINA WAS ACROSS THE CARPET in an instant, cursing, knife in hand.

She ripped the door open, burst through, and almost tripped over her own feet in shock.

Where was the corridor? The balconies and their billowing gossamer drapes? The gleaming walls of gold leaf and glowing amber? The door had taken her someplace else. Lina sucked in a breath. The air tasted tight. Metallic. Like licking the striking side of a matchbox. Dragging her tongue across her bottom lip would end in a mouthful of sparks.

She stood in a room at the top of a storm-ravaged tower. Its roof was caved in, its stained-glass windows shattered, a light rain falling sideways through the holes. Candles, books, and ruined furniture littered a sodden, blackened carpet.

Sudden guilt speared Lina. This was their fault. *Her* fault.

When she'd thrown the bottled spell to summon the storm, she'd seen lightning strike the palace towers. She'd wanted to bring the whole hateful place down, but she hadn't thought—

The door slammed shut behind her.

Lina jumped. "Finley?" She grabbed the door handle, dropping the knife to grip it with both hands.

It wouldn't turn, wouldn't open, wouldn't give.

She thumped a fist on the wood. "Finley? *Finley!*"

Someone groaned. Lina whirled, the door handle digging into the small of her back. She snatched the knife off the floor.

A fallen cabinet against the wall opposite shuddered, throwing up a cloud of dust. Someone was struggling to crawl out from under it, fingernails scrabbling at the carpet. Their blond hair was matted with blood from a deep gash on their forehead.

Lina's heart stopped. Oh God. Had they been in here when she'd brought the storm down? Had anyone else?

"Don't move!" Her slippers squelched as she picked her way through the chaos. She felt like she was going to be sick. "Don't move. I'm coming. Hold on."

"What have you done?"

Her head jerked up at the familiar voice, mouth falling open as she squinted at the dusty, blood-streaked face. "Thomas?"

"What have you *done*?" The words were rasping, thick with pain and accusation.

"I didn't—God, I'm so—" Lina's breath hitched. She slipped

on a leather-bound book and her ankle buckled as her weight shifted suddenly. She crumpled, landing hard, the carpet grazing her palms raw. The knife jolted out of her grip.

She gasped, gritted her teeth, and looked up. "I'm okay. Just…hold still…"

There was no one trapped beneath the fallen cabinet. No one struggling to crawl out of the ruins on bleeding hands and knees. The space Thomas had occupied was empty save for dust.

The hair along the back of Lina's neck rose. "Thomas?" It came out as a whisper.

The air shifted. The slightest gust of wind ruffled the pages of another book, muffled the soft patter of raindrops. Lina struggled to her feet. She was suddenly acutely aware of something, someone, moving somewhere behind her. A whisper of silk. A cat-soft step.

She swallowed hard, steeled herself, and slowly turned.

There was no one. Nothing, save a fading twist of night-dark smoke.

Lina willed her heart to stop racing. She reminded herself of the black pearl she'd swallowed minutes before. She layered her words with the same soft, syrupy sweetness she'd used to compel Finley. "I—I know you're there." She bit her cheek, cursing herself for the stutter. "Why don't you come out? Where's my brother? What have you done with him?"

No answer.

Lina licked the parched surface of her lips. "My name is Lina

Kirk. I'm here for Thomas Lin. I'm here to take him back." Her voice grew louder. "But you knew that, or you wouldn't have conjured that…that illusion, that thing." Fresh anger stirred to life in her stomach, burning away her nerves. "You can't pick the same boy twice!"

The smoky air seemed to pulse with half-heard laughter, as if whispering back: *Who says I can't?*

"Why don't you show yourself?" Lina coaxed, stressing each syllable. The pearl's magic had worked to charm Finley. It worked for the sopranos at the Conservatoire. Why wasn't it working now?

She tried forcing the lock on the door with Finley's knife but only succeeded in blunting the blade.

He was going to be very angry about that.

If he was still alive.

If she ever saw him again.

If the Witch Queen hadn't already fed him to her sea serpent.

In a fit of pure frustration Lina hurled the blunt knife across the room. A panicked tear singed a stripe of fire down her cheek, and she swiped furiously at the wetness.

"Are you still there?" she tried again. "I just want to talk. I—"

There was the softest snick, a key turning in a lock. A drawn-out groan of rusted hinges.

Lina jerked back as the door swung wide, but no one stepped through. The open door merely waited, patient, golden glyphs glinting over its polished wood, the shadows beyond beckoning in silent invitation.

Lina hesitated. Where would it take her this time? Unlikely that it led anywhere good…

But what did she have left to lose? They'd already taken Finley, stolen Thomas. Both were in danger because of her. She wasn't helping either by staying put.

She crossed the threshold. And again, the Water Palace's doors, like doors in a dream, took her elsewhere, somewhere she least expected. It was a chapel, hushed as church. Cold and smelling strongly of incense, its holy walls were decorated with human bones, a chain of skulls grinning above the altar.

Still no sign of anyone.

The next archway—double doors this time—opened into a ghostly salon, pale light falling through thin windows, furniture hiding beneath fluttering white sheets. The door after that led into a crypt where soul cages—lobster pots that sea devils placed along the seabed to lure in the souls of drowned sailors—lined every shelf.

Turning, Lina caught the quickest gleam of two pairs of cat-curious eyes. A flash of two little girls in little black dresses—two witchlings with gold swirls painted on the apples of their cheeks.

Their bare feet pattered. Their black skirts swished.

And then they were gone again.

Lina's heart danced a furious beat. Were they playing games with her? Was this all some twisted form of hide-and-seek? Did they think this sort of thing frightened her? Lina was an *islander*, raised on breakfasts of charms and curses.

She flung open the next door. And the next, and the next, and the next.

For hours, days, maybe an eternity, she searched the palace for Finley and Thomas, for glimpses of a girl made from smoke. There was no keeping track of the time. With each step she grew wearier and wearier. She hadn't slept since before the revel, and there was something hypnotic, nightmarish, to this endless sequence of doors. The rooms all melting together. And her ankle—God she was just *so tired* of hurting. Every day she woke up hoping, and it was still there—this weakness, this stubborn ache.

She was so scared the pain would always be there now, that it would never go away. And she knew she was making things worse by not resting, but she couldn't rest, couldn't stop now.

"Is this the best you can do?" she called out. "I'm not giving up."

She forced herself to push through yet another door, feet sinking with shocked splashes into ice-cold water.

Lina hissed, eyes taking a beat to adjust to the sudden darkness, tongue suddenly tangy with the taste of salt and old seaweed. She was standing knee-deep in the shallows of a flooded sea cave rippling with emerald and sapphire light.

Still water stretched in front of her, craggy fissures in the walls where sea-worn statues stood guard. Moss-covered stepping stones jutted like jade teeth, forming a slippery path through the spill.

Uneasiness curled inside Lina's belly, her mind filling instantly with all the stories Finley had terrorized her with when she was small: Tales of the sea serpent the Witch Queen kept as a pet. The giant monster that snacked on the island's criminals and swallowed mainlander ships, that slept in a cave carved into the flooded foundations of the Water Palace.

But it wasn't like the monster ate just anyone, right? It protected the island, the islanders. She wasn't a criminal… Was it a crime to break into the palace?

Lina started to turn back, twisting to find the door she'd just stepped through. But her attention caught.

Held.

Visions and images chased each other across the still surface of the water, flashing like fish scales. On the island, too, puddles sometimes reflected skies different from the one overhead.

Lina caught a glimpse of skirts whipping like whirlwinds, dancers spinning around a crackling bonfire in a field with mountains beyond. A view of the mainland. They celebrated their own grotesque version of St. Walpurga's Eve, burning black-clad effigies and sometimes, when they caught them, real witches.

Next came a shimmery vision of Caldella, the island's winding water roads and pastel rainbow of tightly stacked town houses, its cobbled squares and secret gardens. Longing stole Lina's breath. Her beautiful enchanted city. The setting of her love story. She wanted to focus the image, to pinch and poke at it until it revealed her front door, until it showed her family, her brother, showed her where Finley was now.

Before she could do anything, the image changed.

Now, the water showed the Conservatoire, its mirrored walls and polished floors the rich, intoxicating color of melted caramel. And a figure, Lina herself, twirling, nimble feet dancing over two crossed swords, performing one of the island's traditional dances, one staged on the eve of battle, that foretold triumph or loss depending on whether your feet brushed the naked blades.

Would she dance like that again? Would she be able to? Her cousin, a doctor, had said she would, but there was always this lingering fear at the back of her mind.

Every injury took its toll. Limited her. Even before she'd broken her ankle, it had been stiff from scar tissue; she couldn't count the number of times she'd rolled it. It was her weak ankle. It was going to take so much work to get back to where she'd been. It had already taken so much hard work to get there, and it *was* hard work, not talent, Lina knew. Hard work and always picking herself up again.

She gave herself a shake.

You've been through this before. You'll get through it again. *Stop feeling sorry for yourself.*

Focus.

She searched the cave, the shadows, voice echoing across the water as she shouted, "How long are you going to keep hiding? Aren't you tired of this game?"

The visions the water had shown faded until the surface reflected only her anguished face.

God, she looked awful. Like something broken and brought in with the tide. Hair matted in knots, kohl smudged under eyes red from lack of sleep.

And then that image vanished, too, the water shivering like someone had stroked a single finger down its back.

Lina opened her mouth to speak again.

It went for her legs. A slick tail lashed out, coiled around her calves, and ripped her from the shallows. Black water swallowed the sound of her screams as the serpent dragged her under.

Lina thrashed and fought and clawed and kicked. But its tail coiled tighter, dragged her deeper, and the black water was everywhere. Behind her eyes. Filling her throat, her nose.

She spluttered, choked, inhaled, choked again. Bloated faces and swollen flesh swirled in a great tide of bubbles. The ghosts of drowned boys come to accompany her to a watery grave.

No.

Strength leached out of her limbs.

No.

Her arms chopped weakly at the current. Her kicks were feeble. A numbness was creeping through her fingers and toes, stealing into her chest. Lina's vision flickered. She saw the bubbles drifting up. Her last breath floating to the surface.

No, please.

11

EVA

"YOU HAD THE DOORS LEAD her into the sea cave? You're going to let the serpent *eat* her?"

"I don't remember dictating what you had to do with the boy." Eva paused in front of the salon door, casting a glance back over her shoulder.

"I locked him up."

Boring. But Eva didn't say so aloud.

Yara caught up. She wore a frown of undisguised judgment, and it looked so much like one of Marcin's that Eva made a mental note to cut down the time they spent together.

"The boy you gave me?" Yara pressed the tips of her fingers together. "I think he'd make a much better sacrifice. Much better than Thomas."

Eva raised her eyes to the ceiling. Would Yara never stop sulking, never be content that Eva had chosen for herself this year? "You don't agree with my choice."

"I think you'll find it difficult to make yourself fall in love with Thomas."

Eva shrugged, a miniscule lift of her shoulders. She took gentle hold of the door handle, smiling faintly as she imagined Lina Kirk's terror as she stumbled into the sea serpent's cave, ignoring the irritating fact that Yara was right.

"Finley's very handsome. And he could play his violin for you."

"You think I will fail," said Eva flatly. "You think the sacrifice will fail again this year."

Because it *would*. The spell that would calm the dark tide was burned into Eva, listed like the ingredients in a cookbook or an old grimoire: *Take the life of the one you love and mix with the tears you shed for them. Add three drops of blood, three strands of hair, and feed it all to the sea by the light of May's first full moon.*

The very first Witch Queen, the girl painted on the Amber Salon's ceiling, had given the boy she was to marry to the sea to save the island, and the tide had developed a taste for such sacrifices. It was only satisfied when given someone the queen suffered to lose, someone she cared about.

It hadn't been a problem for the queens who had come before Eva. They'd loved easily, fallen instantly for the boys they chose, keeping them in the Water Palace until the full moon rose so they could grow more and more attached to them.

But Eva wasn't the type who got attached easily to people; at best, they grew on her in spite of her continued efforts to keep them at a distance. She could feed a hundred islander boys to the tide, one each dawn, each dusk, and it wouldn't matter, because *they* did not matter to her.

Thomas Lin did not matter to her, not in the way that counted. She would not suffer to lose him. She would enjoy chaining him to the pillar and so the magic would fail, and the tide would continue to rise.

"Marcin didn't—" Eva paused. Of course Marcin hadn't objected. Not about this. He wanted to see Thomas drown, and he'd already confessed that he wouldn't mind seeing the city sink.

A part of Eva suspected he liked it when she failed. Preferred it. She used to think it sweet, how he always needed to be the one who took care of things for her, how enthusiastic he was, coming to her with advice. He never seemed to know what to do with himself when she actually succeeded at something without his help.

Yara shifted impatiently, the fabric of her dress rustling like shore weeds.

Eva pushed through the door, starting down a flight of rock-hewn steps leading into darkness. A dull and distant thudding filled her ears, the faint beating of a lost heart, the crash of waves heard from underwater. She felt it more as a force than a sound, the dark tide pounding on walls that glimmered wetly with ravenous, insatiable hunger.

How she *despised* it, this curse that plagued their island. A queen should answer to no one. Not the heavens, not the earth, not the sea. Especially not to something so temperamental as the tide.

Natalia had, of course, laughed the first time Eva told her this. "A queen," she'd corrected primly, "answers to everyone. First and foremost to her family, to her fellow witches. And then to her people, her islanders. What is a queen, after all, without her subjects? A queen of nothing and nowhere."

Eva would be a queen of nothing and nowhere if she lost Caldella, if black waves swallowed the city her sister had entrusted her with. But what was one more year? Surely Caldella could survive for one more measly year. They'd lose parts of the island, yes. Edges. Corners. Some of the islanders would lose their houses and businesses. But the *whole city* would not be lost.

Or so she told herself. And it would be worth it to see Thomas Lin chained to the stone pillar in St. Casimir's Square like he was supposed to have been two years ago. Would have been, if Natalia had not taken his place.

She could hear Yara's steps behind her. She could not expect Eva to just let him *go*. She had honored her sister's memory all this time, hadn't touched a hair on his head. But he'd taunted her, waltzing into the revel with Lina Kirk. It was a slap in her sister's face. Had her sacrifice meant so little to him? How dare he forget her and move on when they were all still grieving? He hadn't cared for Natalia at all, had deceived her from the first. He was out there making her sister look a fool.

Eva pressed a thumb to her bottom lip and bit down hard, then quickly lowered her hand, closing her fingers into a fist so she wouldn't see the nails already gnawed to the bloody quick. Death was almost too good for Thomas Lin. She wanted to take from him as he had taken from her. "It would be weak to change my mind now," she told Yara.

"It wouldn't though!"

They'd reached the bottom of the stairs now, where a dark arch waited to lead them into the sea cave. Eva moved through it, and a bloodcurdling scream greeted her, cut short by a great splash and plume of spray as something scaly and sinuous dragged something smaller into the inky water.

Air caught in Eva's lungs. She stepped down onto a mossy stone. Yara grabbed her arm, leaned in close. "It's not weak to listen to a friend, especially when you know I'm right. You'll show everyone you're a queen who will listen, that you're *willing* to listen."

Eva eyed her sidelong, noting the anxious set of Yara's jaw, the tremble of her lush lips, the ragged hem of her long, glittery black dress dipping into the water. The same dress she'd worn to the revel…

There were times when Yara got so fixated on an idea, so obsessed with a painting or potion or spell she was working on that she forgot to sleep, to eat, to change clothes. She burned so brightly sometimes that Eva worried her friend would burn out. Use up all her magic and fade from existence like a dream upon waking. The way all witches eventually did. There was a reason so few of them grew old.

"Marcin said you haven't been sleeping—" Eva started, tugging her arm free, trying not to let impatience bleed into her words. Trying not to picture Lina wrapped in the sea serpent's coils, her short blond hair fanning out around her head, her blush-pink lips slowly turning blue.

But it wouldn't eat her. Not yet. Eva's pet liked to play with its food.

"I'd sleep better if I wasn't worrying the sea was about to gobble up my home. I may as well use a life buoy as a pillow. Don't you want to save it? Natalia's city? Our city? You said you did." Yara's shoulders were rigid.

Eva's gaze tiptoed past her to the rippling black water. Lina's scream still lingered on her skin, giving her gooseflesh.

"She didn't leave it to you," said Yara, "for you to watch it sink."

Eva stiffened.

A cyclone of wind and shadow whipped the water into spray. Eva raised a hand to shield her eyes. When she could see clearly again, Yara had vanished.

She made a half-hearted attempt to go after her.

But then Lina broke the surface.

Gasping. Trembling. Retching up brackish water. Obvious terror on her face as she thrashed her legs and arms. Her fingers brushed the jagged edge of a stepping stone and she clung to it for dear life. The water was deep where she'd surfaced. The stones floated atop the water by magic.

Eva followed the slippery path they carved through the cave, stealing closer, stopping a step away from Lina. "Did you enjoy drowning?"

Lina's head snapped up. Her eyes were wide as saucers.

"I did hear you screaming—"

"Did you enjoy *listening*?" Lina spat into the pool, gaze darting this way and that, searching anxiously for the sea serpent.

"A little," Eva said, smiling.

"I can't swim!" Lina shuddered, and once she started shaking, she couldn't stop. Her teeth chattered—from cold or fury, Eva couldn't tell.

"Evidently not." Eva crouched and dabbled her fingers in the water, stamping down an odd pang of guilt.

But Lina Kirk had brought this on herself by storming into the palace uninvited. She'd brought out this side of Eva, made her sink to childish pettiness and spite. There was something about Lina that got under her skin.

There was something about her that reminded Eva of Natalia.

They didn't look alike. Lina resembled a drowned rat right now, and Natalia had looked like Eva—or, rather, Eva looked like Natalia. But there was something, some undefinable quality that reminded her of her sister. Something that had driven both girls to dive headfirst into danger to protect the boys they loved.

A seething and sick kind of envy snaked through Eva. Because deep down, she knew that although she might indeed love, she was not capable of *such* a love. Not a love like her sister's. It was not within her. She would always, *always* put herself first.

And why was that so terrible?

Envy mixed and melted into a teeth-grinding frustration. She did not understand. *Could* not understand. What made another person's life more precious than your own? Why would you throw yours away? And if the other person truly loved you back, would they even want you to? If that was love…

The scaly edge of a spine cut the surface of the water. Lina kicked frantically, trying to climb onto the stone she had hold of. Words puffed out between each breath. "Where's my brother? What did you do to him? Where's—"

"Your brother? What did you do to my *palace*? To my sisters who were dreaming peacefully in that tower the doors first took you into?"

"I didn't—" Lina let out a shriek as the sea serpent dove beneath her. "I never meant to hurt anyone. I only wanted—"

"And yet by coming here and trying to take Thomas Lin away, you're hurting everyone. All the people on the island. Everyone in Caldella. Your friends. Your family. A sacrifice has to be made to keep the island from sinking, Lina Kirk, but you would steal mine away and damn us all to save some boy you like." Eva straightened.

Color flooded Lina's cheeks. She hauled herself onto the

stone, dripping, panting on hands and knees. "That's not true. You can give someone else to the tide."

"Oh? So you've come here to offer me someone else? Your brother, maybe?"

Lina stilled.

Eva tilted her head to one side. "He came here with you. He joined our revel."

"He only joined because *you* tempted him," snapped Lina. "Because you promise anyone who does the chance to win free magic and undying love and—"

"Of course we do. You *force us* to. It was originally meant as a reward, to honor those brave enough to volunteer themselves. Like the money we pay to the families for the loss of their sons. But every year, more and more of you grow reluctant. More and more of you forget your duty. Now we *have* to bribe and trick and cajole you into joining the revel, even when you all know a sacrifice is necessary. And now you dare to come here, dare to attack *my* home, *my* family, make demands of *me*. One life a year is all that is asked to keep Caldella safe. That is the deal you islanders struck with the first queen."

"It's hardly a deal if you're not holding up your end," Lina shot back. "We gave you a life last year, and the city's still flooding. The dark tide's been rising since *you* were crowned queen. *Your* magic isn't working."

Eva's composure slipped, her hands balling into fists at her sides. She spoke stiffly. Lied. "The sacrifice will work this year."

Lina scoffed. "Forgive me if I won't gamble Thomas's life on that one-off chance." She rose, wobbling, feet slipping on the moss. "Why him? You could have taken anyone. He already… She was your sister, wasn't she? Your blood sister? Our last queen?"

All witches considered themselves family. But it was a rare thing indeed to be related by blood. "And?"

"And? Don't you care? Your sister loved him, gave up her life for him. She sacrificed herself so he could live. And that doesn't mean anything to you?" Lina looked ready to leap the gap between their stones in order to strangle Eva. Her eyes burned with all the fury of an unleashed storm.

Eva tensed.

"*I* care," said Lina. "I was there that day. I watched them chain her to the pillar. It was the first time Ma ever let me watch. I'll never forget it. Your sister wasn't afraid. Not even a little. Not even when the tide rose or when the black water bubbled up through the cobblestones. Not even when the waves came crashing down. She looked so, so…" Admiration softened her voice, lurked in the bittersweet curve of a sudden faint smile.

Now Eva wanted to breach the gap between them and commit violence. "You speak as if you admire her. As if she did something astounding, some wonderful thing. As if she didn't make a foolish, selfish choice. As if she didn't throw her life away for nothing."

"Nothing? She protected the person she loved. You're the one throwing away her life, her sacrifice, by taking Thomas. She—"

"Would you do it?" Eva interrupted.

Water beaded above Lina's top lip, glinted like glitter at the ends of her lashes. Her mouth opened, but no words came out.

Eva leapt on that hesitation. "Would you take his place? Would you trade your life for his knowing exactly how it feels to drown?"

Lina's chest stilled. For a second she didn't breathe, and in that second, Eva knew Lina would give anything, trade everything and anyone, for the promise that she'd never have to go through it again. That she'd never feel the briny scrape of seawater on her tongue, choking her throat, burning her lungs. That she'd never feel so utterly, entirely helpless as she fought and fought and *fought* and failed to reach the surface.

Still, she wanted to hear Lina say it aloud. She wanted to hear her admit Thomas's life was not worth her own. Eva's voice dipped low. "If you say yes to taking his place, I give you my word I'll let him go." She offered the promise like one would a bribe.

Lina made no move to accept it. She stared, and her fingers twitched against her thigh, but that was all.

Eva smiled. "Not such a romantic vision, is it?" The water slapped, the sea serpent swimming a restless circle around them. "You value yourself more than you think. No boy was worth my sister's life. No boy is worth *your* life." The words flooded out of her. It felt so good to say them, these things she'd never had a chance to say to Natalia. "My sister is not some example to live by, some lesson to emulate. She is not a storybook character to idolize and hold up and romanticize. You should be grateful I've taught you this lesson, Lina Kirk. I won't punish you for attacking my palace. I won't feed you to my pet, and I will even let you go home," she added with an air of great magnanimity. "You can return to the rest of your family. Live a long and happy life."

Tell everyone how generous their new queen is.

Icy trickles of water dripped down Lina's neck and past her collarbone. One of the straps of her dress was slipping off her shoulder.

"Aren't you going to say thank you?"

Salty air whispered through the sea cave. Emerald light danced over the craggy walls.

"My brother."

Eva cocked her head.

"What about my brother?"

Eva didn't answer. She couldn't let him go, too. Either he or Lina would have to be punished for their storming the Water Palace, otherwise the islanders would start to get ideas.

Lina probably knew it too. Her gaze had dropped to the water. She gave a tiny, infinitesimal nod at Eva's silence, consoling herself perhaps. Then she looked up.

"I'll do it. I'll take Thomas's place. And my brother's. Let him go, too. It's enough to punish one of us, right? I'll stay with you and be the sacrifice, so please—" Lina bowed her head. "Please. It's my fault they're here. Thomas joined the revel to help me. You've left him alone before. I'll stay with you instead, I promise. Please."

A wild disbelief flared through Eva. It felt like losing, like they'd been playing a game Eva hadn't known they were playing, and she had somehow lost.

Why did people not have the same love for themselves that they did for others?

She stared at that bowed blond head, speechless, the hollow space where her heart used to be aching, expanding into an emptiness that threatened to swallow her. And it hit her: the sacrifice might actually work this year if it was Lina.

It wasn't love she felt. It wasn't even *like*. But Eva would suffer, and for the dark tide, that might just be enough. It would hurt to watch this foolish life snuff out and know that Thomas Lin had somehow managed to steal another girl's soul.

Someone else seemed to take possession of Eva's body then. Her arm reached out and a voice that was no longer her own whispered, "Very well."

If Lina Kirk was so keen to embrace death, then who was she to stop her? And perhaps this was a better kind of victory; she would take someone from Thomas the way he had taken someone from her.

12

LINA

LINA HEARD HER BROTHER BEFORE she saw him, angry shouts carrying around the next bend in the corridor.

She hurried toward the sound, strands of wet hair sticking to her cheeks as she glared at the witch walking next to her. "If you've hurt him—"

"I already told you we haven't. I think someone's gone and told him you're taking Thomas's place?"

Lina's steps faltered. A scratchy wool blanket hung from her shoulders, enveloping her still-damp clothes. Soft pink petals drifted down from the cherry blossom branches painted on the corridor's ceiling, and one brushed the tip of her nose.

Steam curled from the mug she clutched in one hand. A mug of homey, smoky-sweet fish soup that she'd been shocked to recognize as the local fishermen's favorite Caldellan Stew. If she shut her eyes right now, she could almost tell herself a story, make believe none of this was happening, that she was back on the island, standing at the edge of the North Shore amidst town houses painted pastel shades of orange and blue. A briny breeze banging lemon-yellow window shutters. Silvery bells tinkling as a stooped and scarf-muffled figure shuffled out of the tea shop on the corner that sold egg tarts. Black water lapping at the rickety boards of the wooden walkway people had erected so they wouldn't have to wet their shoes.

"I thought you were desperate to see him?"

Lina's eyes snapped open. She met the gaze of the witch who had given her the blanket, who had insisted that she drink the steaming mug of stew. *You're the sacrifice now; we can't have you dying from a chill before the full moon.*

Yara. A girl with a husky, questioning sort of voice. The kind of voice that stayed in your memory long after you'd heard it. She swayed closer, her long, glittery black dress swishing with a sound like waves washing the shore. Her short black hair was set in the most perfect finger waves. She was draped in pearls, and coral bangles climbed her arms, shining bright against her soft brown skin.

She looked like someone the sea had fallen in love with.

The Witch Queen—Eva, Yara had called her—had left Lina with her. Dumped her like an unwanted puppy in the middle of the sunny music room where Yara had been picking out a frustrated tune on a gleaming grand piano. "You told me to take someone else as sacrifice," was all she'd said before she'd stalked off, skirts and shadows licking at her heels, leaving a flabbergasted Yara staring at a dripping-wet Lina and an equally flabbergasted Lina staring after Eva, a small, outraged puddle forming at her feet.

"Where is she going?" she'd burst out. Very possibly Eva did have some other queenly business to attend to, some prearranged appointment to ruin someone else's life, but how dare she just *walk away*? After all that?

"Oh, that's just how she is," Yara had said. "People tire her out. I'm so glad she changed her mind. She probably needs some alone time."

"Right now?"

A scowl tugged at Lina's lips at the memory. But beneath her frustration, her fury, and even her uncertainty, a savage triumph sang. She'd found a way to save Thomas. She'd gotten him into this, and she was getting him out. Getting her brother out. Saving them both. It was the same elation she felt when she nailed a brand-new sequence, that explosion of pride when she received a curt nod from the Conservatoire's strictest instructor.

So much more satisfying than if Ms. Czajkowska had simply gibbered praise.

Yara reached out to steady Lina as she took a limping step forward.

Lina shied away. "I'm perfectly capable of walking by myself. I don't need a nurse. You didn't have to walk with me."

Yara blinked. "But I did? The doors here like to make mischief.

Marcin says we've fed the palace too much magic, and now the doors have minds of their own. They like to spit you out in the strangest of places."

A small, dark head poked round the bend ahead. A little girl like the two Lina had glimpsed before. Another witchling. She looked a lot like Lina's cousin Ivy. The same cheekbones and overly solemn stare, the same blunt black bangs Auntie Van always cut an inch too high above Ivy's eyebrows.

How old was this girl? She must be one of the last witchlings they'd found. It didn't happen often now, but the queen used to test the island's children for magic, as well as those children who came to Caldella as refugees before the borders closed. Lina had never told anyone, not even Finley—and she told her brother most things—but when she was little, she'd secretly wished the queen would come for her.

Come and tell her she was special, that she could do magic, that she had to come and live with her in the Water Palace. She'd left her window open so the queen would have no trouble visiting even in the dead of winter, because some inner voice had sworn that if she didn't, the witch definitely wouldn't come.

Lina cringed. What an absolute fool she'd been.

"I never thought of picking a girl for E," said Yara, half to herself, long fingers fiddling with her skirts, frowning at the witchling, who quickly ducked out of sight as if she'd been caught doing something she shouldn't.

"Does it matter who it is," said Lina bitterly, raising the soup mug to her mouth, "as long as someone is fed to the tide?"

Yara's eyes were wide. "Of course it matters. The queen has to fall in love with the sacrifice."

Lina choked on a swallow of soup. *"What—"*

Ahead, Finley's voice railed like thunder. Lina winced. A half apology, half excuse spilled instantly from her lips. "He's not usually like this."

Yara raised an eyebrow.

Lina's cheeks heated. "He's a good brother. He just gets a bit worked up sometimes. Wouldn't you be worked up, too, if you'd been locked in here since the revel?"

God, but really, did he have to be so *loud*? Why did he have to embarrass her like this? Why did he have to shout so? Why did everyone in her family? Uncle, even Ma, sometimes. She hated how incredibly small their anger always made her feel, how it made her heart pound, how it froze her feet to the floor.

Lina pulled the wool blanket tighter around her shoulders. "You should have let me tell him."

Would it have made much difference, though? And maybe, just maybe, a tiny terrible, vicious, and vengeful part of her enjoyed the fact that he was clearly panicking about her being named the sacrifice. Let *him* have a taste of all she'd felt on St. Walpurga's Eve. Let *him* wallow in fear and guilt. Let *him* explain it all to their family, explain how he hadn't listened to her.

A light breeze twirled the petals falling from the enchanted paintings on the ceiling. Yara lifted a hand to catch one, crushing it between her first finger and thumb. "I've been taking care of him since I caught him. I had him locked in my room. I gave him dry clothes. He was my pick at the revel. He's very handsome."

Lina cut her a sidelong glance, suspicion starting to niggle. It would be just like Finley. Her brother couldn't go anywhere without some girl simpering over him. He might even have encouraged the attention, tried to charm Yara the way they said Thomas had the last queen. What a bloody hypocrite. Lina took an angry slurp of her soup.

"I was trying to convince Eva to choose him," said Yara. "To drown him instead of Thomas."

Lina snorted. "And here I was thinking you might be a good witch."

Yara smiled in a way that made Lina shiver. "There's no such thing."

Unnerved, Lina strode ahead, the mosaics covering the walls flashing as she passed. Countless tiny squares of shell and mother-of-pearl depicted scenes from Caldella's history.

There was Queen Magareta. The tragic queen. The one who had wanted to make peace with the mainlanders, who had built a great bridge between here and Seldoma. There she was, meeting her end in the mainlander king's black cooking pot. And there were the giant sea serpents that had once terrorized these shores—minus the one that had terrorized Lina less than an hour before. In the mosaic, three girls, three *dancers*, were hypnotizing the beasts while three witches worked the magic to send them away.

Lina stole a little courage from the image.

They faced monsters—you faced one. *All you have to face now is your brother.*

She rounded the bend. Faces from nightmares and dreams were peering out of doors up and down the corridor. Witches of all shapes and sizes had gathered around Finley. Lina wasn't tall enough to see over the heads of the two in front of her, blocking her way, so she stared *through* them instead. They were like wraiths, their bodies shaped from thin smoke, fading from existence in that way a dream did upon waking, their features uncertain and waning, soon to be wholly forgotten. Witches whose magic was very nearly used up.

"How can you not see it?" Finley demanded, appealing to the crowd, voice leaping several octaves. Yara hadn't lied. He looked fine. Even finer than usual in the dry clothes she'd given him. Yara had even managed to tame his cowlick with a handful of greasy brilliantine, which, if Lina hadn't already known, would have been proof enough that she could work magic.

"All of us folk on the island know. It's bloody obvious to everyone that it has to be Thomas Lin who dies." Finley shook a fist at the crowd, blood crusting his knuckles black. He'd probably gone and punched another wall. "The sacrifices haven't worked since the last queen let him live. *He's* broken the magic, and that's why the dark tide is rising. You can't cheat the sea of its prey."

Yara brushed Lina's elbow, slipping past and squeezing through the throng. "The magic isn't broken."

Lina pushed after her, taking advantage of the path carved by the other girl, the soup in her mug sloshing, slopping.

Finley glanced at Yara, then twisted and addressed a tall man with hair like flames. "I thought the queen was trying to fix it all. I was glad when she took him. I thought, *I should've had more faith in her.* Doesn't she want to save the island? How does taking my sister help? Do you want our home to sink?"

An electric current ran through the crowd.

The man with hair like flame stopped lazing against the wall and stood straight. Before, he'd watched Finley with a vague air of amusement. Now his expression was serious. "There *could* be some truth in what the lad's saying."

"Marcin!" Yara reached the man's side. Lina was stuck a few strides behind; someone had stepped on the end of her wool blanket, jerking her to a halt.

"You know it's because Eva didn't care enough for the last boy," said Yara.

"I know Eva performed the last sacrifice perfectly. We don't know for certain what caused the magic to fail."

Several heads snapped toward Marcin, including Finley's. Including Lina's.

Strands of red hair shaded his hazel eyes. "I don't like to think it failed because she's heartless, because she can't make herself care. I want to believe Natalia was right to make her queen. And I don't like how she's doubting herself, changing her mind. I don't like how you're influencing her."

"*I'm* the one influencing her?" Yara's tone was incredulous.

"You chose the last boy for her," muttered a woman near Lina.

"You've been sulking since she chose Thomas," said Marcin. "Been nagging at her to choose someone else, choose this lad here instead, since we came back. It's like *you* want to save Thomas. Is that it? You fell for him back then, too? That's why you went and let Natalia die?"

The witches' murmurs crested like a wave, building to a roar. Wild shadows skittered over the walls like angry spiders. A woman with skin a shade darker than Yara's and long silver locks threaded with bells moved to place a supportive hand on Yara's arm. But the rest... Lina came to the sinking realization that they hated Thomas as much as Finley did.

Her brother's voice climbed above the clamor. "Thomas tricked you once, didn't he? It's all anyone on the island talks about: how he seduced the wicked queen, how he turned a foolish girl's heart for his own selfish ends. You're going to let him get away with it? He tricked her. He tricked you. He boasts about it."

"That's not true! He never talks about it." Lina finally managed to push past the witches in front of her, bursting into the little breath of space at the center of the crowd.

The noise in the corridor cut to deathly silence. Every eye was on her now.

A witchling's whisper carried: "*Lee*-nah. The one who brought the storm. It's never been a girl before. I didn't think Eva liked girls. I didn't think she liked anybody."

Lina's cheeks were on fire. She liked the spotlight, liked being the one dancing center stage, but she wasn't sure if she liked this level of attention. She opened her mouth to continue defending Thomas.

But Finley was already surging forward, his winter-gray eyes reflecting her own anguish back at her. He crushed her into a fierce, overprotective hug. "If they've hurt you…"

He was shaking. Her brother was shaking.

Lina's throat closed. "They haven't. I'm fine. I'm *fine*, Finley. Let me—"

His chin pressed sharp into the crown of her head. Her protests were lost and muffled against his chest as he rounded on the witches, voice tight. "You lost your sister because of Thomas Lin. Please, do not let me lose mine."

13

LINA

THEY WERE GIVEN A ROOM in the south tower. Marble-floored and vast, with daybeds and a balcony that faced the city. Intricately carved screens of amber and gold leaf sliced the massive space into sections, spilling a warm honey glow and afternoon sunlight through their carved cutouts in elaborate patterns.

Lina sank onto one of the daybeds, and in seconds, was fast asleep, exhaustion dragging her into her dreams.

She dreamed of Eva, of Thomas, of drowned cities and funeral bells still tolling below the waves, of drowned boys and black water closing over her head, jerking awake in the claws of such a panic she could barely gasp each breath out.

"How long was I…" She sat up. "Where's…"

Finley put a hand on her calf. "Not long." He was perched stiffly on the edge of the daybed. An untouched platter of dishes rested behind him on the mattress. Lina vaguely remembered someone bringing it in, clucking and pressing food at her like her grandmother.

You're the sacrifice now; we can't have you starving to death before the full moon.

Lina's stomach rumbled.

"I can't believe you *offered*—" Finley scraped a hand through his hair, tearing at it. "Are you mad?"

Lina scowled and fell upon the food, spooning crab mash into her mouth, chewing angrily. Already the relief she'd felt at finding her brother was fading into familiar annoyance. Why couldn't she have found Thomas first? The witches had promised they'd bring him here, too. She wished they'd hurry up.

"It was the only way she'd let him go. The only way she'd let *you* go."

"I don't need you to save me." Finley dragged a hand down his face. "I'm getting you out of this."

"I don't need *you* to save *me*."

"Weren't you railing at me at the revel? For risking this?"

"That's different." Lina swapped her spoon for a fork.

"How is it different?" Finley demanded. He picked at the food on the platter. Dumplings filled with salmon. Herring mixed with sour cream, baked in two little clay pots and topped with onion and cheese. Soup served inside a crusty bread bowl. Crepes stuffed with sweet cheese, dusted with a snow of sugar.

Lina skewered half a crepe with her fork.

"You're going to regret eating that."

Probably. Lina's stomach and milky, cheesy foods did not mix. But she only shrugged. "Well, I'm going to die soon anyway, so I have to live to the fullest."

Finley blanched.

Oh, and the crepe was *good*. So good. Mouthwateringly good. Sweetly cheesy. Creamy. So absolutely worth it.

"Oh, and when you get home," Lina continued airily, waving her fork, wanting her brother to taste more of the anguish she'd felt on St. Walpurga's Eve, "I'm going to need you to find my hip flask and hide it. It's in my bag with my dance shoes, rolled in a pair of tights. And I need you to get rid of the strawberry-flavored cigars behind my dresser. There's this loose bit in the skirting where I shoved them. And…" Lina racked her brain for anything else she wouldn't want Mama and Ma to find. She'd never really thought about it before, all the incriminating things she'd leave behind if she died.

There were so very many things.

"My diary. Burn it. And don't you dare read it first. And you have to promise to take care of Ma and—"

Her throat choked a little. What would her mothers think of her coming here? Would they be proud she'd fought to save the person she loved?

Or would they be horrified? They preferred her and Finley to keep their heads down, had raised them both to never make a fuss.

"Lina."

Lina ran her fingers through the strands of her necklace, touching each bead, like Mama praying her rosary. "I need a shower. And some clean clothes. I'm about to say my final goodbyes to you and Thomas, after all."

And wasn't there something so romantic and tragic about that? The thought of saying goodbye to the person you loved, who you would never see again? The prospect filled Lina with a kind of melancholy ache, a guilty thrill. Would Thomas think of her when she was gone? As a guiding light, as the voice living on inside his head, as the girl who had changed him, saved him?

"You take that look off your face," Finley ordered, ruining the moment. "Stop it right now. This is not romantic. You are not the tragic heroine in one of your stupid fantasies. You are not doing this."

Lina scowled. *Of course* she wasn't going to do it. It wasn't as if she wanted to die. It was just hard to turn this part of herself off. She'd always lived in daydreams and stories, spinning what adventure and romance she could from an ordinary life, from boring everyday happenings.

She would take Thomas's place because it was the right thing to do, because she'd dragged him and Finley into this, but... There was still time before the full moon. And Thomas had tricked his way out of this dilemma last time, hadn't he? Lina very much doubted she could get Eva to sacrifice herself, but that didn't mean she couldn't think of something else, some other way out. As soon as Thomas and her brother were safely away from here.

"Look," Finley pleaded, sucking in a deep breath, trying hard to control his temper. Lina couldn't stop herself from tensing. "I know you want to save his life, but think, all right? What about everyone else's? What about our lives? What about our home? What will happen to Ma and Mama and everyone when Caldella sinks? I told you, the magic won't work if it's anyone else. The sacrifice has to be him."

Lina bit down on her fork. "The witches don't think that."

Back in the corridor, Yara had said last year's sacrifice failed because Eva hadn't cared enough for the last boy. She'd said something similar when they'd been walking together, too. Lina had been so distracted by Finley she'd almost forgotten.

The queen has to fall in love with the sacrifice.

Lina shifted, suddenly uncomfortable.

Well, *that* couldn't possibly be true either. *That* was even more impossible to believe than Finley's stupid theory.

There was a portrait of the Witch Queen hanging on the wall directly above the daybed. Lina's gaze strayed unwillingly toward it; Eva's painted scowl mirrored her own, only the expression suited her better. It fitted with her dark features and sullen kind of elegance. Half-threatening, half-beautiful.

Such an irritating face.

"Some think I'm right. Like that witch with the red hair."

One of Finley's legs jiggled the daybed, making the plates on the platter rattle. "You can't have both. You can't have Thomas *and* the island. You really don't care what happens to anyone else?"

"*You* only started to care about it all because Auntie Iris lost her house and your stupid best violin was in it when it flooded. You didn't care until you started listening to all those delusional rumors about Thomas, hating him just because Ivy told you *I* liked him."

The tips of Finley's ears burned red. His fists clenched.

Lina bit her lip, heart hammering.

The air grew taut.

And once again, they were dangerously close to that moment on the steps of St. Dominic's when they'd fought and Lina's ankle had broken. It seemed that no matter how far they traveled from it, how many days and hours passed, they always somehow circled back to the moment that had split the world into before and after.

He'd scared her. Her brother had scared her. And she knew he hadn't meant to, knew she'd been the one to start the argument, but the memory stayed like scar tissue, thick and unyielding, the body's way of protecting itself. A permanent reminder that while some things healed, they also left a mark. She would always have to push past this.

Finley's eyes dipped from her face to her ankle. "If you're doing this to punish me—"

"This isn't *about* you. I'm not doing it to punish you. And that, it wasn't your fault." Which was only half-true, but his pity, his guilt, was suffocating. A hundred times worse than his anger. Lina couldn't stand it.

It occurred to her briefly that if she did die, he wouldn't have to be so obsessed with putting things right anymore, wouldn't have to feel guilty every time he looked at her. And then *she* wouldn't feel guilty for making him feel guilty for something that was his fault.

She let out a breath. "Stop looking at me like you broke me. I am not that weak. And I have a plan to get out of this. You and Thomas return to the island—"

"You can't think I'd leave you," Finley cut in.

"—and I stay here to await the full moon," Lina continued, talking over him. "Letting them all think I'm going along with it. Letting them think it's all settled. But there's the regatta. It'll be held soon, won't it?"

The spring regatta always took place soon after the revel. If this were any other year, Lina would already be busy preparing; helping Finley decorate his broom boat with their cousins, weaving wreaths of white lilies with all the aunties to set upon the waves, daydreaming about how many falling stars she would catch at sunset and how many sticky toffee apples she could eat before she made herself sick. The festivities were as large and magical as those held on St. Walpurga's Eve.

"Hundreds of boats will be out in the sunken harbor," she

continued. "Thousands of people watching the races and laying wreaths on the water, *including* the witches. I'll be with the queen—the races are held in the sacrifice's honor—and with all the distractions, I'll slip away. You and Thomas just need to get a broom boat right up close to her ship so I can climb down when it gets dark. Then he and I can sail away together."

Just like in her daydreams.

"Oh, aye," said Finley, "and where will you two idiots go?"

Lina hadn't thought that far ahead. And she didn't know Thomas well enough to know where he would want to go. She didn't even really know where he lived on the island. Did he have family? He'd said that the last time he'd been taken, he'd had no one to save him.

Finley's brow was still furrowed, but at least his fists unclenched. "The queen'll come after you."

"She'll be too busy, won't she? Finding someone else to sacrifice."

Someone else to chain to the pillar in St. Casimir's Square.

Someone else to feed to the waves.

Lina swallowed suddenly, an echo of saltwater choking her throat.

It had never bothered her before, the idea of the sacrifice, and maybe that was horrible, that it *hadn't* bothered her so long as it wasn't her brother or Thomas that it was happening to. Someone *she* cared about.

Finley shifted, as if he were troubled by the same thought. "We'll go to Uncle," he said finally. "We'll find somewhere to hide you."

"And Thomas."

Finley didn't reply.

"And Thomas," Lina repeated louder.

Finley gave a noncommittal grunt, lunging in to steal the last salmon dumpling and cramming it into his mouth. "I don't like leaving you. What do you think they'll say if I leave you? Auntie Van. Laolao."

Lina wanted to roll her eyes. She was pretty sure they wouldn't say anything. The whole family spoiled him rotten. Finley got away with everything because he was the boy. The only nephew. The precious first grandson. He'd even been named after their grandmother's cheery, blue-eyed husband. All he had to do was duck his head and mumble, "I'm sorry, Laolao," and she'd melt and thumb his chin with her wrinkled, crooked fingers.

"Uncle'll have my head. I don't like it. I'll stay, too."

"You don't have to! Everyone will be worried. You have to let them know we're okay. You have to get them to bring a boat."

"Lin can take the message. I'll make sure he—" Finley made a shushing gesture as across the room a door swung wide.

Lina was on her feet, heart thundering. It was Yara, and new faces alongside her, but most importantly, a hesitant figure lit by the amber lanterns in the passage beyond. The boy she'd dragged into this, the boy she was here to save. Thomas.

14

LINA

FOUR DAYS PASSED IN QUICK succession. In the end, Finley dug his heels in and remained at the Water Palace. Thomas returned to the island alone, tasked with taking the news to the Kirk family. Lina crossed her fingers that they wouldn't be too angry with him. And she crossed them again, praying that they would listen to the plan he proposed.

They would help her, wouldn't they? They would sail a broom boat close enough to the Witch Queen's ship so that in the dark chaos of the regatta, she and Finley could climb down and escape.

Thinking about it, though, she realized her family had always gone along with the sacrifice, no matter who was chosen, just like everyone else. Her family kept their heads down, didn't make trouble. It's nothing to do with us, Uncle would say.

But surely it was different now that it was her?

Lina could tell Finley was fretting, too, but as always, he hid his anxiety beneath a thick layer of anger and jokes. It leaked out, though, a muscle twitching in his jaw as the days ticked by, new shadows beneath his eyes that were especially obvious now on the evening of the regatta.

The islanders had decorated the city for death.

Bouquets of white mourning ribbons fluttered from every chimney, every window, every wrist. From the red-and-white-striped mooring posts lining the winding water roads, from the crumbling cupolas and rusted weather vanes jutting from the waves in the crescent-curved harbor. Hundreds of festooned broom boats propelled by magic glided in and out of the barnacle-crusted ruins, sailing over the sunken skeleton of the old city, carrying children grasping sticky toffee apples and paper cones of flickering candles. Uncles snacked on pickled gherkins wrapped in strips of salt herring, on sea snails and cold slivers of sugared melon, while aunties reached down, setting wreaths of bone-white lilies afloat upon the black water like freshly fallen snow.

Sunset gilded the petals of each flower. The sky blazed crimson and gold. The cold deepened as the last smoldering light leeched out of the day. But no one was leaving; the islanders would continue to bicker over who should have won the final race and who would surely win it next year. They would laugh and pinch one other to stay awake as they stood vigil in their broom boats, on their balconies, until dawn.

The spring regatta was a funeral watch with all the feel of a night carnival.

There was dancing, of course. Music. Loud and drunken singing. It wasn't a party in Caldella without it. Eva's ship had dropped anchor in the very center of the action, in the middle of the harbor by the remains of the old bell tower. Night-black sails billowed from its masts, snapping in a salt breeze sugared by the scent of candle wax, toffee, and flowers.

Drums were pounding, pipes wailing. Strings played a song Lina was really, really starting to hate.

The Witch Queen comes on wings of night.
The Witch Queen has your heart's delight.
She'll take your lover for her own.
She'll turn his heart and eyes to stone.

It was like hearing a song from one of her old dance numbers, a jolting rush of panicked adrenaline, mind and body flashing back to endless, hellish hours of practice and nerves.

There were some songs Lina never, ever wanted to hear again.

She was trying to avoid looking at where the instructors from the Conservatoire had set up the school's performance pontoon, a mini stage floating upon the water. Dancers were already twirling in circles across the wooden boards with hoops and brightly colored streamers and flashing swords.

Some students were even dancing directly on the water in the glittery shoes the witches had charmed for them, which let them walk upon the sea as if it were solid. Their steps skimmed feather-light across the surface like skipped stones. Everyone was bewitched by the same wild beat that had Lina twirling across the deck with Eva—because of course the queen's sacrifice had to partner with the queen. Witches spun around them both in dark swirls of wicked laughter.

The scene took Lina back to the first time they'd danced, on St. Walpurga's Eve by the light of the thirteen bonfires, Eva in disguise. The dark thrill of being pulled flush against another body. Lips brushing the curve of her ear as words were whispered tauntingly. Lina's cheeks heated at the memory.

As they did now, Eva leaned in close to whisper: "I'm a better dancer than him, aren't I?"

Lina glared up at her as they whipped past a group of witches stomping their feet, smiling encouragingly from the sidelines, looking disturbingly like Lina's aunties when they were trying to match one of her cousins with some nice boy they'd found.

Eva *was* a better dancer than Thomas, but Lina wasn't about to admit it out loud. The way they moved together, like their bodies *knew* each other, like they'd already danced these steps in another life, made Lina hate herself just a little. Her traitorous dancer's heart recognized Eva's skill, and her even more traitorous body enjoyed the sensation far too much.

Sweaty palm pressed to sweaty palm, eyes seeing only each other. Lina turned fast, faster, just to see if Eva could keep up. Her blood sang with a strange exhilaration, each step matched like it was a challenge, both of them breathing hard.

They were a study in contrasts, whirling across deck. Eva, dangerous and elegant, in a tailored suit with her crimson lips and knife-sharp smile. Lina in a flaring dress of palest blue, her hair a short blond halo. She had on a little scarf, too, a silvery thing choking her neck.

"Doesn't it bother you," said Eva, "that Thomas didn't even protest? That he just up and left you here to die? You would think, really, that if he truly cared for you, *he'd* insist on being the sacrifice. But no. He was so relieved, just like he was with my sister."

Lina could feel the other girl's eyes on her as she turned under her arm, impossibly dark and intense. Waiting for a reaction. Hoping for one. Her necklace of blood-coral beads clicked against her breast. Her stomach gave a guilty swoop as Eva spun her out, then twirled her back into a tight embrace.

The witch was a head taller, and she leaned in again to continue whispering: "He did beg me to take someone else. I did enjoy that part. Although it would've gone down better if he'd done it on his knees. He told me he knew of other boys I could take, gave me their names, but he never offered himself. Not even once."

Something in Lina's chest gave the tiniest twinge.

"At least your brother insisted on staying with you," finished Eva with what sounded like grudging respect, her gaze skipping across the deck to where Finley was *supposed* to be on the lookout for Uncle's broom boat but was instead flirting with Yara.

"He's not the perfect brother you think he is," Lina snapped, causing Eva to raise an eyebrow. Guilt pricked immediately at Lina's conscience. But honestly, why couldn't her brother have returned to the island with Thomas?

Eva's arms tightened on Lina's waist. She was still watching her closely.

Lina's heart jumped in an uneven beat. "I need a rest. I shouldn't even *be* dancing. My ankle… I broke my ankle recently and I can't put too much weight on it." She tore away abruptly, dodging the other twirling bodies, the spell of the dance broken, her embarrassment immediate and intense. It wasn't a complete lie, anyway. Her ankle was protesting. It was so frustrating. She had this constant dread lurking in the back of her mind now, never knowing how long or how well her body was going to hold up.

Lina found a spot at the railing, shifted her weight to her strong leg, and tried to calm the panicked fluttering in her chest.

If Eva was insulted by her sudden exit—she did look strangely bereft, a lone silhouette stranded in a sea of dancing couples—she refused to show it. And Lina reminded herself that she didn't care, anyway.

She followed the swing of the other girl's hips as she, too, moved away from the other dancers. The lines of her suit were so sharp she could have been a character cut from a shadow play.

Orange sparks flared as Yara joined Eva. A graceful flick of her wrist and a snap of brown fingers conjured a flame pinched between forefinger and thumb. Eva put a cigarette to her lips and leaned in, looking up through her long black lashes as Yara lit the end.

There was something strangely intimate about the scene that made a fresh flush start to creep up Lina's neck.

Eva glanced back over one shoulder, catching her watching.

The heat hit Lina's cheeks, and she felt suddenly ashamed, exposed and guilty, and not exactly sure why. She turned away quickly, twisting a hand in the rigging and leaning out over the rail.

Wind whipped her cheeks, her scarf, and she squinted into the fading light, searching the broom boats for familiar faces. She caught glances of shock but also relief and admiration, both a thousand times better than the infuriating pity she'd grown used to since she'd injured her ankle.

What did they think, the girls from her class? Her friends and neighbors? Everyone she knew? Had they gasped when the Witch Queen announced her name? Did they think her a fool for taking Thomas's place? Did they think it brave?

She hadn't talked to any of the girls from her class for ages, had actively avoided them even before the revel, because she couldn't bear to sit around and listen to everything she was missing out on whilst injured.

Splashes drew her eyes to a child leaning precariously out of a boat bobbing nearby, sticky toffee ringing their mouth. A man quickly pulled the child back. The little thing couldn't be more than five or six. *She* hadn't been more than five or six the first time she'd attended the regatta. The mainlanders said it was grotesque, what the islanders did here every year, that they were savages for celebrating the sacrifice of their children. But the mainlanders boiled their witches down to the bone, so it wasn't as if they had a right to say anything...

Gooseflesh riddled Lina's skin.

It *was* a little grotesque, though, really. All of this. Tonight. The island wasn't just celebrating someone's courage and sacrifice. It was celebrating murder. Glorifying death.

Why did they all go along with it? *Was* one life truly worth trading to keep thousands safe?

She didn't want to think about it.

She stared at the faint shape of her shadow on the water, tapping the wood three times to banish the thoughts. Then she leaned out even farther, searching anxiously for Uncle's broom boat, for Thomas. Four days now since he'd been let go.

But even now, he might be sailing closer like they'd planned, scaling up the side of the ship. A second shadow joined hers on the water, and Lina's heart stuttered as she half imagined...

Her hopeful glance melted into a scowl when she raised her head and saw black hair instead of blond.

"He won't come," said Eva, slinking up beside her, standing

so close she could feel the heat radiating off the other girl's arm. "If that's why you keep looking out. He's much too cowardly to change his mind and stage a last-minute rescue."

Uneasiness twisted Lina's insides. She and Finley were relying on him. Thomas would come. Wouldn't he? And her family, too. Where were they? Why hadn't she seen their boats? Very soon it would be true dark, and the witches would pluck the stars as they appeared, one by one, dropping them glittering into the water to join the wreaths, raking their hungry fingers through the sky until the night was starless.

Maybe they were just waiting for that darkness?

"I don't understand why you even like him," said Eva.

Irritation and exasperation seared through Lina like flame. As if always hearing it from Finley weren't tiresome enough. "Why, are you jealous?"

The queen has to fall in love with the sacrifice.

Lina quickly banished that thought, too. "I'm going to like him even more if you all keep trying to make me hate him."

"*That's* the reason you like him?" said Eva, supremely unimpressed.

"What? No, that's, it's…" How did you even *explain* liking someone? How did you explain liking someone to a witch who didn't have a heart?

"He piggybacked me home." That was how it had started. "When I turned my ankle on a slippery rock." It sounded so inadequate, really, when said out loud. But how could you capture in mere words the thrill of having the famous, mysterious Thomas Lin kneel down in front of you and offer to carry you home in front of the whole school?

All those slack jaws and sour lips. Pure envy on every student's face.

Resting against Thomas Lin's broad back. Breathing in the surprisingly fruity scent of his shampoo. This older boy who, even before he'd escaped the last Witch Queen's clutches, had been admired as the most talented singer at the Conservatoire.

"Let me guess," Eva said when Lina paused. "He played the tragic victim for you. Acted all scarred and sad and lonesome? So you felt you just had to mend his broken heart, had to save him?"

"I *have* saved him," Lina retorted with no little triumph. "From you." Now all she had to do was save herself, too, vanish under cover of darkness. Because that was how it worked. The boy and the good girl always ended up escaping together.

And the wicked witch always ended up alone.

"He makes me feel," she added, "like I'm…like I'm someone more, someone special."

Eva looked at her for a long, long moment.

The heat was back in Lina's cheeks. "Haven't you ever wanted that, someone to tell you you're special?"

"Why would I need someone to tell me what I already know?"

Lina scowled and looked away, hands fisting in her skirt.

Embarrassed from sharing something so private. Was it such a bad thing to want? It was useless talking to Eva. She should try shoving her overboard, use *that* as her distraction to slip away.

And then she saw it.

Amongst the hundreds of boats anchored in the sunken harbor, one painted a familiar blue, another red and gold. The first crewed by a squad of grim-faced aunties. The second steered by several cousins. And there were Laolao and Uncle in a *third* boat headed this way, struggling to sail through the crowd.

Suddenly, Lina wanted very much to crawl under something and hide.

Oh God. She was dead. She was *so* dead. She was going to be in so much trouble for all of this. Why hadn't she thought of that earlier?

Even drowning at the hands of the Witch Queen seemed suddenly to pale in comparison to the punishments her family would dole out when they got hold of her. Laolao might even bring out her leather slipper. *The* leather slipper. Lina had never seen the legendary weapon in action, but Ma and the aunties all told stories about it.

She could already hear the scoldings: *What kind of child are you? Why do you have to embarrass us?*

Lina's stomach plummeted, and then plummeted further, because the longer she stared at her family's boats, the more it became clear that Thomas was not there. Not with any of them. He was not in any of the boats nearby, either.

Her distress must have been obvious, because Eva leaned out, too, trying to follow the line of her sight.

Lina quickly grabbed hold of her hand. "Dance? Again? Or, the stars are about to come out. Why don't you draw some down for us?" She pulled determinedly, dragging Eva away from the rail before she could spy the boats and guess what Lina had planned.

They both staggered as the ship rocked. Eva threw a hand out to grasp the ratlines, both of them pivoting quickly as a thousand terrified cries chorused over the water.

15

LINA

A GREAT SHADOW SNAKED OUT from under the Witch Queen's ship, barely visible in the dusky water, twining sinuously through the sunken ruins, diving beneath hulls and keels and rudders. The motion raised lily-crested waves, spinning broom boats, sending them crashing against each other with brutal crunches.

Cries pitched into shrieks as a massive tail cut the surface, a plume of crystal spray and a flash of gray scales erupting before the sea serpent plunged deeper, disappearing into the shallows, stirring up centuries of silt. The air reeked with the sudden stench of brine and rotted fish. Of drowned things, dead things, things that had been under the water too long.

There was a high-pitched squeal from a witchling playing on deck. A deep "Oh, hell" from Finley and a husky cackle from Yara.

Lina might almost have laughed, too, a little hysterically, if her heart hadn't been in her throat at the look of horror on her brother's face. *Weren't you the one who used to try and scare me with stories about it?*

Finley was by the bowsprit, waving at someone in the harbor. Uncle? A cousin? His shouted words garbled under the frantic rush of blood in her ears, but Lina was pretty sure it all amounted to something like: *Don't come! Don't come! Look, there's a giant snake!*

She didn't realize how hard she was squeezing Eva's hand, didn't realize she was still holding it, until Eva said, "You don't have to be afraid."

Lina glanced down at their joined hands. So did two other witches standing close by. Marcin, who narrowed his eyes, and a taller figure with muscles to rival Ma's, Omar, who gave Eva a knowing look.

Lina immediately tried to drop Eva's hand, but now Eva was the one holding fast.

"Are you sure this is wise, Eva?" Marcin asked, voice tight. "If you can't control it…"

Seagulls wheeled overhead, cawing, following the serpent's progress.

"I thought Lina would like to pet it." Eva's smile was laced with malice. "I let it out in your honor. And also because I know how it terrifies Thomas. I can just imagine him cowering somewhere out there, all pathetic. I send him nightmares sometimes about it eating him alive, slowly."

"So you *did* think he'd come?" Lina felt a small flicker

of hope. Only she hadn't seen him out there. She picked at her brassiere through her dress. She didn't need to wear one given how flat-chested she was, but it was a useful place to store things. Like Finley's knife, which the witches had returned. She felt better knowing it was there, especially now.

"There's that old story," said Eva, ignoring the question, "about the serpents and the dancers who tamed them. It likes music. It likes you. Didn't you see how playful it was with you in the sea cave?"

"It tried to *eat* me."

"It does that."

Lina finally managed to rip her hand free, stumbling back a step. More than a step, as the whole ship gave a sudden sickening lurch. The masts groaned, and a wave slapped the port side, cresting and spitting spray over the rail, soaking the deck, soaking Eva, who let out a shocked hissed breath. Lina would have laughed if the ship hadn't rocked again so violently that she careened sideways, slamming into the foremast. Pain exploded in a white-hot flare as her temple connected with the wood. She dropped to her knees, clutching her head as she blinked back tears.

Another shudder racked the ship, followed by shrieks from a group of witches carousing at the stern.

"Eva?" someone called loudly, uneasily.

Lina grasped the mast, hauling herself upright. Heart hammering. Vision dark, or was that just the sky?

All the light had winked out of the world. A shadow masked the dying sun, and a wave of heat washed over her.

A drop of water struck the nape of her neck. She swallowed as she looked up.

An eye larger than her torso stared her down, fully black, covered in a viscous film that cast tiny rainbows over its pupil like oil on water. Slit nostrils flared. A sinuous body coiled out of the waves, thick as two trees, covered in crusted gray scales draped with necklaces of rotting seaweed and braided hair. Its flat triangular head whipped sideways. The seagulls that had been circling the ship vanished in a trail of feathers and crimson saliva.

A scream died in Lina's throat.

She hadn't seen it clearly in the sea cave. It was so, so—

Movement to her right. Eva edging closer to the rail, cooing softly, soothingly. One hand stretched out.

The serpent reared back, snapping at the empty air above its head, clearly agitated, strings of red spittle dripping from its mouth.

A hand landed on Lina's shoulder, and she jumped, letting out a cry. Finley and Yara had stolen up behind her. The serpent swiveled, staring down at her. Had it recognized the sound of her voice?

"Eva, if you can't control it," Marcin repeated, louder this time.

"Remain calm," Eva ordered tightly. "Lina, stay where you are."

Lina couldn't have moved if she'd wanted to. Her feet were rooted to the deck with those monstrous oil-slick eyes locked on her. But she chanced a glance sideways as soft music reached her ears.

Eva was leaning back over the rail, singing softly. She had a surprisingly strong voice.

The serpent swayed, its dark gaze still fixed on Lina.

Lina held a breath, then released it as the monster swayed again, scales glistening. As if it were charmed by Eva's singing, as if it were…trying to *dance*.

It likes music.

A measure of tension leeched out of the air. Fear turned briefly to wonder. Somewhere behind Lina, a witchling giggled nervously and clapped. The serpent's jaw gaped and it swayed closer still, its body smacking against the hull, rocking the ship as its head whipped down toward Eva.

"Eva, get back!"

Heat seared Lina's cheek as Marcin hurled a flaming bottled spell at the monster to ward it off. Lina staggered, heard Yara scream. Her nose filled with the acrid scent of burning hair.

The serpent recoiled. Hissed. And snapped its jaws straight for Lina.

Lina threw herself to the deck. Finley knocked Yara aside, shoving her out of harm's way.

More flame flew past, and the foresail caught fire. The serpent veered, keening, oily blood gushing from seared flesh. Marcin was shouting at Eva to control it.

It smashed its head into the deck, against the hull.

The impact shook Lina's bones and rattled her teeth. She rolled as the monster's shadow loomed over her.

The ship pitched. A gray tail lashed around the foremast, snapping it in two with a thunderous *crack*.

A section of the rigging dropped free, whistling past Lina's head. Finley cried out as a double block struck him in the center of his chest. Time slowed. Everything moved in slow motion as Lina fought her way to her hands and knees, to her feet, as he pitched backward, over the rail.

She caught his wrist.

Felt the weight and pull before it lessened. Cold fingers sliding through hers, torn from her grip. There was terror in her brother's eyes as he slipped beneath the churning water and vanished.

16

E V A

EVA THREW HER ARMS AROUND Lina's waist, hauling her back, keeping her from plunging over the rail and following her brother overboard.

Lina thrashed and shrieked, flinging herself forward, hand still outstretched, fingers still grasping, clutching air. "Finley!"

"Stop! You can't help him, it's too late."

Lina twisted, the crown of her head smacking the underside of Eva's chin, the impact jarring through her skull in a brutal flash of red. Eva stumbled, hip knocking the ship's boom, vision exploding into shards of fractured light.

Too late.

Just like she had been too late to save Natalia. She knew that yawning emptiness, that absolute refusal to accept that the person you loved was gone, had been ripped right out of your arms.

And nothing you do will ever bring them back.

Fury sang through Eva. She kept her grip vise-tight on Lina's waist. Her sea serpent was vicious when it was angry. And Marcin had made it very angry, throwing fire, making it strike out at Lina. Eva could still taste the magic on the air.

Shouts shivered the salt breeze. The water was roiling, frothing, foaming. But no sign of boy or serpent. Her pet had disappeared below the surface.

Violent sobs racked Lina's body, traveling through her to Eva. "*No. No, no, no no no.*"

Would they find parts of Lina's brother washed up days later? A torso. An arm. A leg. Flesh pale and bloated. Blue. Tangled with seaweed. Nibbled by crabs.

A life ring whistled past Eva's ear.

Finley Kirk broke through the surface with a gasp.

So did the serpent.

It shot up from the depths, water flinging from its scaly coils, from its wicked triangular head, fangs bared. A whip-thin tongue flicked out.

What a beautiful thing her monster was.

In Eva's arms, Lina went deathly still. Eva's grip slackened. The ship creaked and groaned, then seemed to hold its breath. The whole world held its breath as the boy flailed hopelessly for the life ring, as the serpent's jaws gaped wide, wider, saliva dripping from serrated teeth.

The moment was shattered by a great splash and a crescendo

of throat-scraping screams. An elderly man had leapt from a red-and-gold broom boat to help and was floundering in the water.

Why in hell had he jumped in if he couldn't swim?

Lina tore free of Eva's embrace, staggering forward, reaching down the front of her dress and drawing out a small knife. She was shouting. No, *singing*.

Loudly. And badly. Voice shaky and painfully off tune. Eva wanted to clap her hands over her ears. Had Lina Kirk gone mad? Did she have a death wish? Did she think her singing so terrible it could send even monsters away?

Did she think she could fight the serpent with her tiny knife?

Eva ripped a bracelet of black hair and red string from her wrist, ready to tie into knots, to trade parts of herself for the power to reshape the world.

Lina waved her arms, raised the knife, and slashed a deep gash across her forearm.

Eva froze, string floating free of her fingers, glowing red like sunset, like the lit end of a cigarette just before it went out.

Blood oozed from the line of the cut Lina had carved, dripped onto the wooden deck in thick crimson splashes.

Something in Eva recoiled. The serpent swiveled toward Lina, slit nostrils flaring.

Lina rose onto one foot, staring straight ahead at the serpent, at the sea. Eye to eye with Eva's monster. Her expression smoothing into something that was almost peaceful. She placed both fists on her waist and bowed deeply. Then her hand swept out, palm rotating to face the sky, pinching the air, sweeping up above her head. She sprang onto the ball of her foot, and her other leg lifted and flicked out.

She spun on the blood-streaked deck of the ravaged ship, dress flaring, one arm lifting and then the other. The movements flowed from her, building to a rhythm only she could hear: A heel drummed wood. A fist pressed to a heart. A sweeping flourish of sun-kissed arms. An elegant spin and an impossibly high kick.

Swift, audacious motions, full of defiance, full of daring. A fling meant to be danced upon a shield, beside a sword. The waves jumped and surged as if they were applauding, as if the sea itself longed to move with Lina, the turn of her body contagious. Magical.

The serpent swayed slightly, caught in the dance's thrall. The silent melody chained it, held it captive, held it mesmerized.

As Eva was mesmerized.

Something stirred in the hollow inside her chest. She knew Lina was dancing for her brother. For that old man who had leapt into the sea. To buy them time, to aid them, save them. And she wanted suddenly, selfishly, for someone to dance that way for her. The scorching, soul-deep ache for it crept up her throat.

Drums beat across the waves, musicians on the floating stage spying what was happening, raising pipes and violins.

One slip. One misstep…

Eva tore her eyes away from Lina. Nodded curtly to Yara

and Omar, to the witches struggling with the chaos that was the *Carterhaugh*'s sails, the tangled rigging and shattered foremast. She held a hand up as Marcin ran forward.

Eva vaulted from the deck to the surface of the water with impossible grace, landing like a cat upon the cresting waves. Her shoes were charmed as the Conservatoire dancers' shoes were, spelled to cross the sea as if it were solid.

The tide licked at the points of her boots. Eager. Hungry. A thousand eyes weighed heavy on her, islanders watching with frantic hearts from broom boats and balconies. A thousand candles glimmering as true darkness fell and the scene turned blue-violet with shadow.

Eva's steps were quick. Light as smoke. The air hummed with magic as she tied knots in another red string bracelet, calling up a wave that swept Lina's brother and the elderly man into a red-and-gold broom boat. A group of women frantically hauled them in.

The dancing figure flashed in the corner of her eye, a whirl of pale blue and gold. The serpent's head followed Lina, keening as it swayed, a hair-raising sound between a hiss and a wail.

Lina did not falter.

Neither did Eva as she approached it, taking advantage of its trance, reaching out a tentative palm. Her monster. Her beautiful, vicious pet. The reek of rotting flesh and fish was almost overpowering. She wanted to gag.

But a queen did not gag.

Eva stroked the undulating gray scales and sinuous muscle, smooth and slick and shockingly hot. Whispered quietly, soothingly. A tremor ran through the serpent as she brushed the seaweed snared around its long neck, the seared flesh from the fire Marcin had thrown.

Blood blackened her fingertips, stained dark crescents beneath bitten-down nails. Molten fury blazed through her.

Then with a sharp cry, Lina slipped.

Fell.

Her body slapped the deck, a deafening wet *smack* that seemed to echo, that made the planks of the ship shudder.

The serpent reared back.

Fangs flashed toward Eva. Jaws slammed closed inches from her chest. She felt the serpent's rancid breath as she barreled to the left, sprawling onto her stomach, undignified, losing a shoe. Scrambling to get up, gasping, cursing. A knee and then her hand stabbed holes through the surface of the water, plunging into icy, empty nothingness. With only one charmed shoe, she lost control of the magic holding the sea solid beneath her.

She choked on a mouthful of spray and was blinded as salt burned her eyes. Jaws snapped at her heels, her legs, curved teeth catching, tearing through the hem of her trousers. She kicked back, clawed at the water. Crawled.

With a thousand eyes watching. A humiliation worse than the terror of death itself.

The serpent whipped its head back and lashed it down. Eva rolled sideways fast, but not fast enough. Fangs shredded fabric, skin, flesh.

An explosion of fire overhead. Heat and agony ripping through her right thigh. The serpent shrieked, enraged, and Eva wanted to shriek too at Marcin to stop throwing fire.

She twisted onto her back, looked up as that gaping maw streaked down.

Was this death, then? This moment, impossibly suspended? This mad second when she felt so impossibly, infinitely alive, aware of every shuddering breath, the *thud-thud-thud* of blood in her ears, the arctic chill of the water?

Was this how her sister had felt? Was this how she would go down in history, a failed queen eaten alive by her own monster?

The sea heaved. Black eyes looked into black.

Don't you dare.

The waves trembled. The serpent swerved abruptly, unnerved. Zigzagging, neck uncoiling, striking instead for easier prey, for the golden-haired dancer struggling to stand on the deck.

Eva felt the air catch in her throat.

She slammed a fist down on the surface of the blood-thick water. Summoned waves that swelled in a great curving arc, forming a wall between ship and monster.

An inelegant kind of magic. Brutal. Enchantment worked with blood.

The serpent reeled, body stretching up out of the water.

The tide swept Eva to her feet. She ripped off her last remaining red string bracelet, using the magic within it to shape the sea to her will. She lashed a dark wave at the serpent as if it were a whip.

There was a crack as loud as thunder.

She felt the blow as if she'd struck herself. A pain that set every nerve end screaming.

The serpent gnashed its great fangs. Writhed. A line of fire was carved across its scales.

Eva lashed it again, driving it into the depths of the sunken harbor.

A pained keening split the air. Fathomless oil-slick eyes turned on her, bewildered. Wounded.

Piercing her more sharply than any weapon ever could.

Her monster writhed, but weakly now, sinking its bleeding, blackened coils into the water. Spearing her with one last stricken glance before it slipped into the deep.

17

LINA

THERE WAS SO MUCH BLOOD.

Garish crimson staining her summer-blue dress, painting the ship's deck raw with magic, dripping in little bread crumb trails down the stairs leading into the captain's cabin. More blood than anybody could really stand to lose. Lina couldn't tell if it was her own or Eva's. "Is she...is she going to be okay?"

No one answered.

Lina was bundled down the stairs by broad-shouldered Omar. She twisted, catlike, straining in his arms, protesting. Her family's boats were still out there. She'd seen her aunties hauling Finley into one, thank God. And Uncle, too. She still couldn't wrap her head around him jumping into the sea to save Finley when he couldn't swim himself. She needed to make sure they were both—

Grim faces crowded the stuffy, dimly lit space. Omar set Lina down firmly on an old buckled sea chest. Somewhere in the cabin, a witchling was sobbing, a sound that made Lina clench her teeth. Her legs trembled. Her heart hammered with panic, with indecision.

Blood soaked sluggishly through the scarf she'd wrapped around the gash in her forearm, leaking down her wrist, crusting between her fingers and under her nails. Omar touched her arm, and Lina flinched.

Her gaze skittered back and forth, back and forth across the cabin, from Eva to Omar's concerned face to the stairs leading up to the deck to Eva. The queen was propped up on the captain's bed on the opposite side of the cabin, supported by an anxious Yara and ashen Marcin.

Eva was barely visible through the curtain of witches busy with bandages. A part of Lina knew she shouldn't be so worried, shouldn't care if Eva was hurt.

But the other girl was such a deathly gray. Her hair straggled out of its tight crown of braids and hung about her face, a sheen of sweat glistening on her skin.

This was not—this was not how tonight was supposed to go.

Lina bit her lip hard as Omar started to peel the scarf away from her throbbing forearm. She hadn't given it a thought, had just drawn the knife down, splitting the skin like a fish's belly.

Her whole body was an ache. A bruise. But she couldn't just… She needed to…she needed to move. To help somehow. To run away. She couldn't sit here all useless, helpless.

A hand on the wall, Lina rose to standing, not even sure what she was planning. Omar objected loudly, his voice distorted, the words sounding like they were coming from underwater. But she had to…she had to—

The world spun violently, viciously. Her stomach heaved.

Someone called for a bucket.

Lina sank back down quickly, retching, body shaking ever more violently. From belated fear, from shock, maybe, from the delayed terror of dancing for a monster.

How strangely good it had felt, though. To leap. To spin. To sway. To dance as death stared her down. How *alive* she had felt in that moment. She'd held a monster captive with the turn of her body, the stamp of her heel on deck. A different kind of magic than the one Eva wielded, maybe, but magic all the same.

A second boy knelt beside the sea chest, singing and humming an eerie, silky tune, knotting hair and string as Omar cleaned her wound, working a healing charm to ease the pain.

Some of it was fading. She stopped shaking. Omar smeared some horrible herbal concoction over her cut. It smelled just like the teas Ma made her drink, which tasted exactly like dirt. As soon as he was done bandaging her arm, he stood and headed for the captain's bed and Eva.

Darkness ate at the edges of Lina's vision.

She clutched her knees, shut her eyes, and breathed deeply, the way she'd been taught to do when she was seasick.

In for three, hold for three, out for three. Repeat.

The air in the cabin was suffocating, stale and sickening, scented with sweet jasmine perfume, healing herbs, and the harsh, metallic note of freshly spilled blood.

In for three, hold for three, out for three.

The world receded.

In for three, hold...

"You have a death wish," said Eva quietly.

Lina's eyes fluttered open. She must have blacked out for a second. A minute. More. The cabin was less crowded all of a sudden, practically empty. Most of the witches were gone. Yara was hitching up the hem of her dress, clattering up the stairs to the deck. Marcin followed, throwing a troubled glance at Lina over his shoulder.

Eva was perched beside her on the old buckled sea chest. In this dark corner of the dark cabin, she could have been a shadow, a mere piece of the night itself.

She scowled at the bandage on Lina's forearm. "You could have bled out. Or fainted. Your arm will probably still fall off from infection. I'm not wasting anyone's magic to heal you." The words came out in a rush, as if Eva had been holding them in all this time. She'd left a careful distance between their bodies. Pale smoke twisted from the end of her cigarette. "I think I finally understand you. This isn't about Thomas at all, is it? *You* just have a death wish. *You* just don't want to live."

"Of course I want to—"

"Is it because of your injury? Because you worry you can't dance the way you did before?"

Lina stared. And then something sparked deep inside of her, an ember that grew into an inferno, seething through her body like wildfire. Her nails dug deep crescents into her palms. "How dare you."

"I could have let the serpent eat you."

"Why didn't you, then?" Lina's voice spiked.

Eva took a long, shaky drag from her cigarette. She had a blanket wrapped around her waist, but the bandages on her leg flashed as she crossed one ankle over the other. She winced, pressing a hand to her thigh. "I can't have you dying before the full moon. I need you as this year's sacrifice." There was a pause, and her voice dipped lower. "It has to be you. I don't think it can be anyone but you."

"Should I be flattered?" Lina spat. A shiver traveled through the ship. Her ears pricked at the grinding, at the creak and squeak of timber, footsteps falling above their heads, the scrape and thump of rope. The familiar sounds of a ship setting sail. "Wait, where are we—"

"Did it make you angry," said Eva, "that Thomas didn't come to the regatta? That he was too cowardly to risk himself for you the way you did for him?"

"I don't care!"

"Don't you?"

Lina was silent for a beat too long. Why hadn't he come? Why hadn't he been there? Had the thought of the sea serpent scared him that much? Or did he really not...

Eva met her eyes, seeing far too much of her hidden thoughts. Her smile was a knife's edge in the dark. "I tried to warn you. Selfish, and a coward through and through. The first time I snuck him into the sea cave to see the serpent, he fainted dead away."

"So? Boys can be weak sometimes. They're allowed to be scared." Lina didn't mind being the strong one, the one who did the rescuing. She could be brave enough for both of them. Although she wouldn't have minded too, if it had been the other way around, if he had been the one to come rescue her, if only to know she *was* someone he thought worth rescuing. "I imagine your sister would have been so pleased with you luring him down there."

Eva's smile didn't falter. "Natalia was livid. More furious than I'd ever seen her. She threatened to turn me on her knee like she used to when I was a witchling and spank me."

The revelation was so unexpected, the image it conjured so astounding, that a startled laugh burst out of Lina. She immediately bit the inside of her cheek as punishment.

Eva's eyes had gone a little distant, fixed on something far in the past.

Curiosity got the best of Lina. "What was she like?" She wanted to know, wanted to know everything about the queen she'd watched drown, the girl whose story she'd admired and stolen courage from for so, so long.

Eva didn't immediately answer. She flicked ash off the end of her cigarette. "She was everything. She was my best friend. And she was foolish and selfish. You have a brother who clearly loves you. Did you consider how he will feel? What it will be like to lose you?"

Lina fingered the blood-coral beads Finley had given her for her seventeenth birthday. That she'd worn every day since. "Oh, he'll be fine. We're always fighting, anyway. I'm just a burden to him. The fact that he always has to walk me home from dancing is like the great tragedy of his life. Give it a month, and he'll forget all about me."

"There isn't a day that passes when I don't think of Natalia. Don't disrespect your brother by thinking he wouldn't mourn you."

Lina's cheeks heated. "I wasn't disrespecting him."

"Your brother will remember every insult he's ever uttered toward you. He won't be able to walk past the Conservatoire without thinking of you. It will happen every time he sees someone dance, whenever he hears music. This morning when I woke, my first thought was, *I have to tell Natalia...*" Eva cut off.

Lina stayed quiet. But Eva didn't even *know* Finley. Finley was a fool. Finley would be fine.

And she wasn't planning to let herself be sacrificed, anyway. She'd just have to find another way out of it.

"Give me that," she snapped, suddenly needing to do something, needing to say something to break the silence. "If you're going to smoke in front of someone, the least you can do is share."

Eva blinked, dark brows knitting in confusion. She hesitated, then held out the cigarette.

Lina took it, deliberately nonchalant, heart beating faster, trying not to think about her own lips closing over Eva's damp lipstick prints. She wasn't really a fan of smoking; when girls at the Conservatoire took breaks, she always made the excuse that she preferred cigars. It sounded cooler, classier, and was easier than just saying no. She tried to keep her expression casual, to infuse a loftiness into it. The same indifference Eva so easily summoned.

"Oh."

The smoke didn't taste of tobacco. It tasted bittersweet, like broken dreams, like longing, like dark, sour chocolate and citrus tea gone cold. A shiver tingled all the way to Lina's toes.

Eva was watching her with undisguised wariness. Eyes narrowed, tension coiled beneath her skin, a snake about to strike. There was something almost funny about it. A reversal in their roles that made Lina feel strangely powerful.

She blew a cloud at the cabin roof. "Thank you, anyway. For saving Finley. I saw what you did."

"I didn't do it for you." Eva was scandalized. "I didn't do it for him. It's my pet; if I'm going to let it eat anyone, it's going to be someone I *want* it to eat. Like Thomas Lin. So I can enjoy it."

Lina shot her an exasperated look. "The way you keep bringing him up, it's like you're the one with feelings for him."

Eva didn't bat an eyelash. "What can I say? He left a very large hole in my life."

Smoke curled sour off Lina's tongue. She passed the cigarette back, gaze drawn to the curve of Eva's neck where it dipped to meet her collarbone, the sharp planes of her face that were illuminated as she raised it to her red, red lips. "Will it be okay? The serpent?" Eva's face had been terrible when she'd forced it below the waves.

"It will be fine once I've fed it the witch responsible for this disaster."

"The witch...the person who threw fire at it?"

Again, Eva didn't immediately answer.

"It's complicated."

Complicated? How was it complicated? Marcin was the one who had thrown fire. The one who had attacked the serpent when Eva was trying to calm it. But maybe Lina understood. All witches were family regardless of blood. And things with family were *always* complicated.

"And stop doing that," said Eva. "Thinking of everyone else before yourself. Worrying about the monster that tried to *eat* you." She sucked in one last breath and stubbed the cigarette out. "I'll have someone prepare a cold compress for your ankle. Did Jun tie a charm for you for the pain? If your arm starts to hurt, I'll have him sent down to you."

"I thought you said you weren't going to waste magic on me."

"I also said I can't afford for you to die before the full moon."

Lina scowled, glancing down at her ankle, twisting her injured arm. "It's fine. It isn't a deep cut. It's not going to get infected. You don't need—"

But Eva was already gone, nothing left beside Lina on the sea chest save shadow. The witch might never have been there at all. She could have been a dream, but for a single waning twist of black smoke.

Lina let her head thump back against the cabin wall. "I really hate it when you do that. I really, really *hate* it."

18

L I N A

LINA SLEPT FOR A LONG time after the ship returned to the Water Palace, waking only when a witch came in to change her bandage and urge her to eat and drink. A whole day drifted past, and then half of another. They'd given her the same room as before, the one with the marble floor and amber-and-gold-leaf screens and pillow-packed daybeds.

She was so tired. She'd been going, going, going nonstop since the night of the revel—maybe even before then, worrying about her brother, about her ankle—and now her mind and body were giving out, giving up...

Or maybe it was just the witches' magic luring her into this daze, ensnaring her in sleep like a princess placed under a curse. Her chest gently rising and falling, rising and falling, trapped in the rhythm of a deep and dreamless slumber.

Every time Lina's eyes fluttered shut, a little more magic snuck into the room.

A tingly body balm to ease her bruises and aches appeared on a nearby shelf. A little striped reef snake with iridescent scales slithered across the daybed and curled around her wrist and up her arm like a bracelet. Handfuls of those licorice-black pearls that made your voice siren-sweet spilled from a bowl on a side table.

Burrowed so deeply beneath a heavy blanket that only the tip of her nose peeked out, Lina watched as a tiny silver spoon stirred three sugars into a steaming cup on a silver tray without her having to ask.

But she didn't want any more of the witches' milky tea or any of their other treats. Too much rich, greasy, milky food was turning her stomach. What she was really craving was a piping hot bowl of rice porridge with ginger and chicken broth, the kind her grandmother made for her when she was sick, the kind she got at home.

She started to curl farther under the blanket, a crab burying itself in the sand. But she stilled at a faint patter of footsteps.

A shiver of anticipation chased up her spine. The same breathless feeling she got while waiting in the wings before a performance. Lina let a count of eight pass, as if listening for her cue. Another count. She pretended to sleep, gave a little snore, and then…

Something touched the blanket. She flung it back, heart thundering, searching for a flash of black braids, the hem of a dusky dress, a whisper of cold smoke.

She found no one—so far she'd only managed to catch Eva once.

But heaped on top of the daybed, on top of the heavy blanket, on top of *her*, was a pile of dresses. Silk, chiffon, taffeta. Slinky, scandalous slips in sea greens and stormy blues. A sugar-pink feather boa. Lacy fingerless gloves. And at the very bottom of the bed, a charmed pair of silver dancing shoes, glittering all over with diamonds.

The most perfect dancing shoes Lina had ever seen.

Her eyes widened.

She slipped off the bed, wincing as her joints cracked liked an old woman's. She was so stiff—she hadn't stretched or done any of her strength-building exercises. She tiptoed around the bed, stepping over and around all the other trinkets and gifts that had appeared, all as silently and anonymously as the clothes.

Guilty delight shot through her as she brushed her fingers over shimmering amber rings and necklaces set with fallen stars, over spells to banish bad dreams, bottled in smoky jars. There were seashells in a velvet drawstring pouch that whispered dark fortunes and the secrets of those you held dear when you lifted them to your ear. A black case containing a gleaming violin carved from caramel-colored wood that played itself, played the songs Lina loved to dance to. As well as darker melodies. Lyrical, calamitous nocturnes and twisting sonatas. She couldn't help but wonder if they might be Eva's favorites.

Did Eva realize the secrets she was giving away about herself with each new gift? Was she hidden somewhere, watching for Lina's reaction to each one?

Lina plucked a crimson lipstick from the chaos, rolling it across her palm. It was the exact shade Eva always wore, and her heart beat off-rhythm as she popped the lid and drew a wicked bloodred bow upon her own lips, checking her reflection in a little shell-shaped mirror, imitating Eva's haughty expression, her scowl.

She knew what the gifts were: morbid reminders. The queen always made sure the sacrifice's final days were filled with as much magic as possible.

And yet she couldn't quite quash the thrill of it—the thought of Caldella's infamous Witch Queen plying her with gifts, racking her brain to think what Lina would like best, like next, thinking of nothing *but* her.

Because each gift was strangely thoughtful, fitting. She couldn't help basking in the attention, couldn't help feeling just the tiniest bit *special*.

Lina threw down the lipstick and mirror, hating herself.

She started to pace, all the tension that had drained out of her rushing back. Here she was again at the palace, taking Thomas's place—Thomas, whom she hadn't even glimpsed at the regatta. Had he meant to come? Had the sea serpent really scared him off? Or had he decided she wasn't worth the trouble? After all, she *was* the idiot who had dragged him back into all of this. Maybe he thought her too stupid to rescue.

A hot lump choked Lina's throat. She cursed softly, and then again louder, words that would have made most people blush—her mothers were sailors, after all.

Every night, the moon grew fatter and fuller. She was running out of time.

A crisp breeze blew in from the balcony, the pale drapes hanging in the archway leading onto it rippling, making it seem as if ghosts were dancing in and out of the room. The little reef snake that had curled around Lina's wrist and up her arm, then slithered off and disappeared somewhere beneath the blanket, poked its head back out, thin black tongue flicking out.

"We thought we were going to have to kiss you to wake you up."

Lina jerked, whirling toward the singsong voice.

A witchling peered at her from the other side of the daybed. A wee thing with bouncy brown curls and freckles dotted in a thick band across her nose. She gave Lina a leering vampire smile, made so by the fact that she was missing her two front teeth. "Like in a fairy story."

"That doesn't actually work," said a second voice, acid and monotone. "I told her we should pinch you."

Lina didn't jump this time, only scowled as a second witchling popped up behind her. Another little black-clad ghoul. She had the same olive skin as Eva and long dark hair, which she'd braided in obvious imitation atop her head. Lina took an instant dislike to her, to both of them. Where was Finley when she needed him? Her brother was the one who turned all gooey over children.

The main door was still closed. There was nothing to indicate whether they'd materialized from thin air or blown in with the breeze from the balcony.

Miniature Eva climbed onto the daybed and pinched the lipstick, smearing crimson all over her mouth.

"Don't do that!"

"Why? You did."

"That's… Were you spying on me?"

"We wanted to see what presents Eva gave you." The freckled witchling joined her friend on the bed, the mattress dipping beneath their weight. She poked at the dresses. "They're not as good as Natalia's presents. She gave much better things to Thomas."

A current of irritation surged through Lina, and she wasn't sure exactly at whom she was annoyed. "Like what?"

Miniature Eva smacked her newly red lips. The witchlings traded glances and spoke as one. "Kisses!" They burst into uncontrollable giggles, Miniature Eva crawling toward the silver dancing shoes.

Lina slapped the girl's hands away before she could smear her lipstick-stained fingers all over them. Curiosity once again got the best of her. "What was she like? Natalia?" She'd asked in the ship's cabin but hadn't really gotten answers.

"She looked like Eva."

Lina's overly helpful imagination instantly conjured the memory of Thomas and Eva kissing at the revel. His lips on her lips. His hands on her waist. His hands sliding up into her hair.

Heat swooped through her stomach, crawled up her neck. What did it feel like to kiss someone like that? What was it like, kissing a witch? Someone so powerful they could slay sea monsters with string and strands of their hair?

Lina hadn't even had her very *first* kiss—that time with Josef when she was eight didn't count, and neither did practicing with the girls at the Conservatoire, because that was just practice.

A pang cut through her. What had *she* shared with Thomas save those few shy smiles? A handful of words. A stolen dance whilst searching for her brother. A piggyback ride when she turned her ankle on a slippery rock. Interactions so innocent, so childish. She suddenly felt very small, and somehow lesser. In that heartbeat, she would've traded all those moments for something darker, more grown up.

"Natalia was kind." The freckled witchling gave Lina another gap-toothed grin and wound a curl around her finger to chew on the end. "And very sad."

"No, she wasn't," said Miniature Eva.

"Yes, she was! Not all the time, but sometimes. You'd be, too, if you had to keep feeding the boys you loved to the tide."

"No, I wouldn't. It's romantic, falling in love with a boy who's doomed to die."

Lina opened her mouth to say something and stopped.

"The magic doesn't work if the queen doesn't love the sacrifice," the freckled witchling explained. "It's not a proper sacrifice if it doesn't hurt her."

"The tide aches to taste her sorrow," said Miniature Eva with ghoulish enthusiasm. "It hungers for her tears."

"It's a stupid magic." The freckled witchling made fists in Lina's blanket. "Even Thomas said it wasn't fair to us. That's why Eva said she liked him."

"Eva *liked* him?" Lina sat on the edge of the daybed. "When?"

"Before. Last time. He made Natalia laugh."

"We liked him, too, a little," Miniature Eva admitted grudgingly. She picked up one of the silver dancing shoes.

Lina was too distracted to protest. "If she liked him—"

"He used to play his music for us," said the freckled witchling. "And sing. While Yara played piano. None of the other boys did that. They were always too afraid. They spent all day on the balcony staring at the city and all night watching the moon."

Lina didn't think that was in any way surprising.

"She tried to save him."

Lina's jaw nearly hit the floor. "*Eva?*"

"She wanted Natalia to be happy. Because she really, really, loved Thomas. Eva said a queen shouldn't have to answer to the sea. She tried to find another way to calm the dark tide. Thomas helped. And Yara. They looked up all this old magic, dug out the first queen's old grimoires, wrote to foreign witches and traded our bottled spells for their spells."

Lina didn't understand. "Then why does she hate him now?"

"Because Thomas is a liar," said Miniature Eva.

"Because he was only pretending to care," said the freckled witchling.

A shiver of foreboding snaked through Lina, and for all her earlier curiosity, she suddenly didn't want to hear the end of this story. Didn't want to hear how Thomas and Eva had once been friends, allies, of a kind. Didn't want to know what they had attempted together and how they had fallen apart, when Natalia died.

The freckled witchling pinched the bracelet of strung shells around her bony wrist. Lina had had a bracelet just like it when she was younger, as had Finley. It was a common charm to keep children safe from harm. A talisman against ill luck and misfortune.

"They tried it all," the little girl said. "All the spells they found, but nothing worked. The tide kept rising. Natalia was scared about what would happen to the island, and it was almost the full moon. They were running out of time. So Eva tried one last spell. A blood spell. She works with hair and knots usually, but she thought if she let the tide drink her blood…"

"She gave too much of herself to it. She lost consciousness, started to bleed out. Not just blood—that wouldn't have mattered so much, it's awfully hard to kill a witch. But Eva was bleeding her magic into the sea. She might've faded away like the old witches do, like a dream does, but Natalia found her. She put Eva in a healing trance, and then she snuck Thomas down to the lower levels of the palace and let him escape in a broom boat. And then she sacrificed herself so no one could protest about it. All while Eva was unconscious. Natalia had the others chain her to the pillar. She said there was a passage in one of the grimoires Thomas had read that said her sacrifice might calm the tide for good, an act of true love to break the curse. Only later, no one could find where it said that. Thomas didn't try to stop her. He let her do it. Eva might have forgiven him if he'd taken Natalia with him and fled, no matter what it meant for the island and everyone else. But he didn't fight for her at all."

"Because it's what he wanted all along," cut in Miniature Eva, voice like venom. "He only pretended to love Natalia and made her love him *too* much. He doesn't care about anyone but himself."

"You can't know that." Lina's tongue flicked out to wet her lips. Her heart hammered against her ribs, beating as if she'd run a race. "You can't know he was just pretending, that he didn't care."

But wasn't that what everyone on the island had long suspected? Wasn't that why so many admired him? He was the boy who had seduced a queen. The boy who had tricked a witch and won his freedom. The only boy the Witch Queen had ever let go. Wasn't this why she had gone to him for help, asked him how to make a witch fall in love? Because she'd wanted her brother to do the same if he was taken?

Why, then, did it feel like someone was clawing out her heart?

Why was it so different hearing it now?

The breeze carried in the crash of the tide from the balcony, a dull and rhythmic roar.

Lina tried to remind herself just who it was that she was feeling sorry for: Caldella's wicked Witch Queens. The queens who stole faces and chained boys to pillars to drown on full-moon nights. She shouldn't feel bad, shouldn't care that one of them had traded everything to save a boy who might not have loved her back. Even if she'd admired Natalia—

Eva and Natalia were still witches. Living nightmares.

And she hated them suddenly, hated everything about this. Their story had taken something from her, something she didn't know if she could get back.

Was it even true? Had Eva sent the witchlings here to tell her this? Was this *another* gift?

"And now he's doing the same thing to you," said Miniature Eva, the reef snake slithering sinuously across her lap. "Using you. Doesn't that make you hate him? Doesn't that make you angry?"

Anger *was* flooding through Lina, hot as coals. "Did Eva send you here to tell me this? Did she?" It was *easier* somehow to be angry with Eva, easier to cling to that familiar fury.

The witchlings must have sensed the change in her mood, heard the lethal edge in her voice, because both slipped away suddenly, bodies and black dresses dissolving into sea mist.

They left the daybed all in a rumple. The dresses wrinkled.

Lina didn't care. She didn't want *any* of these twisted, macabre gifts. The enchanted violin. The little reef snake. The perfect silver dancing shoes.

She snatched the shoes up, carried them out onto the balcony. And, chest heaving, breath so choked it felt like someone had wrapped a hand around her throat, she hurled them high into the air, into the sea.

But she could not make herself look away, could not stop watching as they fell, sparkling with white fire, sinking to their watery grave.

19

L I N A

THERE WERE NO NEW GIFTS after that. No trays of treats or magical trinkets. No sinister, black-clad visitors tiptoeing closer to the daybed when Lina's back was turned.

Or at least she didn't wait for any to appear. As soon as another day broke, she left the room.

Whatever Eva had hoped to achieve by having the witchlings tell their story—to make Lina regret her choice, to make her hate Thomas—Lina was pretty sure it had backfired. Because after a night of turning the tale over and over in her mind, only one part of it occupied her thoughts now, and that was this: Eva had tried to find another way to calm the dark tide, one that didn't require the sacrifice of an islander's life.

And if she'd tried once, if she'd believed there was a chance once, then why not try again now?

You didn't give up simply because you failed at first. You tried again. And again. And again. You kept at it, through the setbacks and the bad days, never giving up, because defeat was unacceptable.

Which was why Lina wasn't giving up now. Gnawing her cheek in frustration, she jiggled a brass door handle. The Water Palace doors were still playing games with her, leading her in circles, rearranging the rooms to their own inexplicable whims. She could wander this labyrinth forever. Lost. Alone.

But, Lina had to grudgingly admit, never bored.

Flowers blossomed as she pushed into a sunroom that doubled as a secret garden, fresh greenery sprouting wherever she stepped. Each hesitant footfall conjured ghost flowers and violet hollyhocks, blushing anemone and sunset-orange marigolds. As if she were the May Queen, the spirit of Spring itself. Dancing in to wake the winter world, come to rouse the barren earth.

Sweet-smelling gardenias trailed her like footprints in damp sand. Roses bloomed where the tips of her fingers tapped a cold stone wall three times for luck. Peach azalea and butter-yellow trillium sprouted in rings around her heels as she twirled, her new sugar-pink dress fanning out, chin tilting to the ceiling, giddy with guilty wonder. The air was lush with the scent of rain-wet leaves, heady with the sharp tang of a wild vine crushed under boot. She trod softly, fearing her slippered feet might scorch the floor.

She crossed a covered walkway next, strung through the air like a necklace linking two of the Water Palace's towers, a crisp breeze gusting through the bridge's spindly columns. The stone swaying like it was made of rope.

And then she was passing the wall mosaics in the corridor she'd found Finley in: images of dead queens and dancers taming sea serpents fashioned from glimmering chips of shell and mother-of-pearl. Scenes from Caldella's colorful history.

Smiling at the serpents now, Lina hummed as her eyes focused on a new mosaic. One depicted the story of the girl who had refused to hand her lover over to the Witch Queen. The girl who'd held on when the queen used magic to try and steal him away, never letting go, even when the boy was transformed into a sea serpent, a monstrous bear, a raging wall of fire.

Hide him, hide him, out of sight. Hold him, hold him, hold on tight.

She'd danced the part of that girl once at a summer performance—she could still remember the steps even now. It was a role she'd fought tooth and nail to win, because it was exactly the kind of story she liked to imagine herself in when she was daydreaming through a boring class or worrying if Mama and Ma would ever sail home.

Sometimes she wondered if she constantly escaped into stories, dramatized situations, merely to keep her mind busy. Her imagination was such a vast and anxious thing that if she didn't keep it active at all times, the ugliness of the real world threatened to creep in. Disappearing into stories was a way to keep all the frantic thoughts and fears at bay.

Lina reached to open another door.

Her hand froze an inch from the handle. A will that wasn't her own pulled on her fingers. They splayed wide, wider, then gave a little wriggle as she gasped, as if she were playing piano on the air. Her fingers bent themselves so far backward that she cried out, a flare of agony shooting up her forearm.

Whatever will or magic held her let go.

Lina cradled her hand to her chest, eyes stinging with tears.

"Oh, it's you. Our little dancer." Slippers scuffed behind Lina. Marcin peered down at her, licks of red hair falling across his pale brow, large blue shells stretching chasms in his earlobes. He was handsome in that effortless way her brother and Thomas were, but there was something about him that set the fine hairs at the back of Lina's neck prickling. She got the distinct impression that he didn't like her, which made her anxious, because she couldn't help always wanting everyone to like her.

"You don't want to go through that one," he said. "Where are you trying to get to?"

"I wanted to find Eva." Her voice came out shy, and she hated the sound of it. "I need to talk to her."

"Maybe she doesn't want to talk to you."

Lina bristled.

"I can open a different one for you. Send you straight to the Queen's Tower." Marcin tipped his head toward a shimmering door set between the mosaics farther down the corridor. It was next to the final image in the story Lina had been following: a girl and boy engulfed in flame.

Burning alive. Burning until there was nothing left.

Because the girl hadn't loved the boy she was trying to save enough to keep him.

Lina looked away. "Really?"

"If you give me your blood-coral as payment. Your necklace."

The glossy red beads made a little shuffling snick as Lina clutched the strands. She'd been gifted so much magic of late that she'd forgotten there was usually a cost. Forgotten that magic was damn *expensive*. The necklace Finley had given her—she couldn't part with it.

Marcin smiled. "Or a kiss."

Lina tensed.

"Or an eye. You have very lovely eyes, little dancer. Just like the storm clouds gathering outside."

Lina's heart beat a cadence of panic.

"Wouldn't want you to wander our palace forever; it's not long now before the full moon, is it? You don't have much time. If I were you, I'd be focusing on trying to get away from here."

"Away?"

"Let me know if you change your mind." Marcin started in the opposite direction, slippers slapping the floor, the sound growing smaller the farther away he moved.

Lina bit the inside of her cheek, then turned and advanced

on the door beside that flame-bright image, running a hand over the golden glyphs shimmering restlessly across the polished wood, pleading with it.

Please.

Pretty please, take me to where I want to go.

She thought she'd failed again when she found herself in the dark, stepping down onto a slippery, moss-grown stepping stone, a gasp of cold air scraping the top layer of her skin, conjuring gooseflesh.

But then her eyes adjusted to the sea cave's murky emerald light, and her ears recognized the soft *shusha-shusha* of saltwater. Her nose wrinkled at the pungent stench of fish. A soft cooing echoed off the sea cave's walls, then cut abruptly into silence.

Eva looked like one of Lina's small cousins when they'd been caught with their hands in Auntie Iris's enchanted biscuit tin: flustered, embarrassed, their lips sticky with crumbs tasting of lost kisses and chocolate-coated laughter.

She was poised atop a stone in the center of the ink-black water, in dark trousers and a waistcoat, leaning down with parted lips, clearly frozen in the act of baby-talking to her pet sea serpent.

"Aww," said Lina, drawing out the sound, layering it thick with sarcasm. "You're so disgustingly adorable when you're with it."

Eva straightened.

Lina took a very careful step onto the next stone in the trail leading through the water. They were slippery, and she couldn't risk another fall so soon after her last one on the deck of Eva's ship. She'd had to strap her ankle. But she was having a good day today, savoring the absence of any kind of ache. "How is the monster? Eaten anyone today? All healed up?"

"I don't know," said Eva, and she sounded so forlorn, so lost, that had it been anyone else, Lina would have done something utterly ridiculous, like try to wrap an arm around her. "It won't come to me anymore."

"Oh." Oh, that wasn't…that wasn't what she wanted to hear at all. A strange feeling of loss and pity hollowed out Lina's stomach. The sea serpent was terrifying, but it had liked her dancing. And there was the awful way it had keened, so bewildered, in so much pain as Eva had forced it below the waves. That terrible grief on Eva's face.

Reaching the stepping stone nearest Eva's, the natural instinct to offer comfort still lingering in her skin, Lina couldn't stop herself from reaching out.

Eva tensed, staring at Lina's hand like *it* was the serpent come to bite her. "What. Are you doing," she snapped, voice too flat to make it a question.

"I—" Lina flushed. *I get this stupid, overwhelming impulse to make other people feel better when they look sad.* She dropped her hand, tucked a strand of hair behind her ear. "I was thinking I would push you in, and then you could swim down and make up with it. Or you know, get eaten. With any luck."

Eva stared at her, eyes as dark and unfathomable as the sea at midnight. And then the corners of her mouth lifted in the tiniest curl. "Maybe I should make *you* swim down to it. As I said before, it took a liking to you."

"That's because I am irresistible," said Lina.

"Irritating is the word I would have chosen."

"How long has it been—a hundred years? More?—since a dancer last managed to tame one?" said Lina, smug and relieved to be back on familiar footing, trading barbs. She didn't need to feel sorry for the other girl, couldn't let her guard down. But her smugness faded abruptly, shriveling like a sea slug doused with salt as her gaze dipped from Eva's face down her body to the sparkle of her shoes.

A familiar pair of silver dancing shoes, glittering all over with diamonds.

"You didn't need to fling them off the balcony if you disliked them," said Eva. "You're so needlessly *dramatic*."

"Because you can talk?" Lina shot back. Vanishing in a whirl of dark smoke, slinking about in the shadows, the black clothes, the bloodred lipstick. "You fished them up from the bottom of the sea just to annoy me."

Eva's hint of a smile became a wide and wicked one. "It worked. If you didn't like them, you could have asked for something else. Is that why you're here, to ask for something else?"

"I'm here because the witchlings told me a story," Lina started, gaze skating over the ink-dark water, attention catching on the visions flitting across its surface.

Shock stole the questions she had come to ask before she could ask them.

She saw her brother. Dark circles lurked beneath Finley's winter-gray eyes; rough stubble shadowed his jaw. He was dragging a hand down his face, stamping his foot down on the bottom of his broom boat, sending it surging through a soup of thick mist, sailing round and round the Water Palace.

Trying to find a way in to steal back his little sister.

A hot lump choked Lina's throat. How long had he been out there? How many sleepless nights had he spent trying?

The scene was crystal clear, like staring through a window, like the murals painted on the walls down by the floating markets that you could reach into and take things out of.

If she touched the water, would she fall straight through and arrive dripping by the stern of his boat?

There was a tiny splash that might have been the sea serpent stirring. The resulting ripples washed away the image of Finley and his broom boat, made it into something new.

"Don't gaze too deeply," Eva warned, looking out, searching for her pet.

"I'm not an idiot," Lina said, even as she sank to her knees and leaned forward.

"The visions can drink you in. Drive you mad, like a sailor who's stared too long at the water."

"Like I said, I'm not an idiot."

"Experience would dictate otherwise."

Lina made a rude gesture with her hand, one she'd learned from Finley. In the new vision, she was dancing.

A glimpse from the past? The future? How did the witches tell?

"You're very good," said Eva slowly after a moment.

"Good?" Lina was indignant. *Good?* She was far better than *good*. She couldn't afford to be good, even very good. She had to be amazing. She had to be the *best*. How else would she justify becoming a dancer to Ma and Mama and Uncle instead of becoming a sailor like them?

She glared at Eva with such ferocity that the Witch Queen actually backpedaled.

"It was the wrong word. You are... It's why I gave you the shoes. A dancer as talented as yourself deserves a pair worthy of her skill. On the ship, when you danced for the serpent..." Eva hesitated, pausing. "It was moving. Breathtaking. Almost magical. And incredibly foolish," she added, sharp, not quite meeting Lina's eyes. "But I've never... I've never felt that way watching someone dance before."

Heat rushed to Lina's cheeks. Her entire face was on fire. And her ears. And her neck. "That's..." She didn't understand why she was blushing so badly. Wasn't this what she'd wanted? Wasn't she always complimented on her dancing?

But never by someone who was by all definitions an enemy.

Never by someone as remote and cold as the heartless Witch Queen herself. Somehow a compliment from Eva felt like it meant more. Like she'd won something.

I've never felt that way watching someone dance before.

"It wasn't... It was messy. So messy." Lina was babbling and couldn't seem to stop. "I'm out of practice. I haven't danced properly in months." She looked away, looking for... looking for anything, really, anything so she wouldn't have to look at Eva. Or the silver dancing shoes that Eva thought she deserved, thought were *worthy* of her.

She focused on the water, on the shifting images flickering like a fish's scales. The color that had rushed to her face left as quickly as it had come.

Now the water showed her standing at the top of the steps of St. Dominic's. Finley was there, too. Each of their shouts, each harsh breath turning to fog on the frigid air. Half the island had heard them going at it, some stupid, pointless argument about Thomas Lin.

God, but she was almost sick to death of hearing about him.

Finley's voice rose up in her memory, clear as a bell.

"What kind of man lets the girl who loves him go to her death and does nothing? What kind of man lets his queen go to her death to save him and does nothing? Thomas Lin is no man, Lina. How can he live like nothing's happening? Like our homes aren't flooding, knowing he could be the cause?"

Her older brother wasn't about to let her moon over the boy who had caused the sacrifices to stop working.

But Lina wasn't about to let her brother tell her who she was allowed to like. In the watery image, she shook her head, stormed past him, starting down steps still slippery from high tide.

As she knelt on the stepping stone, Lina's hands squeezed into fists. She knew what was coming. She did not want to relive it. She did not want to remember. She wanted to scream, to shout, to warn herself.

But the black water was unforgiving. All she could do was watch as events unfolded unchanged. Watch as Finley grabbed after her, that beloved face turned brutal and ugly with fury, her brother towering enormously tall, determined to make her stay and *listen, goddammit.* Fear climbed up her throat and she ripped away, twisting, ankle rolling, slipping, feet finding only air.

She looked like a rag doll falling. Hair the color of the sun on the sea flying out in a halo, blue scarf and coat whipping wildly. Pink lips parting in a perfect O.

Her ears echoed with the wet crack of bone.

"Is it terrible that a part of me doesn't want to forgive him?" Lina didn't realize she'd spoken aloud until Eva responded. And then she was painfully aware that Eva was *there* and had seen everything.

"I'll never forgive Natalia."

Yes, but that's because you're terrible.

Lina caught her lower lip between her teeth. Sometimes she

wished *she* could be a little more terrible. It would make life so much easier. And she really wished she could forgive Finley wholly, and not only because she so badly wanted him to stop feeling guilty. But even despite knowing how far he was willing to go to try and fix things, despite the whole family constantly, relentlessly reminding her how hard he was trying to make amends, how it wasn't *all* his fault…

The more forgiveness was demanded of her, the more she balked.

Why should she have to forgive him? Why did *she* have to be the bigger person? Wasn't *she* the one who'd been hurt? Even if he regretted it, even if it tortured his dreams. He wasn't the only one who had to live with the scars.

"Do not let anyone make you feel like you owe them forgiveness. Not even family." Eva glided gracefully from stepping stone to stepping stone. "You don't always have to make nice. This is what you meant when you said you broke your ankle?"

"It's nothing. It's fine. My brother has a temper. He never means to hurt anyone. I can handle it." She'd handled her family's anger all her life. She was strong. She was used to it.

"Just because you can handle it doesn't mean you should, doesn't mean you have to." Eva's eyes sparked with the tiniest evil glint. "Would you like me to punish him for you?"

Lina snorted. But the words soothed an ache deep inside of her, one she hadn't even known she was carrying. "Is that another gift? Should I start thanking you for them?"

"You can kiss my feet if you really feel the need."

"I'd rather shove a fishhook up my ass. And you're a hypocrite. You say all this, but have you punished the person who threw fire at your serpent, or is that still too complicated?"

Eva didn't answer.

The image in the water changed again. Glimpses of the island flashing by so fast this time that Lina could barely catch them.

Black water bubbling through the cracks between cobbles. A skinny dog stranded on a red-tiled roof. Smoke and seething clouds on a dawn horizon. A ring around the moon.

Eva had been moving farther away, but now she moved closer.

Lina could taste rain and feel, as when she'd held the bottled storm, the phantom patter of raindrops on bare skin.

Caldella couldn't weather a serious storm. Not now. Not with the dark tide hungrier than it had ever been, rising faster than it ever had. And if the sacrifice didn't work this year...

"Eva."

"Lina," she replied, almost like a joke. But the Witch Queen's voice had gone distant, cold. Any hint of earlier playfulness sealed in ice. "I know. I can see it."

20

EVA

EVA HAD REACHED HER LIMIT for human interaction.

She could feel the climbing tension in her muscles, the sharp stab of irritation every time another person spoke, the rising desire to pluck one of the hairpins out of her braids and shove it through someone's throat.

The audience chamber echoed with the wind-chime tinkle of messenger spells. Words carried on small spiraling winds sent from the city. Grievances. Complaints. There were stories of a wild storm brewing—the one she and Lina had glimpsed. Accusations and reports of further flooding, of looting on the evacuated North Shore, a hard thing to fathom in such an enchanted place as Caldella. The islanders were demanding restitution, money and magic, for the damage their broom boats had taken from her sea serpent in the chaos of the regatta. They were demanding to know what was happening, demanding that she return Lina, and also that she give Lina to the tide *now*, that she perform this year's sacrifice early.

As if the ritual itself were unimportant, as if Eva could afford not to wait for the full moon.

As if she were ready to let Lina Kirk go.

She could feel everyone in the audience chamber judging her, these well-dressed witches weighing her with their eyes, thinking her a poor substitute for the sister they had loved, the queen they had lost.

Because of her.

Because she had not been strong enough to break the dark tide's curse, not strong enough to find another way to save her sister.

"But you don't have to be Natalia?" Yara had told her once in that husky, questioning voice. *"They would love you just as much if you let them know you. If you let them in."*

But Eva didn't know how, didn't think she could, and didn't *want* to. She was not that type of person.

"You'll have to find another way to rule them, then."

She was trying. She raked her bitten-down nails over the arms of her throne and leaned back into the black velvet cushions. She did not sit here often, preferring to do what Natalia had jokingly referred to as "the housekeeping" from a small salon in the Queen's Tower. Natalia's ghost had a habit of poking its head over Eva's shoulder in here, whispering in her ear that it was undignified to rest a foot on her knee, to sit sideways, to smoke, to look bored and snap at stupid questions.

There were some things she did not miss about her sister, although she would never admit it aloud.

More tinkling, this time from the bells woven into Cyla's silver locks. The woman tossed her hair back over her shoulder, shooting a pointed look at Eva as she squabbled loudly with Jun, who took a frustrated drag on his cigarette and blew smoke that became a creature prowling the air. Omar scratched his stubbled chin and adjusted the bandages he used to bind his chest. His voice boomed out above the bickering.

"The islanders are angry. They don't like that we're taking their daughters now. They sound like mainlanders, the things they're saying about witches. Won't be long before they band together against us. The men are scared."

Because that *was an acceptable excuse.*

Marcin smiled at Eva's souring expression, ignoring Jun, who was trying to get his attention.

"Marcin, I think we need to consider…"

Eva crossed her ankles. Recrossed them. Crossed her legs at the knee instead.

I have to get out of here, or I will murder someone.

But no, she was queen. Why should *she* be the one to leave?

"Enough." She raised a hand before they could go on. "Everyone out. All of you."

Heads turned.

Eva inclined her own toward a small round table on the dais beside the throne. Seashells were scattered across its dark wood surface. "I've seen what's coming, and I want to listen. The sea always has answers."

Of the nine witches present, three read her mood instantly and retreated, and three hesitated, swapping frowns as they packed up deliberately slowly, waiting for her to change her mind. The seventh and eighth of her siblings had the gall to look to Marcin.

He waved them off and remained after the rest withdrew, the grating *click-click-click* of their heels cutting abruptly to quiet as the audience chamber's doors groaned closed.

Silence was such a gift.

Eva rose from her throne, from Natalia's throne, and trailed her fingers through the shells scattered across the table. Cockles and periwinkles. Cuttlebones and small spotted cowries. Abalone glowing with the brilliant rainbow iridescence of mother-of-pearl. White snail-curled moon shells.

She pressed the pad of her thumb to a conch's needle-sharp spire, relishing the pain. Its outside was buttercream, its inside a soft salmon pink. If she lifted it to her ear, what truths would the sea whisper? What secrets, what dark fortunes? The day and manner of her death? The name of her true love or that of the person who would one day betray her?

Marcin came to stand by her side, red hair and the jet buttons on his black wool vest burning bright beneath the amber lights. He gave the fat braid slinking down her back a playful tug, like he used to when she was but a witchling. "You should be in bed, sweet thing. Resting. Your pet took a great bite out of your thigh, if you recall. And how much magic did you spend attempting to tame it? You need to be more careful. You're making us all worry."

"If I wanted a lecture, I would have asked for one." She was beyond tired of people telling her what to do. She did *not* need to rest. What she *needed* was for everyone to stop second-guessing her every choice, to stop undermining her. What she needed was to know who might make trouble if she punished Marcin for throwing fire at her sea serpent.

Eva pressed a cold moon shell to the curve of her ear. She shut her eyes, chin angling toward the ceiling as if she were tipping her head back underwater, soaking in the sensation of the universe muffling, the world going quiet.

Eva listened.

For the secrets the sea sang to those who would hear.

For the scurrying footsteps and anxious murmurs creeping through her palace.

For everything they were saying about her. Her siblings' hidden thoughts and fears, their doubts and whispered desires, the weaknesses they admitted to only in the dark.

There was the deep pulsing rush of the ocean, a familiar drumming beneath her feet, a ravenous heartbeat rising up from the levels of the palace that had been swallowed by the sea. The tide whispered:

You can have the city or the person you love, but you cannot have both.

Eva's eyes flew open.

Marcin circled the table to stand opposite her. Maybe she should punish him now, quickly, while they were alone with no one to see.

He drew a map from his vest pocket and unfolded it.

Natalia had taken tithes from the other witches when they made trouble, like the queen before her had done. Snipped off their hair or the tips of their fingers. She could use this magic instead of her own, so she didn't use herself up.

Just the thought of it sent a chill snaking down Eva's spine. Because that was what the mainlanders did: cut witches into pieces and stole their power. Boiled them down and carved their bones into charms. Made amulets of their teeth, used their hair to cast curses.

It was the only way to have magic if you didn't buy it and it didn't grow within you.

Marcin brushed the seashells aside and spread his map over the table, businesslike. The craggy coastline of the mainland and Caldella's sharp crescent were etched in charcoal.

Eva's gaze strayed to the last two fingers on his left hand. Or the space where two fingers should be. Fingers he'd lost to hungry mainlanders when he was thirteen, before he and Natalia and Eva had been rescued by the reigning Witch Queen.

They'd always been inseparable, Marcin and Natalia. Fire and smoke. Neither complete without the other.

If it had been anyone else, Eva would have punished them already, but Natalia's death had broken Marcin as much it had broken her. They were different people now. Colder. Crueller. It had been two years, and Eva could barely remember the person she'd been before. It was all of this and the fact that he would never forgive her if she stole pieces of his magic the way the mainlanders had.

And if she took more of his magic, how much would he have left? He was already so much older than her, had spent so much already and always used it sparingly. When she was younger, he used to trick her into casting spells for him. He did it still to some of the witchlings, said it was good practice for them. Eva didn't know if she could bear the thought of him fading out of existence.

In her head she could hear Lina call her a hypocrite, and in her mind's eye she could see Marcin, panicked and stupid and shouting at her from the deck to do something about the sea serpent. After he'd made it angry. He hadn't even bothered spending magic to control it. He'd put everyone in danger. And now her pet wouldn't even come to her.

"We need to start evacuating."

Eva blinked twice. "Evacuating?"

Marcin tapped a star on the map. "Seldoma. The closest mainland city. I've dreamed of a ring around the moon—a wild storm is coming. It might break in another day or two or three, or even tomorrow. Jun says he can already smell it. We'll go there."

"We're not leaving."

"The island is lost, Eva. You heard the reports. The East Tower's completely flooded. The tide's stealing back the levels below us. We can't stay here. We need to sail before the storm breaks." Marcin smoothed the map. "We need to get our family to safety."

"And the islanders?"

Marcin shrugged. "They can come with us if they wish, if they'll work for us. We'll rebuild, take over Seldoma first."

"You want to start a war with the mainlanders."

"I want to lead us home. We were born on the mainland. I want to take us away from this cursed place. The mainlanders may even offer to help us."

"And if they don't? If they still hurt people like us? If they don't want us there?"

Marcin had this frustratingly mercurial attitude toward the mainland, one day hating it and everyone who lived there, the next longing insatiably for home. Other witches who had fled from there refused to talk about it at all.

Eva placed the moon shell she still held on the table atop the map, grimacing at the sight of the three nails she'd bitten bloody. Natalia would have known how best to respond. Marcin would never have pushed her like this. A wave of longing filled the hollow inside Eva's chest. The confession slipped out before she could seal her lips.

"I miss her."

She wanted to snatch the words back. But it was, in fact, the cleverest move she could have made. The soft words went in like a blade through butter. The fire banked in Marcin's eyes, leaving only shadows swirling through his hazel irises.

Strange how even weakness could sometimes be wielded as a weapon.

Marcin massaged the scar tissue on his left hand. He looked suddenly older. Creases pinched the corners of his eyes, fading into blue veins peeking through the soft skin at his temples. He was a creature made from porcelain, riddled with cracks.

"Why?" said Eva. "Why did you throw fire? I had the situation under control. Did you want the sea serpent to attack Lina? Attack me? Never has a queen looked such a fool."

"Well, that's not true. What about that year the sacrifice jumped from the ship at the regatta and tried to escape by swimming to shore? I can still see Natalia's face."

Eva cut him off. "Yara was almost hurt! *I* was hurt!"

The air in the audience chamber thickened. They held each other's gazes. Marcin was the first to break.

"I thought I was helping. It certainly didn't look like you had it under control. Why did you have to let it out in the first place?

You wanted to scare Lina? To show off for her? You seem"—he paused, glancing down, smoothing a crease in the map—"interested in her, in a way you weren't with the last boy."

Interested?

Eva stiffened. Heat rose in her cheeks.

"Even now you're still slinking off to play with her, showering her with gifts and magic."

Of course she was. She was doing what was expected of her, to please the rest of their family, and to make sure Lina's final days were filled with as much magic as possible, as the queens had always done. It wasn't because she was *interested*. She wasn't Natalia, falling in love with the boys she took. The very thought was absurd.

But maybe not as absurd as it should have been.

Eva tried to ignore the tiny part of herself that was even now recalling the ache of watching Lina dance for the sea serpent.

She'd known in that moment exactly what Thomas Lin saw in her, had known the reason he'd dared to love again after Natalia. She had always understood Thomas. Deep down, they were alike, both cold and selfish creatures. Both people who would do anything: lie, pretend, sacrifice anyone to ensure their own survival. It was why she hated him with such a passion, because she knew she would have done exactly as he had, had their roles been reversed.

But Lina was different. Fearless. Selfless. Foolish and completely infuriating. Eva now understood Thomas's urge to warm his hands on that courage, that flame, to try and steal a little of it for himself.

He did not deserve her. And she could just imagine the look on his face if he found out that she and Lina were...

She kind of liked the thought of taking Lina away from him in that way, stealing someone he cared about from him like that. She liked it *a lot*.

"I couldn't bear the thought of you starting to care for her too much. I worried you would end up making the same mistake Natalia did. You even let Thomas Lin go free. After he spat in all our faces dancing into the revel with her. After all Natalia did for him." Marcin's expression was darkening.

Eva wondered if this was the true reason he'd lashed out, like a child throwing a tantrum because he had lost his favorite toy. Marcin was going to lose his precious chance to watch Thomas Lin drown.

Eva sliced a dismissive hand through the air. "I let him go because I wanted him to know what it felt like to have someone he truly loved stolen from him. But if you hate him so much, I'll let you feed him to my serpent when this done. Does that make you happy?"

A flash of uncertainty crossed Marcin's face. It was so very rare that she surprised him.

"I promised I wouldn't use him as this year's sacrifice, I promised nothing else." And really, Lina was a fool for not having considered that, for not even asking. But foolishly good people so often made a habit of thinking everyone was as honest and foolishly good as they were.

Marcin was staring at her hard. Eva kept her emotions in check, not a flicker of feeling on her face. Was he seeing her or merely searching for Natalia in the set of her features?

I am not my sister. I will not make the same mistakes.

The silent vow passed through Eva's mind as quick as light, but at the same time a bubble of doubt dredged up from the depths of her being. Because she was and always would be a creature of all or nothing. She didn't care at all, or she cared with everything she was.

Caring like that got you killed.

"And here I'd almost forgotten," said Marcin slowly, "that you'd thrown away your heart."

Eva adjusted her collar. She wished Yara were here to back her up. But she'd gone to speak with Lina's brother, to convince him and the rest of Lina's family to stop sailing pointlessly round and round the Water Palace.

Yara's presence would likely have set Marcin even more on edge, anyway. Natalia had spelled him to sleep the night she'd sacrificed herself so he couldn't stop her. Eva, too. And Yara had tried to talk Natalia out of it but failed.

A deeply buried part of Eva couldn't forgive Yara for that, just as she couldn't forgive her own failures, and she knew Marcin never would either.

"I know what I'm doing." She would care enough, but not too much.

"You wouldn't have to do any of this if we left."

Eva's temper frayed. She peeled the map off the table, scrunched it slowly into a ball. Natalia had made *her* queen, not him. She had to believe her sister had done so for a reason. "We are not evacuating. We are not going anywhere." She set the ruined map on the table. "The sacrifice will work this year. Have Jun weave more witch's ladders so we can send away the storm. Tell the others to strengthen the spells on the lower floors against further flooding. Seal the doors. We will not abandon our sister's city."

21

LINA

SCORES OF CANDLES HAD STRANGE shadows dancing across the walls of the book-lined study. Together with the flickering flames, they kept Lina company. She tapped a finger on the spine of each book as she tried to decide which might help, which of the countless grimoires might hold an answer. The only sounds in the room were that and her breathing, a distant but steady *plink-plink-plink* of water dripping, and a sudden muffled shuffling that might have been someone's shoes marching across the carpet.

Did your mother never teach you not to wear shoes indoors?

"What do you think you're doing?" Eva gritted out. "What have you done to the study?"

Lina smiled without turning. "It's getting late. I just lit a few candles. It was so gloomy and dark in here."

"I *like* the dark."

Lina hauled a heavy tome off the shelf and sank cross-legged onto the carpet, back against the edge of a low lounge, flicking carefully through the pages. More books made untidy towers on either side of her, dusty hundred-year-old diaries, leather-bound grimoires, and tide charts, their pages folded or bookmarked. "I'm researching."

"In my *private* study."

Now Lina did turn, looking up, gray eyes wide and innocent.

Eva wore a real crown, a narrow thing of scorched steel and spikes, and her hair was loose. Long, long, dark fairy-tale hair rippling down her back in impossible waves. Lina had a sudden terrible urge to tangle her hands in it.

She cast a glance around the study instead, soaking in everything: The faint lingering scent of bittersweet smoke, the record player in the corner, turntable still spinning. A brass telescope for stargazing. A discarded coat and a stray slipper, a message sealed inside a cloudy bottle.

Tiny forbidden glimpses into Eva's life.

There was so much Lina still didn't know about her. But it satisfied her in some small way to know Caldella's infamous Witch Queen was as messy as she was. The fact brought her down to Lina's level.

"The doors brought me here. I didn't know it was private." Although she had realized, with no small amount of glee, that she'd finally managed to find her way into the Queen's Tower. After that glimpse of the coming storm in the sea cave, Eva had vanished as abruptly as she always did, before Lina had had a chance to ask any of her questions.

"Is that from Jada's shop at the floating markets?" She pointed at the bottle with the message sealed inside. It was not the kind of bottle you'd expect to find in a witch's house. Not a round-bottomed spell bottle filled with baby teeth and wishes.

The bottle in question was old. Ancient. Cloudy green and crusted over, stoppered with wax and cork. The type of bottle that might have been brought up from a shipwreck like sunken treasure or discovered buried in the sand along Caldella's rocky shore. A bottle filled with crumbling love letters or murderous confessions rolled and tied with twine. Never meant to be read, cast into the unforgiving depths of the sea. Decades, even centuries old.

"I love going there," said Lina. Each of Jada's bottles had its own secret story sealed inside.

Eva looked startled, then uncomfortable. "Me, too."

"Really?"

"I've always thought there was something…"

"Romantic," prompted Lina.

"Tragic," said Eva, lip twitching. "Macabre. About sealing something inside a bottle and casting it into the sea. Or maybe I just worry my own bottle will wash up there one day."

"Your bottle?" Lina couldn't picture Eva writing anyone a love letter. A murderous confession, on the other hand…

The thought crossed her mind in jest, but it spoiled as it lingered, bringing her back to herself, to the reason she was here.

It had been so easy for a moment, in this shadow-filled, candlelit room, with a dusty grimoire on her lap, to pretend that they were just two witches discussing spells.

So easy to pretend she wasn't a prisoner here—a prisoner of her own making—and that the moon wasn't growing fatter and fuller, and that every breath wasn't another grain of sand trickling to the bottom of an hourglass. Her life, running out.

A fresh wave of panic made Lina's skin flash hot and then cold again.

She stabbed the pages of the grimoire in her lap with her finger. "I'm finding another way to calm the dark tide. One that doesn't require someone dying."

Eva glided away from the low lounge and Lina. "There is no other way." The words had the ring of an adage oft repeated, a finality, a tired note of resignation.

"Maybe there *is.*" Lina caught the singlet strap slipping off her shoulder as Eva stopped before one of the book-lined walls and very deliberately started snuffing out the candles resting on the shelves, pinching the flames between her thumb and forefinger. A moody silhouette in a long, cascading black lace dress. It was quickly becoming apparent that she was allergic to color.

Lina had taken several books down from that shelf; they were on the floor to her left, on top of an illuminated text from the mainland, a tome so large Lina could have curled up inside its gilded covers and drawn the pages over herself like a blanket.

She had grabbed anything and everything she could find that had to do with human sacrifice. And animal sacrifice. Bloodless sacrifice. Offerings made to stave off drought, wildfire, storms. Libations to placate earthquakes and volcanoes. Sacrifices made for good fortune, for good harvests. To please malevolent gods and vengeful spirits.

"Here." Lina held up a different grimoire, flipping to a page she'd marked. "A different kind of sacrifice. 'The witches of Skani sheared the fair locks from their skulls and with them wove a net of hair to cast upon the waves, calming the vengeful sea,'" she read out.

"You want us to shave off all our hair," said Eva flatly.

"There's also teeth!" Lina grabbed a gold-edged grimoire. "Witches on the desert continent used to brew a potion, there's a list of ingredients here. They'd add a few teeth and pour the mixture at the foot of Mount Coroban every solstice to stop the volcano from erupting."

"Not to stop it from erupting, to *honor* it. The volcano is their goddess. They don't see destruction in the eruption, only beauty. Strength."

"Well, there are more things, too," said Lina, determined. This bored detachment was not the reaction she'd hoped for. A tiny part of her had even wanted Eva to be impressed she'd thought of this, to leap at the opening she was giving her. "There are plenty of other examples: witches giving up their voices, their beauty, trading away their memories, sacrificing their—"

"And why is it," said Eva, eyes narrowing dangerously, "that in all your grand schemes, it's *we* who have to give something up? Our hair. Our teeth. Our voices."

Lina pressed both palms to her bare knees. "And how many of *our* lives have we given up? Every year. Every May. For hundreds of years. It's only we islanders who—"

"Only you? Are you forgetting my sister? The girl you so admire and aspire to be like? I've been meaning to ask, is your life truly so boring that you're determined to live hers for her? Even going so far as to pine pathetically over the boy she loved?"

Heat scalded Lina's cheeks even as the words set her mind racing. Natalia had sacrificed herself, and that had settled the tide for a time. Would the sacrifice work again with another witch?

Why *didn't* the witches ever pay the price with one of their own?

"Every year, our queen surrenders pieces of herself," said Eva, as if she could read Lina's mind. "Only the destruction of the city or her suffering can quench the tide's hunger. Her tears. *Our* magic. We spend ourselves, trading pieces until there's nothing left. Until we have no magic left and fade away. *We* already give enough. *We* have saved this island."

"And in doing so, you made the sea a monster!" Lina flipped open yet another book, rising to standing. "I've been reading these old diaries." She probably should have paid more attention before now instead of just rolling her eyes in class and when Finley gibbered on about his theories as to why the island was sinking. She should have listened to her aunties, who talked about the tide like it was some kind creature cultivating its power. "The island was already flooding two hundred years ago, yes, and it *was* almost lost. But the tide wasn't like this before the first queen cast her spell. You witches gave it life. You gave it power. And now you keep *feeding* it."

With more lives, with sorrow, nourishing it with tears.

"In the past, there didn't even have to be a sacrifice every year. An islander was given to the tide once every decade or so." Lina slammed the diary closed.

Eva had gone still as stone. It was possible that Lina was about to be cursed, or worse. Eva might summon the wind or sand to scour the flesh from her bones, scrub them smooth as sea glass.

Lina dropped her gaze. "Sorry. I just… I have to find another way."

I really, really don't want to die.

"I offered to let you go," said Eva tightly, running her finger up and down the edge of the shelf, her back half turned. "You asked for this. You wanted to take Thomas's place. I *told* you to put yourself first."

She had, and the same frustration painting Eva's tone was tying knots in Lina.

"I don't regret it." She'd made her peace with it. Even after hearing the witchlings' story about how Eva had nearly died trying to find another way to calm the tide for the sake of her sister, for whom she'd even fought to save Thomas. The same way Lina had fought for Thomas and for Finley.

The way Thomas hadn't fought for Natalia or, it seemed, for her.

Thomas, who maybe wasn't who she'd thought he was.

But what he'd done and was doing now had no bearing on her choice. Maybe he wouldn't risk his life for her, as she had done for him. Wouldn't trade his life for hers, as Natalia had done for him. But that was him and what he could live with.

"I'm not going to be made to feel bad for saving someone's life. No matter how afraid I am now, I would still make the same choice. I'd rather die knowing I saved the person I loved than live knowing I abandoned them to save myself. But that doesn't mean that I *want* to die." Lina twisted her necklace into a stranglehold. "I want there to be another way. I need there to be."

Eva pressed a thumb to her bottom lip in thought, in frustration, in an eerily familiar gesture.

Familiar because it was a gesture *Thomas* always made. A gesture, Lina realized with a jolt, that Eva must have picked up from him. Or was it something Thomas had picked up from Eva when he'd been here last?

She shook the thought free, gnawing the inside of her cheek.

If she *didn't* find a way, if she didn't survive this…was there a part of her Thomas would take with him? A part the next girl he kissed wouldn't know belonged to Lina Kirk? Her habit of chewing her cheek? The way she hummed when she was nervous?

What part of me are you going to share with someone else once I'm gone?

Her eyes followed Eva's hand as it dropped and the other girl bent down, picking an open book off the carpet, fingers standing out against the yellowed pages.

What parts of you have I known through him?

"I will find another way," said Lina.

Eva shut the book with a clap and drew a circle on its dust-clouded cover, fingertip coming away with a silver film as if she'd pinched a moth. "Do you think you're the first to try? Do you think it a coincidence that there happen to be so many books and letters here on the topic? Accounts and grimoires from all over the world, all here in my study." Her voice was soft, even, deadly. "Do you think so little of us, that we haven't tried it all before?"

"I know you tried." Lina's voice was just as even. "The witch-lings told me what you did, what you tried. But *you* gave up. You failed, and then you stopped fighting."

Eva's eyes flashed with such fury that Lina shrank a little inside her skin. Eva's anger could put even Finley's to shame; it seethed like the tide in a tempest. "I do not need to be told that by someone who never fought at all before this. There are islanders who have protested the sacrifice, islanders who petitioned Natalia, yet I never saw you or your name listed among them. You were happy enough to let lives be taken until it was the life of someone *you* cared about. Until it *was* you. And now you dare lecture me? You, who've never fought and lost anyone? You, who never tried to change anything?"

Lina's heart pounded. Her mouth opened and snapped shut. A pang of shame twisted her stomach.

Because it was true, and she really wished it *hadn't* taken Thomas being chosen and being trapped here herself to realize that maybe they should try to find another way. Instead of merely accepting the yearly sacrifice as something that was necessary. Never questioning it, because this was the way things had always been done.

"You know nothing," said Eva. "You heard one story, and you understand nothing."

"Fine." Lina threw her hands up, slumping back down to the floor, tucking one leg beneath her. "Fine, I don't. But I will. I'm going to keep searching for a way. I know I should've before. I know it's probably too late now. But I'm not giving up."

"And you think I'll just let you stay here all night, picking through all my private belongings?"

"If you want me to leave, you'll have to carry me out," said Lina, tensing a heartbeat later when she started to wonder if Eva really would try and drag her out of the study.

But a second heartbeat passed, and then another. From over

by the bookshelves came a long and exasperated exhale. Lina relaxed a measure, yanking a stack of folded letters into her lap, ruffling through their crackly pages.

She discarded them when she realized they were written in another language, one she didn't recognize. She reached for another diary instead.

Anger was still singing through her, and the words were almost a blur. Though to be fair, words often looked that way to Lina: fat paragraphs of black letters squiggling eel-like, attempting to swim off the page. She loved stories but preferred hearing them or watching them danced out onstage. She was not a big reader.

She chewed her cheek, trying to concentrate. But buried below that song of anger was a sharp, stabbing disappointment. Why had she thought Eva anything more than a heartless nightmare? Why had she gotten her hopes up? Why had she wanted so badly for her to be something more?

She couldn't stop herself from chancing a last glance across the room.

Eva had slouched ungracefully into a high-backed armchair and was gnawing on a thumbnail, staring studiously at the ceiling and ignoring Lina.

Lina looked at the ceiling, too.

And then back.

And then away again quickly as she caught Eva doing the same, stealing a glance at her.

Their eyes caught for the briefest awkward beat.

Lina's cheeks heated, and she *really* focused on the text this time, searching for clues, for magical solutions hidden in delicate lines of curving script as the candles slowly melted down to stubs. Rubbing her stinging eyes and humming to keep herself awake.

The Witch Queen comes on wings of night.

The Witch Queen has your heart's delight.

She did fall asleep at some point, jerking awake minutes or hours later, drool making ink weep through a page. Eva was very likely to drown her just for that.

But the armchair was empty, and when Lina sat up, a blanket smelling faintly of smoke slipped off her shoulders.

Twists of dark smoke were dissolving in exactly the space where someone might have stood if they'd tiptoed close to tuck it gently around her.

Lina blinked, heart falling into a strange, unsteady rhythm. She clutched the blanket, not knowing if she wanted to tear it off or draw it snugly around herself. In the end, she did draw it snugly around herself, lit fresh candles, and continued to research.

22

LINA

SHE DIDN'T FIND ANY ANSWERS in Eva's study. No solutions or spells to try, because they had already *been* tried.

So she begged the Water Palace's doors to take her elsewhere, anywhere, to anyplace within its walls where she might uncover a new kind of magic to calm the dark tide. She used the black pearls that steeped her voice in syrupy sweetness, cajoling, complimenting each one on its pretty shining, shimmering glyphs and polished dark wood frame.

Apparently the doors responded well to flattery, because with only a few mischievous detours, they led her to more bookshelves, let her into hidden workrooms, into bedrooms where grimoires were tucked secretly beneath feathery pillows.

She ventured into dripping vaults and dusty archives, was chased out of both by angry witches wielding brooms. But she didn't let it stop her.

After all, whenever a particularly irate witch threatened her—like Marcin, whose precious handwritten journals she might have borrowed without asking and then spilled tea all over—Eva appeared to rescue her.

Lina was this year's sacrifice; it wouldn't do to let anyone *else* put an end to her.

Ducking inside a smoke-hazy salon as footsteps drummed an ominous approach, Lina clutched two books to her chest and smiled. The first was a tattered diary containing a scrawled spell of transformation she thought might work, and the second...well, she hadn't picked that book herself.

Over the past few days—days she could ill afford—odd books and stray unopened letters had found their way into her hands, tumbling innocently off the shelves she was searching, adding themselves to the bottom of the stacks she was carrying, slithering beneath scrolls she'd just set down.

Lina hated letting herself hope, but she was almost sure she knew who was behind it.

It was as if, deep down, Eva really wanted to help, wanted to continue the search she'd started two years ago, but she was too afraid to let herself. Lina couldn't decide if this made her even more frustrated, or amused, or angry, and even the slightest bit sad.

She could feel herself walking in Eva's footsteps. Half the time she'd discover Eva's notes already scribbled in the margins of the grimoires she took down. She'd get distracted then, tracing that perfect handwriting with her fingers, each carefully penciled line so faint it was as if the words were the other girl's whispers breathed onto the page.

A hesitant knock sounded on the salon door. Lina slipped hastily past armchairs and a low lounge, halting when an arm suddenly snaked out of nowhere and dragged her into a shadowy alcove.

"Do I even want to ask who's chasing you this time? You know Marcin spat in the face of the last person who angered him and turned them into a bird."

"Oh, how sweet. It's almost like you actually care what happens to me." Lina's back was pressed against the wall. She was pinned between it and Eva, a blush creeping into her cheeks, suddenly painfully aware of her own heartbeat.

She blamed it all on the books she'd been reading.

While searching desperately for solutions, she'd also looked for that passage the witchlings had spoken of, the one they'd said Thomas had read to Natalia about how if she sacrificed herself instead of him, it might calm the tide once and for all. Forever. The passage no one could find afterward.

Lina hadn't found it, either.

But she'd read repeatedly that the queen had to love the sacrifice in order for the magic to work. She had to care enough for that person that she wept genuine tears over them.

So why, back in the ship's cabin, had Eva said the sacrifice had to be Lina? That it couldn't be anyone but her?

"Maybe," said Eva. "I just don't want to go down in history as the queen who had to sacrifice a seagull. But on the other hand, it would mean I'd get to keep you in a cage until the full moon, so perhaps I should let whoever it is catch you."

Lina adjusted her grip on the books she was holding, expression turning mischievous. "Ah, but are they trying to catch *me*?"

For the first time, Eva looked vaguely disconcerted.

Lina pushed off the wall, moving forward into Eva's space. "I'm not running from anyone. I was looking for you. And a little witchling tells me a certain queen likes to hide in here and smoke when she's supposed to be—"

Eva pressed a cold fingertip to Lina's lips as another loud knock sounded on the salon door.

Lina's heart skipped a beat. "I found a spell that could work," she whispered. "I want to try it."

"What part of 'be quiet' do you not understand?"

"It's a spell of transformation." Lina held up the diary.

"It won't work."

"You can't know that. Look." Lina grabbed Eva's hand, the one she'd used to press quiet into Lina's lips. "If you give me a lock of hair and some of your red strings, your bracelets, I'll try it myself. I can work knots. You saw, yesterday." The storm had broken the morning before. Lina had paused her search to help two witch aunties weave a giant web of witches' ladders, holding the loops as they tied knots to direct the worst of the wind and rain away from the island.

Lina had looked up halfway through and caught sight of Eva, watching her, an unreadable expression on her face—a look that had turned quickly into one of undisguised amusement when Lina decided to show off a little and instead tied herself into the web.

She got carried away like that sometimes when she knew people were watching. Mostly other girls. The older, cooler girls at the Conservatoire. She couldn't stop herself from doing stupid things like talking really loudly, dancing about, flaunting her skills.

She couldn't stop herself from blurting out now: "Ma jokes I could have been a witch, I have such a good memory for knots."

Eva raised an eyebrow and canted her head to the side. "When were you born?"

Lina deflated a little but didn't let go of Eva's wrist. "Morning. Midmorning." When the summer sun was shining highest. She wished sometimes that magic were a skill you could master if you only worked hard at it and not something that happened to bloom within you by chance, depending on the hour when you were born. "When were you—"

"Midnight. At the stroke." Crimson lips curved into a crescent. "On the longest, darkest night of the year."

Of course she was.

A true nightmare, then. Yet it seemed strangely fitting, mirroring the way they faced each other now. Morning challenging midnight.

"It won't work," repeated Eva.

"How do you know before we even try it?"

"Because I've tried everything before." Eva swept out of the alcove, Lina hot on her heels. The salon roof was a drum for the rain, but thick drapes drawn across all the windows hid the storm raging outside. Lightning flickered through a gap and Lina twisted toward it. "So you'll just hide in here and smoke? What happened to sending away the storm? You gave up on that too? Don't you care what happens to the island? The flooding's already so bad, we can't survive this."

It felt like Caldella was caught between two monsters, fighting off a ravenous storm *and* sea. But if the sea was a monster that swallowed its prey whole, then this storm was a beast that stalked the city's streets, crunching its victim's bones.

Thunder crashed, the great boom of a drum loud enough to wake the heavens, a deafening sound Lina felt shiver through her teeth. "Can't you let me try?" She hugged the books to her chest.

Eva stopped at a desk against the wall, back to Lina, gathering up loops of red string and long black hair, winding it all through the sharp teeth of a mother-of-pearl comb.

"Are you afraid to fail again? Is that it? Like you did the last time? Like your last *sacrifice* failed?" There was acid burning at the back of Lina's throat. And fear. That wasted life—a boy her brother's age, her age, who had never had the chance to grow up.

His voice seemed to whisper to her, a fellow sacrifice-to-be, his clammy fingers wrapping around her heart.

A life stolen before it could be lived. An innocent life sacrificed for nothing. Because Eva had to have known she didn't love him, didn't she? As she chained him to the pillar, as she fed him to the tide? You could tell when you loved someone, couldn't you?

You drowned an innocent boy for nothing.

As *she* would be drowned for nothing.

"If you won't try the spell I found," Lina bit out, "then tell me how yours is supposed to work. Because I know you actually have to care about me for the sacrifice to do anything."

Eva turned around. "Did you come here just to irritate me? Because that seems rather a sad way to spend your final days."

"Maybe I thought we could spend our final days together, seeing as you're going to let the tide drown us all. We can braid each other's hair, trade stories about our self-destructive tendencies."

Eva's expression soured. She threw the mother-of-pearl comb at Lina. Lina dropped the books as she scrambled to catch it.

"If you *waited* for a breath."

Lina blinked.

"Well? Don't you want the magic now?" Eva dug a witch's ladder out of a desk drawer: a skein of silvery cord tied with shells and gulls' feathers. "You assume I won't let you try simply to shut you up. You assume you know my feelings." She pulled two bottled spells off a shelf and left the desk, ripping aside the drapes to reveal windowed doors leading out onto a storm-ravaged balcony. "Are you going to stand there and continue to insult me, or are you going to show me you can work string well enough to be called a witch?"

23

LINA

LINA PAUSED ON THE THRESHOLD of the balcony, amidst the fluttering black drapes.

Lightning laced the heavens, lit the low clouds from underneath, leaving the sky glowing like the pale underbelly of some gigantic beast. Eva's hair flew out from her head like a flame, streaming behind her in the howling wind. Yet the rain itself dared not to touch her. No raindrops glittered on her olive skin, kissed the stark line of her neck, pooled in the dark dip and curve of her collarbones. Her black dress stayed dry as she leaned back against the hip-high balustrade, untying a knot in the witch's ladder, features shadowed and sharp with sudden mischief.

Lina could feel the ebb and flow of magic rolling off of her, a steady pulse that set the pace of her own heart, that thrummed through her fingers where she clutched the mother-of-pearl comb wound with loops of red string.

"What are you waiting for?" Eva's voice was half drowned by thunder. "A spell of transformation, wasn't it? Shape a net. And this time, try not to get tangled in it."

Lightning cracked.

Lina took a tentative step forward. An icy pitter-patter drummed the top of her skull, plastering her gold hair to her cheeks. She skittered back beneath the balcony's awning.

A wicked smile tugged at Eva's lips, the same smile she'd worn on St. Walpurga's Eve just before she vanished in a vicious howl of smoke. "Are you scared?"

"No!" *A little. And I don't understand you. What did Eva mean by "You assume you know my feelings?"*

"I just don't want to get wet." It was more self-consciousness now than fear. Her fingers felt suddenly clumsy, clammy, overly large and all thumbs with Eva staring so intently. Lina wanted to snap at her not to look as she freed a loop of red string twisted with strands of black hair, tucking the comb down the front of her dress and into her brassiere.

"A net."

"I *know*." A flush crawled up Lina's neck. The strands of Eva's hair were slippery as silk, the red string far more delicate than fishing line, a thousand times finer than rope. Together they were as much a tangle as her thoughts, as the emotions twisting and twining through her head. It was like trying to play cat's cradle with cobweb.

Lina cursed as the strings slipped and snarled. The witches made it look so damn easy.

"Don't rush." Eva's tone was surprisingly patient. She unstoppered one of the bottled spells, placing the bottle on the floor and stepping back as curls of pale smoke spiralled up from it to feed the clouds, in the hope that it would satiate them.

Some of the tension leeched from Lina's shoulders. Something like excitement crept in. What charm was Eva having her work? If she proved she could do it, would Eva help her with the spell in the diary? She started again, brow furrowed with concentration. Keeping the long strings parallel, weaving one of the simpler shapes in the Witches' Game, the fisherman's net. "Why red string?" She'd always wanted to know why some witches worked magic one way and others another. "Why hair?"

"I have a lot of it," said Eva with such a straight face that it took Lina a second to register it.

"Did you just make a *joke*?" She almost dropped the loops of string.

Another tiny smile tugged at Eva's mouth, but a real smile this time, not taunting or spiteful or wicked, the kind of smile that appeared no matter how hard you fought to hide it.

Lina's stomach flipped with a strange, uneasy kind of pride.

"It's personal preference. There are even foreign witches who dance their magic. They slit the balls of their feet open with knives. Some like to say there's more power in blood and spit and bone, but it's a risk spending so much magic at once. And it's messy. Strands of hair mix well with Caldella's traditional knot magic, and the red string is… Good. You'll need to form the fish next, and then the tower."

Lina pulled the loops taut, hating the helpless, intoxicating thrill that shot through her from head to toe as the strands glowed hot.

"Now the tower," said Eva, "for change and transformation."

"What are we transforming?"

"The rain, seeing as you are so concerned about it."

And afterward, the tide, Lina promised silently.

So much power at the tips of her fingers. She couldn't quite believe she *was* working magic. Like a witch. With a witch. In a tempest at the top of a tower, alone but for the vengeful sea crashing far, far below and the Witch Queen watching her with eyes that glinted like the moon on dark water.

"Do you have to stare like that?"

"Like what?"

Like you're planning to eat me.

Lina ducked her head and focused solely on forming the final shape. She and Finley had always lingered at the markets when the witches sold the wind to Ma in twists of string and hair, had tried to memorize the movements of their fingers.

Her brother would love this. If Eva let her keep the comb, she'd save some of the remaining loops of string for him. She half wished he were here now, even if got angry and frowned and called her a fool for enjoying working magic with Eva. She couldn't remember a time without Finley. Couldn't imagine a future where they weren't close.

The wind picked up, plucking at her dress, fanning the black drapes behind her.

"Are you going to hide in the curtains forever?"

Lina shot a glare at Eva. The tower she'd shaped between her fingers glowed bright as burning coals, as the lit ends of cigarettes. Her ears filled with a roar, a new kind of thunder coming from everywhere at once. Her skin tingled. Her heart raged. But it was a rush. A fever and thrill that set her alight. Pure magic.

And then the light winked out, the strands of hair and red string burning away to ash, to nothing.

Lina looked from her empty, tingling fingers to the sky.

But it hadn't changed. Lightning still danced coquettishly through desolate clouds. Thunder still rumbled.

Her stomach sank. *She'd* failed.

Eva held out a hand. Lina reached forlornly to take it, joining her at the balustrade, hunching, braced for the wind, for the icy chill of rain.

Something hot landed on her bare shoulder. She flinched, but the heat merely melted into her skin, sending out little ripples of warmth. Something blindingly bright struck the tip of her nose. Fire greeted her when she flung her head back, eyes going wide.

Tiny teardrop flames dripped from the sky, tiny sparks in place of rain, winking out as soon as they hit skin or balcony stone.

The patch of sky directly overhead was ablaze, a single storm cloud weeped orange and crimson and gold. Lina opened her mouth, catching falling fire with her lips, on the tip of her tongue, hot and peppery.

Eva brushed against her side, a different kind of heat, leaning in to be heard above the rumbling thunder, hair wild in the wind. "A little more exciting than braiding each other's hair, no?" Her tone was so smug that Lina wanted to shove her off the balcony.

But she couldn't stop playing with the fiery rain tumbling over them like falling stars. She cupped her hands together and tiny tongues of flame pooled between her palms.

"There's no reason we couldn't do both. Couldn't we do this with the tide, change it into something else? What if we worked together like this? I can help you. *Let me* help you."

Fire was pooling between Eva's palms too, little orange teardrops dancing. "You never give up, do you?" Her tone was both exasperated and something else. "Don't you ever rest?"

"No." *Fear doesn't let me.*

And she had to hold onto her fears, to stay focused, because it was so easy to get distracted here, by all of this, by all her unanswered questions.

Why did you say the sacrifice couldn't be anyone but me?

Eva shaped the flames she'd caught into a band, a shifting,

dancing circlet of fire that she set on Lina's head. A crown of light to match her dark one. "For a would-be witch." There was something so solemn, so deliberately grand about the gesture that Lina almost laughed.

Instead, her stomach turned over. They were standing too close. Eva's hands on the circlet, grazing her temples, framing her face. Eva's chin angled down, her own tilted up. Almost as if…as if they were about to… Eva's breath hitched as if she too had just realized…

"Why did you have to come here?" She sounded angry.

"What did you mean when you—" said Lina.

A mouth pressed to hers. Soft. Firm. Insistent.

Oh.

Eva's hands tangled in Lina's hair. Lina's lips parted in surprise. Heat swooped through her center. Her heart was pounding so hard she could feel it through her entire body.

She sucked Eva's bottom lip into her mouth, blood coursing through her like flames when Eva inhaled sharply. Something dark and violent curled low in her stomach. A thrill, vicious and shocking as victory. Her hands gripped Eva's hips hard enough to leave bruises. Fingers clenched and knotted in Lina's hair, almost painful, pulling her impossibly closer. And something inside of her broke free, the lock wrenched off a door she hadn't known existed, endless possibilities spilling out. Why hadn't she ever thought of this? She was the rain—transformed. Floating and burning and falling, falling, falling.

The scrape of nails sent tingles racing across her scalp. Their noses bumped. Flames were raining down all around them. Lina couldn't catch her breath. She didn't know if she was doing this right or if she—

Eva nipped her lip, and a jolt snaked through Lina like lightning. The soft, curving pieces of her seemed to slot and fit and *press* into the soft, curving pieces of Eva as if that's what they were made for. She was on fire, dizzy with the sensation of Eva's mouth closing over her own, the climbing need. She needed to get closer, she needed—

Lina pulled back for breath. Eva stared down at her. Lips swollen. Eyes wide. Black hair a wild tangle, swept back to expose her shocked face. She stared at Lina like she was something astounding, something strange, like nothing she had ever seen before.

Lina's lips throbbed. Her heart beat a painful rhythm.

What are you doing?

What are you doing what are you doing what are you doing?

She was almost grateful for the scream.

It made them both jump. A faint, piercing cry from somewhere inside the Water Palace.

Lina tore away from Eva's touch, racing inside, stumbling through the thick drapes and across the hazy, smoke-sweet salon, speeding past the desk, the low lounge, unsure if she was running toward the sound or away from Eva. Her heart thudded against her rib cage.

What are you doing what are you doing what are you doing?
Oh God.

She didn't want this. She didn't want to feel like this. This was all Eva's fault.

The scuff of her stockings on the carpet became a squelch.

Lina halted, looked down.

The carpet was wine-red, deepening to the color of old blood as water oozed through the crack between the floor and the salon's shimmering, glyph-engraved door, a great half moon bleeding outward.

Eva rushed past, the silver dancing shoes she was still wearing stepping lightly, sparkling with diamond fire as she flung open the door. It didn't misbehave for her. A wall of cold horror and sound hit them as they burst through, bodies colliding with a flock of shrieking witches and witchlings fleeing down a murky corridor as towering ink-black waves crashed round a bend.

The dark tide had come to reap what it was owed, to take what it was promised, what it had been denied for two long years.

Blood drained from Lina's face. The water moved like a living, breathing thing. Serpentine and ravenous. Pouring itself down the corridor with deliberate intent, gushing eagerly over the floor, reaching, touching, tasting. Liquid darkness clawed forward on wet black fingers. Teeth of froth and foam raked along the walls, cresting white and biting down.

Lina didn't move fast enough. Waves smashed into her

head-on with strength enough to sweep her off her feet, to drag her under, to swallow her whole. She tumbled into a ball, saltwater flooding her nose, her mouth, her ears. She sloshed and slapped against other screaming, squirming, drowning bodies.

Rough hands seized her by the hair, tearing at her scalp, hauling her up. She gasped as she burst from the water's hold. She gripped Eva for dear life.

"Marcin!" Eva was shouting as red hair flashed past. The water seethed, hissing its hunger, roiling and swirling around their knees, their waists. Light rippling off its pitch-dark skin, webbing over the ceiling.

Marcin was struggling to stay upright against the swell, fighting the fierce push and pull of the waves. He fished a witchling out of the flow, hauled the small boy over his shoulder.

Eva's grip loosened on Lina's hair. She shoved Lina roughly back through the door they'd just come from, a small wave going with her, spewing into the salon, soaking more of the wine-red carpet.

Lina stumbled, catching herself against the back of the low lounge.

Eva grasped the edge of the door, face grim as she heaved it shut. "Stay here."

24

LINA

LINA DIDN'T STAY.

Inaction was agony. There wasn't a force on earth that could have kept her still. Her fingers curled around the door handle a heartbeat after Eva shoved her through to safety.

She fled the salon, fear chasing her through door after door after door, through rooms blissfully free of that writhing, living tide. She ran until she found herself back in her marble-floored bedroom, stumbling past the amber-and-gold-leaf screens, collapsing, shivering, onto a daybed in shock.

No one chased after her.

Minutes passed. Then hours. Hours where her mind refused to stop spinning. Her thoughts flooded with too many terrible scenarios to banish with a magical bargain or a tap on the wall.

Had it been like this for Thomas when he was taken? Had he felt this lost and alone, this damn frightened? This confused? This helpless? Lina's eyes burned. She swiped furiously at her face as a tear escaped to scald her cheek.

The little reef snake Eva had gifted her slid from beneath a pillow, coiling its stripes around her wrist and fingers as if to squeeze her hand.

Lina prised the little creature free, pacing up and down, up and down, ignoring the growing hot ache in her ankle, almost enjoying it, because she deserved pain and because at least that was familiar—that she could handle. Her eyes skimmed unseeing over the chaos of magical gifts as she struggled to think of something, anything, other than what had happened on Eva's balcony before the dark tide had come to claim what it was owed.

To claim her.

What the sea wants, the sea shall have, as sailors said.

She suddenly couldn't stand the still-damp clothes clinging to her. It felt like she'd been licked, swallowed, tasted, and then spat out. Lina stripped, shimmying into a short, glittery green shift with matching gloves. She tied her blood-coral beads in a double knot around her neck and felt a little more in control. The familiar ritual settled her nerves. It was like putting on makeup before a performance, like putting on armor, like prepping for war.

She combed her bangs out, brushed the sleek, damp bob of her hair, wincing at the state of her roots. Put on lipstick, rouged her cheeks, painted her eyes with shadow.

Keep moving. Do something. Don't think.

Don't think.

A hum sang through her skin as she picked up the comb Eva had given her, thumb sliding over red string and silken black strands threaded tight through the shiny teeth. Heat flooded Lina's cheeks, and she hesitated, then shoved the comb back into her brassiere. A gift was a gift. And a piece of emergency magic was always useful to have, no matter where it came from.

No matter the witch it came from.

Where was Eva now? Had those black waves washed her away, drowned her in the dark corridors of her own palace? Drowned all the witches? Maybe Lina was the only one in here left alive.

Maybe that was for the best. Now that she was calmer, Lina didn't think she could face anyone ever again, especially Eva.

Her fingers reached up questioningly to trace her lips, as if she could recapture the feeling of the Eva's mouth crashing down on her own.

What even was that kiss?

And why had she *enjoyed* it?

Lina knew what love was supposed to look like. She knew what she was supposed to want, *who* she was supposed to want. She'd been brought up on sweeping tales of soft, sweet caresses, stories of hand-holding, butterflies fluttering in stomachs, and epic, tongue-tied romance.

She didn't want to hold Eva's hand. She wanted to shove her up against a wall and scream, "What have you done to me?"

She'd wanted to bruise her hips when she'd kissed her. She'd liked how *powerful* she'd felt. When she thought of Eva, there were no butterflies; only this heated swoop in her stomach, like a thrill, like adrenaline. This violent uneven rhythm of her heart.

Trying to reconcile what she was currently feeling with all those soft, sweet tales, with all the scenes she'd rehearsed in her head, with all she knew… She didn't know anymore. What if what she thought was love wasn't what anyone else felt when they said the word? How would she ever know if what she was feeling was right? Was truly love?

Lina paced out onto the balcony. The rain was still falling, but as mist now, not as fire. Ordinary gray clouds roiled and readied themselves for the next brutal onslaught.

The shadow of a lonely seabird threaded through the gloom. Lina gripped the hip-high balustrade, the only thing standing between her and the sea below.

Did the waves look closer than they had a day ago? Was the inky water climbing higher?

And what of the moon? Last night, the storm-ravaged sky had hidden it. How full and fat had it grown?

She tried to distract herself with a story, seeking refuge in fantasy and wild imaginings, envisioning herself in a different time, a different place.

It didn't work.

The balcony faced the city, and even in the overcast gloom

Caldella was clearly visible, a faded pastel tapestry of town houses and winding cobbled streets. The crescent isle looked fragile somehow, slim, like the moon the day before it went dark. Waves with white teeth gnawed at its edges, swallowing districts piece by piece. Black water snaked toward the city center in sickly, swollen veins.

Something caught in Lina's throat. Her beautiful fairy-tale city. Her sinking city. Her home.

Drowning.

She backed away from the balustrade, knuckles white.

At least if Eva... Did Eva really care? Was it possible she truly...

Was it terrible of Lina to want to believe it, to want it, for her stomach to flip at the thought? To think that she of all people could have captured the wicked Witch Queen's heart? A girl people claimed *had* no heart?

Lina's own heart skipped a beat.

She shook the thought away.

At least if the magic worked, her death would mean something. Finley was out there, and Uncle and Laolao and all her aunties and cousins, and Ma and Mama were sailing home. Ensuring their happiness and survival—that was less a sacrifice and more her duty, wasn't it? If she thought of it that way...

No. She shouldn't be thinking of it that way. She should be thinking about how she could *use* Eva's affection to her advantage to save herself. If Eva cared for her, how could she choose between saving the person she loved and saving everyone? It would be like with Thomas and Natalia.

And yet, just thinking that, thinking of taking advantage of someone's feelings like that, someone *she* might even...

Something inside of Lina rebelled. A burst of panic like a caught bird fluttering inside her rib cage.

A voice drifted out onto the balcony, calling her name. Lina whirled around, fighting her way through the balcony drapes, gossamer lace catching like cobwebs at her arms, her face, blind-folding her before she stumbled into the warm embrace of the room.

A boy was weaving past the amber-and-gold-leaf screens, a boy with sea-tanned skin and sun-kissed hair. A boy in soaking, storm-wet clothes. The boy who'd once carried her home when she turned an ankle.

Lina stopped cold. Thomas rushed forward. Amber lanterns swinging from the ceiling faded the scene like an old photograph.

He didn't feel real. He looked like someone from a dream, someone she was struggling to remember, to grasp the shape of. Who *was* Thomas Lin? How well did she really know him?

He stopped before her. "Lina."

The way he said her name, like a prayer or a wish, turned her legs to jelly. All her old shyness flooded back. A thousand questions raced through her mind, a thousand things she longed to say, wanted to shout. A queer part of her wanted to *apologize*. But what came out was a question. The very last she expected herself to ask.

"Did you care about her at all? Natalia?"

Did you love her? Did she kiss you? Did you like it?

Or am I the only strange one, having all these confusing feelings for a witch?

Thomas's face shuttered. His gaze dropped to the floor. He was silent for a long, long moment.

A moment in which Lina could hardly breathe.

"I don't know." Thomas scraped a hand over the back of his head. "Truly. But what else could I do? I thought if I made her care enough for me, she wouldn't go through with it, and I quickly realized I *could* make her care. I know what girls like. I know girls like me. And she was easy. Even though she was the Witch Queen and people said she was wicked. She was quiet and a little shy."

Something inside of Lina splintered.

"At the beginning, I hated her. At the revel, I thought I was kissing this girl I liked, and then Ula's face changed, and then I was *here*. Trapped. Waiting to die like all those other boys. I think... I think hated everyone then. Everyone just lets this happen year after year, and no one tries to stop it. They just accept it, celebrate it, like we have no other choice. But later..." Thomas's expression was pained. "When you're acting like you're in love all the time, it's impossible not to...to...it all starts to blur, what's true and where the lie ends."

Play a part long enough, and it starts to turn real.

Lina swallowed past the lump in her throat. She knew the truth of that from dancing, knew it from the fantasies she spun for herself, when she stole courage from the image of Natalia holding strong against the tide, when she hummed the song of the girl who'd held on to her lover through enchantment and fire, pretending she was brave until she *was* brave.

She knew the power in pretending.

Thomas breathed out. "They said they wanted it to stop, too. Eva tried to find another way to calm the tide so I wouldn't have to be sacrificed, so I could stay with Natalia. We all tried, Natalia and Eva and another witch called Yara and I. It tied us together, that desperation, more than anything else could have. But Eva's different now. Colder."

Because of you, Lina wanted to say, but didn't. It sounded too much like an accusation.

And maybe it was.

"I never expected—I never thought things would end the way they did. I thought if I made Natalia care for me, she'd let me go. That was all I wanted. I tried so hard to be strong, but God help me, I was so *afraid*. I didn't want to die. And when nothing was working, I thought if I told her… Those books said so many things. She promised she wouldn't let me…" Thomas's voice cracked.

The ache started somewhere deep in Lina's marrow.

Thomas stepped closer, clasping both her hands in his,

calloused palms warm through her gloves. "I *know* I'm not a good person, Lina. Not like you. And when it happened all over again with you, I was still a coward. I still didn't want to die. I couldn't make myself move. I let you take my place like she did. But I want to change. I failed you at the regatta, but I won't fail you now. Finley has a boat—"

"Finley?" Lina put a hand to her mouth.

Finley in his broom boat sailing desperately round and round the Water Palace.

Because her brother was just as stubborn about not giving up as she was.

For a flicker, Thomas's expression turned rueful, and the slight discoloration beneath his left eye suddenly looked a lot like a fading bruise. "Your brother has quite the temper. But he wasn't going to refuse the help. I know the palace best. He's distracting Yara while I fetch you." He tugged on her hands. "Come, we have to hurry before the storm picks up. It's almost a full moon."

Lina's feet were rooted to the floor. "But the *island.*"

"Sacrificing yourself won't solve anything. Saving Caldella only means another sacrifice next year. And the year after, and the year after that. More innocent lives. This island is cursed. It will never end. Do you really want to be a part of that?" Thomas's cheeks darkened with color. "Come with me. At the revel you said you would hold on to me. I know we've never... I didn't have the courage to say how I felt before. But I need you, Lina. You came after me, didn't you? You were willing to give up everything for me."

Lina's heart pounded. "I—" For a second she saw it, dreamed it, lived it, a version of the world where she took his hand and left the palace, escaped the wicked witch and the hungry tide, the cursed island, and sailed away with the boy she—

Loved?

The words stuck in her throat.

Oh, why hadn't he come sooner? Why hadn't he come for her before things had gotten all confused?

"Lina?"

A distant rumble of thunder saved her from answering.

Thomas shot a wary glance over his shoulder. "We need to go now." He crossed to the daybed, rummaging through her gifts. "They gave you presents, didn't they? Magic?" He threw a dress on the floor. A spell bottle crashed after it, shattering. The little reef snake let out a scathing hiss.

Thomas jumped and flung a pillow at it.

Lina flinched. "Don't!" There was something violating about him tearing through all the things Eva had given her.

"Here, we'll take these." He snatched up a palmful of the black pearls and caught her hand again. "They're good for charming the doors. Here." He handed her a wooden oar he'd left leaning against one of the amber screens. Broom boats didn't need them; had he brought it as a weapon?

"Come on, your brother's waiting." He smiled softly then, so proud and so full of hope. "We've come to rescue you."

Lina couldn't make herself say anything as he pulled her across the room and out the door.

25

E V A

SPLASHES, AND THE SOFT WIND-CHIME jingle of bells reached Eva before Cyla hurried into view. Black water was bleeding under all the closed doors on this level of the palace, one of its lowest. Puddles blooming darkly, eating up the floor. Amber lantern light glimmered off their glassy surface.

The tide licked at Eva's heels, at the glittering silver dancing shoes she had yet to kick off. She'd warded this floor, hadn't she? Sealed these doors? Come down here only minutes ago? Scattered salt, poured sand mixed with her siblings' blood in deliberate circles, pushing the sea back with sheer savage will as it fought to take over the fortress the third Witch Queen had raised from the depths and made their home.

She'd been at it for hours and hours. The anxious rush of water lived within her now. It was all she could hear, that cursed susurration, that drumming of waves pounding on a far-off shore.

"We need to hold the ritual. Perform the sacrifice." Cyla's face was pinched with worry. She scooped her silver locks over one shoulder, splashing through the puddles, coming closer.

"It's not yet the full moon."

"It will not matter. The tide is ravenous, Eva. Marcin has half the palace packing to leave. If you want us to stay, if you want us to follow you and not him—"

A surge of irritation set fire to Eva's blood. She'd *told* Marcin they were not abandoning the island. She'd *told* him to ward the doors against further flooding. And yet, when her next words escaped, there was no real heat or conviction behind them. Her arms and legs were leaden, heavy anchors weighing her down. Her crown was a band of pressure growing tighter and tighter as it circled her brow.

She was so bone-achingly tired.

"To offer a sacrifice without the full moon to draw on, without a natural amplifier, without the moon's sway over the sea," she started. "It would take too much from me."

Magic wasn't inexhaustible. You had as much as you had, you were as much as you were, and when a witch used herself up, she faded from existence like the wisps of a dream upon waking. Jun, who was of course on Marcin's side, had protested loudly when she'd ordered him to send the storm away, saying it was too violent, too vast. "Magic of that size and scale? It would burn me up to banish it all. I can calm parts of it, maybe, with help. I'll need everyone to weave ladders for me."

Eva, too, had used too much magic of late, had been reckless with it. She had always been reckless with it, refusing to take tithes because she was vain enough to think she had so much magic she didn't need to steal from others.

She'd been using it constantly to impress Lina. Because she liked the way Lina looked at her when she did magic, like she *was* pure magic. It was so terribly easy to get addicted to eyes that looked at you that way.

Eva glanced down at the sand she'd been scattering, as if trying to read its lines for portents and signs. For the thousandth time, she tried to *forget* Lina. Every time she thought of the other girl, her body reacted as if she were caught again in that moment on the balcony, fire falling like rain all around them, skin coming alive wherever they touched, Lina's heart beating so fast, so hard she could *feel* it. A shared thunder that filled the hollow inside her chest. As if Lina's heart were beating for them both.

"We can help you," said Cyla. "Lend you our strength, our magic. Take some of the burden. We used to, with Natalia. It's you who never lets us help you."

Cold sweat dripped down Eva's back. The puddles lapped at their shoes. She could see Lina suddenly in that eerily undulating water. Those storm-gray eyes eaten by crabs, that sun-gold hair tangled with eelgrass and oyster shells, reams of old fishing line. Lips painted a cold corpse blue.

She blinked, and the vision vanished.

"A sacrifice must be made to appease the tide," said Cyla. "Choose rightly. Do not make the same mistake your sister did."

Eva flinched. She wouldn't. She would never make the same mistake. She would do as all Caldella's queens had done for centuries: sacrifice her heart to save her city. Pay the blood price to protect her home, protect her family, her subjects.

It doesn't matter what I feel, Natalia had often said. *I am the island's queen. I have a duty.*

A duty to sacrifice one life to save thousands of others.

Eva had always known it would come to this. Hadn't Lina known it, too? Hadn't she brought this on herself?

Hadn't she been desperate to find another way? Hadn't she said she didn't want to die?

Eva had a very strong feeling Lina was going to find some way to come back and haunt her. But that, at the very least, would make life interesting.

Even bearable.

Eva swallowed around the swell of emotion in her throat. "Ask Yara if she will come to me." Her voice wavered. She suddenly needed Yara. Needed her badly. She did not know if she could do this alone, did not want to be alone when Lina...

It shocked her, because she always wanted to be alone. Preferred it. Eva did not like people.

But there was also a small part of her that ached to be known, that ached for company in small lapses in between months of contented solitude. It would burst upon her like sunshine after a storm, this sudden fury of longing.

What *was* Yara doing? Where *was* she? She'd sent her to deal with Lina's brother, to turn his broom boat back, to remind him that what he was attempting was treason. A sacrifice was *necessary*. Lina had offered to do this.

Eva pressed a thumb to her bottom lip, biting down hard. Hadn't Omar said the islanders were turning on the witches? If Lina's brother had dared attack Yara…or was Yara merely distracted by his handsome face?

Cyla laid an insistent palm on Eva's forearm. "Make the right decision. You know what's at stake."

"I know. I *will*," Eva snapped.

This, all of this, was why she had cast away her heart. Because despite her best attempts not to let anyone in, irritating people kept sneaking through the cracks somehow. She *still* cared, still loved.

Still hurt.

"Natalia made you queen for a reason," said Cyla.

Because her sister must have believed her strong enough to do this. She had entrusted Eva with the island she had loved.

Yet a part of Eva couldn't quite believe Natalia had willingly trapped her in this cage she'd been so eager to escape herself.

Eva moved to the closest door, gripping the handle deathly tight, giving a single sharp nod. "Gather whatever is necessary, whoever is necessary. Prepare to leave for St. Casimir's Square. We'll perform the sacrifice early. I won't let our home sink. I'll bring Lina Kirk myself."

Relief showed plainly on Cyla's face.

Eva opened the door, stepping through with a little gush of water, heels clicking on the cold marble floor, ignoring the agonizing ache in the hollow where her heart had been. Her gaze lifted unwillingly, skipping past amber-and-gold-leaf screens, skating over the empty daybed. Noting the bottled spell shattered on the floor.

A wave of uneasiness washed through her.

Cyla checked the balcony. Returned, the bells in her hair chiming in her wake. Chiming like funeral bells. "She's not here. Where would she go?"

Eva bit the tip of her thumb again. "I don't know. Just find her."

26

L I N A

THE DOORS WEREN'T COOPERATING.

It didn't matter how Thomas pleaded with them while Lina stood mute by his side. It was as if the Water Palace knew what was happening and was rearranging its rooms to stop its guests from escaping. As Lina stepped from an empty tea room into a familiar balcony-lined corridor, her gut pinched with the tiniest hint of guilty relief.

But isn't this what you wanted?

She clutched the wooden oar to her chest, trying not to imagine what would happen if Eva caught them running away together. Trying not to feel guilty that they *were* running away. She shouldn't feel guilty. Eva was the one who had told her to be more selfish, more terrible, to put herself first. This was what Eva had wanted.

Doors dotted the wall opposite the line of balconies. Thomas reached for another brass handle, but it tore from his grip, yanked open by someone on the other side.

Lina could not have said who looked more surprised, Thomas or Marcin.

A bolt of lightning flashing outside lit his red hair, glinted in his wide hazel eyes. "Well, this I was definitely not expecting."

As the door clicked closed behind him, Marcin's gaze flicked past and then between them, his lip curling. "But I suppose I did tell you," he said to Lina, "to focus your energy on getting away from here. And Thomas Lin, you really cannot stay away. This is good. No, excellent. I would have hated to leave the island without giving you the goodbye you deserve."

Thomas tensed.

"Leave?" Lina moved in front of Thomas, pulse spiking. "What do you mean, leave? And you can't touch him. Eva promised."

"Eva promised you could take his place as this year's sacrifice. Nothing more. Nothing less. And she promised me that I could feed him to her pet serpent as soon as you were dead." Marcin smiled as the color drained from Lina's face.

It wasn't true. He was lying. Eva wouldn't.

"Our lovely queen has no heart, little dancer. She tore it out." Marcin flapped his hand, shooing her aside.

Lina didn't move. Her grip tightened on the wooden oar. She reached behind her back with one hand, finding Thomas's forearm, pressing an urgent message into his skin: *Go.*

He only needed to open another door. The next one down the corridor. She'd keep herself between him and Marcin, a shield. She was still this year's sacrifice. They still needed her. Marcin couldn't hurt her.

An exasperated sound rumbled from Marcin's throat. Real anger crept into his voice now. "Are you really going to waste yourself on him? He isn't worth it. He wouldn't do the same for you. He left you here."

"Maybe." Lina drew a breath. "But he also came back, and even if he hadn't—" Even if he hadn't, it didn't matter. She was doing the right thing, protecting someone because she had the power to do so. It didn't matter if he would do the same or if she was or wasn't in love with him. "Do you really think I'm going to just stand here and do nothing? Do not *insult* me." She pressed her fingers deeper into Thomas's arm, irritation surging through her when he didn't move.

Marcin's gaze didn't leave hers as he dug into his pocket for a hip flask, took a long swig from it, and swallowed. His motions were tight and controlled. Then he licked a finger and painted a shape in the air so quickly she almost missed it. Magic rippled through the air like heat. Reaching for her, reaching past.

"Lina." The fear in Thomas's voice tore through her. He let out a pained gasp and doubled over, knocking into her shoulder blades, throwing her forward.

She swung toward him, then back to Marcin, pivoting,

spinning with all the fluid grace of dancer. Hitching up the oar, wielding it the way she would a blade in a battle dance.

The flat of it sliced the air, catching Marcin's jaw with a deafening *crack*.

A grunt burst from his lips as his head snapped back. He staggered against the door frame, dropping the flask, cursing, blood staining his teeth. He caught the oar in a white-knuckled grip as Lina swept it up a second time. His other hand lashed out, catching her by the hair, slamming her face-first into the stone wall.

Lina's vision exploded in sparks. Fire and agony burst through her forehead, her nose. Her legs folded under her, the world spiraling into black. Hot blood gushed furiously from her nose, over her lips and down her chin.

Across the floor, Thomas moaned.

"Just for that..." Marcin yanked Lina's arm up, ripping her glove off and spitting into her hand. Drawing a symbol in the hot saliva, drawing magic on her palm.

Lina tried to roll sideways, to use momentum to wrench free, crying out as he twisted her wrist viciously. Blood filled her mouth. His grip was iron. "You can't." Her words were thick. Her face throbbed. "Eva needs me. It has to be me as sacrifice. The island will sink!"

"Let it." Marcin's clipped words carried an echo of Thomas's from earlier. "This city is cursed. It can all end right here if only we let it."

Lina kicked at Marcin's shins, making him stumble and fall half on top of her. "Eva won't—"

"Eva doesn't even have to know you're gone," finished Marcin for her.

A terse knocking sounded on the door that had closed behind him. Lina opened her mouth to shout.

"Don't speak," whispered Marcin.

Her palm burned like a brand. A hundred tiny hooks sank through her lips and sealed them tight.

"Don't fight."

The order slithered through her ears, burrowing deep into her marrow, tugging at every fiber of her being. Like when he'd stolen control of her hand, yanking her fingers backward; a will that wasn't her own pulled on muscle, on blood, on bone.

No.

Lina craned her neck. Thomas was sprawled on the carpet but was dragging himself up.

Marcin spat into his own hand and clenched his fist.

Thomas's lips parted, pressed together, formed the shapes of words, but no sound escaped. His eyes turned frantic. A hand flew to his mouth, his throat.

"Look at me," said Marcin.

And Lina did, something inside of her snapping, stretched to the breaking point. She turned her head.

The terse knocking came again, hammering in time with her heart.

The scene swam, rippled, *changed*, the way it had at the revel after Eva had worn her face and kissed Thomas. The hard edges of Marcin's features softened. Smoothed. The violent welt blooming at his jaw vanished. Pale lips blushed pink. Pale cheeks warmed to a sandy hue. Hazel eyes turned a cold storm gray, red fading from short hair until there was only gold.

Blood bubbled from Lina's nose, dripped from her horrified lips, her chin. Deep crimson speckled the creamy carpet, blossoming like flowers. His face was a mirror of her own, minus the blood and anguish.

"Coming!" Marcin called, and his voice was hers now, too, high-pitched and lilting. His black suit was transforming. He leaned in close, breath hot and wet against Lina's ear. "See? No one will know you're gone. That balcony over there? You're going to crawl to it. And then you're going to cast yourself *off* of it, into the sea. Understood? Now nod."

Lina nodded, and when Marcin let go of her arm and turned toward the door, turned to smile sweetly at Thomas, she started to crawl toward the balcony.

27

EVA

WHERE HAD SHE VANISHED TO, where had she gone? Eva had *told* Lina to stay put. Had told her to stay safe in the salon with the balcony where they'd... She'd thought Lina had returned to her room, but she wasn't *in* her room.

Was she hiding?

Was she running?

A part of Eva was almost glad.

"Oh!" exclaimed Cyla, looking back up the wide curving staircase they'd just climbed, then retreated down after finding the double doors at the top locked tight.

It was rare for any room in the Water Palace to be locked to Eva. She half wished she hadn't told her siblings to seal the doors in the flooded sections of the palace. It meant taking detours now. It meant the doors themselves were confused and couldn't usher her through their usual passages.

The doors at the top of the staircase sighed softly now as they swung open; Lina spilled out in a sea-green dress and gloves, cheeks flushed, eyes bright with mischief.

"Where?" Eva burst out, and the word was like a dagger thrown, exploding out of her, flung at the closest target. She was at the foot of the staircase in an instant, brushing past Cyla, splashing through the dark water swilling an inch deep across the floor. "Where did you go? Why didn't you stay where I told you to?"

Lina blinked. "What's got you in such a mood?"

You.

Always you.

Since the night of the revel. Since the day you stormed my palace.

Natalia had spelled Eva to sleep when she'd sacrificed herself, and it had always felt to Eva as if she'd never entirely woken from that spell. It had held her here in stasis, paralyzed with fury and drowning in grief. The whole world had gone down with her sister, sinking into the deep, and Eva had lain there dreaming ever since, coming apart like a shipwreck slowly rotting into pieces.

Until Lina had forced her way in and started the story moving again, a prince dashing into a castle to break a curse. Ripping Eva from her slumber, making her remember, flinging the blankets back and dragging her hissing and flinching into the light.

Lina came down the stairs, pausing on the bottom step, dipping a toe into an inky puddle with a distasteful expression. "It's very wet in here, isn't it?"

Eva clenched her teeth, twisting her hands in the fabric of her dress just to have something to do with them. Water weeped from the ceiling, dripped saliva-like down the mirrored walls. "Cyla," she called. "You can gather the others now. Tell Marcin he is to stay behind and stem this flooding by himself."

"Marcin," said Cyla.

"Marcin?" asked Lina. "That's the handsome one, right? Where are you all going?"

Handsome.

Eva's eyelid twitched. "The *useless* one, you mean." She'd told him to ward the doors, told him they weren't leaving the island. Why did he have to fight her? Why was he making their family panic, using their fear to turn them all against her? Convincing them to leave because he wanted to leave? This was why Natalia had not left him in charge—because he did not love the island the way she had. He could not be trusted to protect their home the way Eva would.

"Tell him if he doesn't, I will take such a tithe of magic from him that he'll have nothing left."

Lina stiffened.

Eva would snip off the tips of his remaining fingers. She would shear off the strands of his fire-red hair. Take pints of his blood to drip into bottled spells, as Natalia had done to the witches who made trouble for her. She would take all his magic. She raised her chin toward the ceiling and shut her eyes. No matter how much she loved him, she would punish him this time, even if it killed a part of her to do so, even if it killed another part of him.

Cyla murmured something inaudible and left, hurrying up the staircase, disappearing through the doors at the top.

Eva let out a long breath, recoiling as cold fingertips dusted her cheekbone, swept a strand of dark hair away from her face.

Lina tucked the strand behind Eva's ear, fingers brushing her crown. That heavy thing of scorched steel and spikes that Marcin had once laughed at her for choosing. He'd given her braid a playful tug and pinched a spike, lifting it off her brow. "Why would you wear a crown someone could so easily rip off your head?"

"Because I'd rip it off my own head first," Eva had snapped, slapping his hands away, "and stab them with it if they even thought to try."

Lina dropped her hand. In the other she clutched a silver flask, lifting it now to her mouth.

"Where did you get that?"

"This? Didn't you give it to me as one your gifts?" Lina took a long sip before offering it to Eva. "You look like you could use a pick-me-up."

Eva's nose wrinkled. "Did you just spit into it?"

"No. Why would I do that?"

Eva took the flask and savored the heat as malt whiskey burned her throat. She willed herself to be stone, made her face a mask.

You can do this. You have no other choice.

She'd already sent Cyla ahead to gather the others. "It's almost the full moon…"

Maybe it was because they were alone in the cold and dripping ballroom, surrounded by icy mirrors, the high ceiling soaring into shadow, but the words seemed to echo with an awful finality.

Like last words.

Eva took a second sip from the flask, biting her lips together. They were tingling. Her skin prickled, flashing hot-cold-hot-cold with nerves. She was suddenly afraid that she'd say the wrong thing, that she'd tell Lina to go, to run, afraid that she would decide to let the world drown to save the girl in front of her.

She shoved the thought down. There was no time for this, for grief, for regrets. "It's almost the full moon and the tide is… You have to understand, I can't, there is no other way…"

Eva swayed. Staggered. Her tongue was numb. The world was tipping, tipping, tipping. "What did you—"

What was in the flask?

She dropped it, metal hitting the floor with a crash. Lina steadied her, an arm around her waist, holding her upright with surprising strength.

How long had she been planning this?

Eva's legs buckled, knees striking the floor with a crack she didn't. The puddled water soaked her dress, soaked through her sheer silk stockings as Lina helped to lower her and laid her at the foot of the staircase.

She took Eva's face in both hands, a grip that was almost painful. "I would have taken you away from all this. I wanted to so badly, but you are *so* stubborn. I tried to steer you toward the right choices. I tried to hold you up. But I can't take your weight any longer, Eva, not if it means keeping my own head above the water. Not if it means keeping all of us from drowning. I can't watch this island destroy you. Can't you see what it has done to you? It's eaten you alive like it did Natalia."

Cold lips pressed a kiss to her forehead. "You would even have taken my magic. Cut pieces from me willingly. Do you know what it feels like to have your magic stolen from you? To watch as your bones are ground down to dust and sprinkled into potions? You made me do this. You gave me no choice."

Eva's eyelids fluttered, the words not making any sense. Consciousness was a guttering candle. Yet she couldn't help but smile, a last bittersweet twist of her lips, a strange triumph singing through her veins as she slipped slowly into the dark. Hadn't she said from the very beginning that caring only got you hurt, that caring got you killed?

There was a certain savage satisfaction in knowing she was right, even now, at the very end.

Because it was the end. Lina crossed the floor, wrenching open the doors at the opposite end of the ballroom, letting in a great gushing wave of black water, pausing to welcome in the tide.

Eva could smell old seaweed, old fish. The tangy scent of the sea cave. The door must have opened into it. Her vision dipped in, out. She focused one final time on Lina as she rushed back past, chased by the water that was now crashing over Eva, escaping up the staircase, leaving her to drown.

28

LINA

LINA COULDN'T FIGHT IT.

That balcony over there? You're going to crawl to it. And then you're going to cast yourself off it, into the sea.

Marcin's will was like a weight pressing heavy on her body, rough fingers forcing their way into her mind, wrenching control of muscle and bone, commanding her to crawl, forcing her to keep going.

She couldn't stop herself. She couldn't stop her body. She was a prisoner inside of it, screaming herself hoarse. Terrible things were happening to Thomas, to Eva, and there wasn't anything, anything, she could do to stop it.

Why are you so weak? Why are you letting this happen? Fight it. Fight.

Lina's dress dragged across the rain-slick stone, knees and palms scraped raw. Why couldn't she stop this? Why wasn't she as strong as the girls in the stories?

But this wasn't a story. This was really happening, and she was too damn *weak*.

Her nails splintered and bled as she fought to dig them into the floor, to claw them into some crack, trying desperately, fighting every inch of movement as her body dragged itself to standing and clambered onto the slippery, icy balustrade.

For the space of a breath, she halted there, seated astride it, as if she'd merely skipped outside to idle and kick her legs over the storm-dappled sea. Wet hair plastered her cheeks. Every nerve screamed *no*. Rain slipped between her lips as she swayed, tilted, buffeted by the wind. She looked down and knew, knew she was going to shatter when she hit that roiling liquid darkness far below. Knew she would feel it, hear it, that terrible wet crack as she broke across the waves.

Please. Don't.

Her body didn't listen. There was no one there to help. Lina tipped forward, legs and body sliding, slipping off the balustrade with a whisper, a regretful sigh of silk.

She fell like a star, faster than the rain, plunging, plummeting toward midnight-black water.

Moments passing in rapid heartbeats, wind shrieking in her ears. Plummeting down, down, down. The sea rushed up to meet her, the inky surface separating into white-crested waves, each tiny individual ripple cast by the rain.

The tide rose up. Eager. Hungry.

From the depths, two great watery arms shot skyward, slim and elegant as waterspouts. The outline of wrists and hands shaped from water and sea foam, delicate half-moon fingernails etched in sea lace. Two giant palms cupped, catching Lina as she had once caught flame.

She pooled in the liquid curve of those palms for an instant, another agonized heartbeat. The strangely solid sea was cool and alive against her bare skin, pulsing as if blood raced through it.

The dark tide was so eager to taste her that it hadn't waited for her to fall but had plucked her from the sky like some ripe fruit.

But it didn't swallow her, didn't gulp her down. The hands gently lowered and dropped her with a small wet smack into the bottom of a familiar red-and-gold broom boat. A puddle pooled beneath her shocked body, saltwater washing the tears from her eyes.

"Well, now," said Finley shakily. "Don't you look like absolute shit." But his voice broke. And *his* eyes were glassy.

The water puddling beneath Lina swirled and gathered itself, receding over the broom boat's rail as if from a sandy shore. Her body was her own again. The vile weight of that twisted will had finally let her go.

And Finley, Finley was here. Her brother drew her into the warm circle of his stupid strong arms, crushing her to his hard chest so tightly that all the air squeezed out of her lungs and her throat burned with the scent of that awful overpowering perfume he poured on by the bottle. Vanilla and smoke and spicy cedar. Because he thought it made him irresistible to girls.

Lina started to cry. Not tears of frustration or fury, not one or two tears escaping to slip silently down her cheek, but rasping, strangled, full-body sobs. Wrenching and raw and aching. Her nose was a tender mass of swollen flesh. It felt like someone had taken a hammer to her face. Pain throbbed through her when she tried to breath. Everything hurt so, so much. She'd been so, so scared.

Finley held her tighter.

"What was she thinking?" A husky voice was asking him. "Was *this* your plan to rescue her? What happened to her face?"

Lina blinked rapidly, the blurred shadow looming over her and Finley spiraling slowly into focus. Darkly painted lips against brown skin. Black hair set in perfect finger waves, sculpted to frame a questioning face. A long black dress fluttering in the wind.

A witch.

Lina's chest constricted. Paralyzing fear turned her entire body to ice, vomiting up her throat before recognition clicked. Yara. Yara, who'd said her brother was handsome, who had made sure no harm came to him at the palace.

"Why in hell would you jump from there?"

Finley tensed. "Don't you yell at her!"

"I'm not yelling." Fat drops of rain spat from the sky, trailing down Yara's neck like tiny diamonds, dripping from the end of Lina's nose.

In one white-knuckled fist, Finley clutched a length of braided hair and twine, knotted and threaded through with mother-of-pearl and bone. The witch's ladder he'd won all those nights ago at the revel for Mama and Ma, a charm for sailing safely through storms.

The broom boat rocked as he struggled out of his raincoat, draping it over Lina like a blanket. A small white puff of a dog wormed between his shins—Auntie Van's dog, Tam, shoving his icy wet nose into the crook of Lina's knee, sniffing, sniffing, sniffing.

"I just want to know what happened?" Yara's voice, that voice that pitched at the end of every sentence, making every phrase sound like a question, didn't fit with the intensity in her eyes, the anxious rigidity of her spine. She perched at the prow like a mermaid figurehead, both fierce and fragile. "You said Thomas went in to get her."

Cold fingers squeezed Lina's throat. Tears blurred her vision. "Marcin. It was Marcin. He wants the island to sink. He wore my face. He said Eva—he took—" She choked on the words, on Thomas's name.

Yara's face was grim. Her black hair melted into the rain-shrouded shadow of the palace beyond, its wicked spires crowning her. She cursed loudly, fluently, then bent to rap her knuckles urgently against the side of the boat, attempting to steer it, to urge it forward.

But the little skiff was enchanted to follow Finley's orders, spelled to listen to him and Lina and Ma and Mama alone.

Shouts and sharp staccato barks, louder than thunder, trembled in the air. Lightning scorched the scene into Lina's eyes: Tam scampering from one end of the boat to the other, tail wagging madly. Yara beating her fist on the wood, shouting at Finley that he owed her for the magic she'd just done, for saving Lina. Finley shouting back that Yara owed him for his saving her from Eva's sea serpent. Amber lantern light winking in the palace windows ahead like guttering candles.

"We're not going in there," Finley bellowed. "I'm not taking her back there. Lina, Uncle's evacuating. Don't worry, we're not going back."

Lina did not want to go back.

The broom boat rolled on the waves, the sea sloshing against its sides. Water slapped the hull, burst over the bow. She could fall asleep to that familiar cadence. Wanted to so very badly. She wanted to curl up here in her brother's strong arms, blanketed by the oilskin raincoat, and let Finley sail her home. She wanted to let her eyelids flutter shut and sink into peaceful blackness, to not think, to forget everything, to imagine it had all just been a bad dream.

But she didn't. She couldn't. She reached out with a shaking hand and rapped her knuckles against the broom boat's side.

LINA

THERE WERE TOO MANY STAIRS in the Water Palace. Too many stairs and too many doors and too many endless flooded corridors for someone still recovering from a broken ankle. Someone who'd just rolled that ankle for the hundredth time as she rushed indoors. Someone with a broken nose. Someone whose whole body was aching.

Lina cursed as they climbed a spiral staircase, cursed as they crossed an empty landing beneath a ceiling set with milky stars, cursed as they flitted past framed portraits of frowning witches only to find *another* flight of stairs twisting skyward, another useless empty room, another spiteful, glyph-engraved door.

She cursed the world and whatever stupid person had built this palace, cursed the witches for dredging it up from the depths of the sea, for feeding the doors so much magic that they'd acquired minds of their own. She cursed herself and her body and her utter uselessness right now. Cursed Yara for speeding away as soon as they'd raced indoors without telling them which way to go.

"You're not even the one doing the damned work!" Finley huffed out, panting, sweat pouring from his temples, down the back of his neck, his handsome face flushed an angry red from piggybacking her through what felt like half the goddamn palace.

Lina adjusted her monkey grip on his shoulders. "Could you go any *slower*?"

"Could you lose any *weight*?" he shot back, sounding exactly like one of their aunties.

Lina resisted the extremely tempting urge to lock her arms around his throat and strangle him.

But then who would carry her?

"Please." She shut her eyes, bit her lip. She had not fought this long and this hard for nothing. Thomas. Eva. Marcin.

What was he doing while wearing her face? Would he hurt Eva the way he'd hurt her? Would Eva stop him from hurting Thomas? Was Thomas…

Don't think.

The roar and rush of water, voices high and low, angry and frightened, filtered through the walls. The drub of running steps. The unmistakable sounds of panicked arguing. All conjured up images, each one darker and more horrific than the last.

Lina tried not to think, and then tried to think of nice things to block the bad thoughts out: being named Best Dancer two years running; winning a solo in the autumn performance; the fact that Finley was here, that he'd come to rescue her; working magic with Eva; slurping steaming cups of Caldellan stew with Ma on the wharf; Thomas's promise-filled smile.

But her mind had never been cooperative or skilled at holding on to the good things. The memories morphed into nightmares; her shining awards turned into bloodstained weapons. Thomas's smile became a scream.

The stairs curved up and up and up.

"I know you hate him. I know you might hate Eva, too, but she only made me the sacrifice because I—"

"Lina," Finley gritted out. "I'm *going* as fast as I can, all right?"

Lina jolted up and down as her brother took the steps two at a time. Her rain-soaked clothes stuck to her skin. Every breath felt like she was inhaling needles.

"And I, about Thomas—" Anguish deepened her brother's voice. "I still don't like him. And he's still too old for you. He deserved that black eye. Oy, don't slap!" Finley's grip tightened on her knees, hitching her higher on his back. "But he came looking to rescue you. He should have come a damn sight sooner. But he admitted that, too. And I know how it feels to want desperately to make up for something you've done that's unforgivable."

Lina leaned her forehead into the back of his head.

"I would've taken the devil's help if it meant saving you," Finley said.

The door at the top of the stairs had no brass knob to turn, no gold handle to jiggle. It was sealed by no visible lock or bolt. Lina clung on as Finley slammed a shoulder into the shimmering dark wood.

The door scraped, gave a little, stuck fast.

Lina let out a snarl of pure animal frustration. Guttural. Raw. The echo dwindled into the sound of Finley's ragged breathing.

He threw his whole weight against the door. Lina beat on it with her fists above his head, pleading, flattering. It didn't budge.

Finley cursed, pressing his forehead to the wood, chest heaving. Lina sucked in a deep breath.

And remembered.

She dug a frantic hand down the front of her dress, into her brassiere, digging out the mother-of-pearl comb wound with Eva's red string bracelets and ink-black hair. That curious sensation, that hum that seemed to sing through the strands like a plucked string, prickled her fingers and chased up her arm. "Put me down! Put me down!"

"What?"

"Now!"

Finley knelt, and Lina half fell, half scrambled off his back. Her fingers were busy teasing a loop of string free, trying not to think of the last time she had worked magic with Eva's hair out on the balcony in the storm.

"Where did you get that?" breathed Finley.

"You're not the only one who gets gifted magic." Lina stretched the red string taut and racked her brain. A knot would be quicker than making shapes, like those Eva had tied in her witch's ladder during the storm. But what knot did you tie to force open a door? What knot did you tie to will it to take you where you wanted? A reef knot? A bowknot? A tiller's hitch?

She could tie any of those with her eyes closed. She had an elephant's memory, the Conservatoire's instructors liked to say. She never had to be shown a set of steps twice. But she didn't know what each knot meant. She didn't know how to speak to magic. It was like knowing the words of a foreign language but not what order to put them in.

"Let me."

Lina twisted away from her brother, pinched the strings between her fingers, shut her eyes, and recalled the sensation of doing magic with Eva. That intoxicating, terrifying thrill. That tantalizing feeling of absolute power.

Please.

She threaded a loop. *Please. Please open, please take me to where I need to go.*

She imagined the soft scrape the door would make as it swung open. Willed the charm to work with everything she had.

The door stayed closed.

Finley glanced back and forth between her and the door as he pushed. The patterns decorating the darkly polished wood shimmered and shifted restlessly. Mockingly.

Rage and despair choked Lina, and she swallowed them both down. She slammed a palm against the wood, throat tight, eyes burning. She tied a blood knot and held her breath as string and hair started to glow a fiery orange.

It started at the tips of her fingers: a faint prickling like pins and needles, blossoming into searing heat. Full-blown fire. Lina let out a cry as it engulfed her. There was a flash of blinding white, the heat at the very center of a star.

Please, she whispered to the magic.

And this time, it listened.

Lina leaned her weight into the door and fell through it as effortlessly as sunlight falling through glass—catching her balance at the top of another grand staircase. There was a pained "Hell!" as Finley followed her and stumbled. The door had vanished completely, leaving only an empty arch. The blinding light of the magic was fading, revealing details: a glowing amber chandelier, pale stairs running down into a ballroom flooded with black water. The swell slapped against the stairs, rising halfway to the top, to where they stood.

There was something swimming in it. Something scaled and dark and sinuous, something keening horribly as it tried to nudge something smaller and equally dark onto the steps. A body facedown in the dark water, head crowned with scorched steel and spikes.

No.

Lina flew down the staircase while Finley grabbed for her, trying to stop and steady her.

"Don't you dare. Don't you *dare!*" She fell to her knees, dragging Eva onto the stairs, her upper body out of the water. The sea serpent's breath was hot on the back of her neck, stinking and rotten. Its endless keening made her shudder. "Finley!"

Eva's head lolled. Water ran down her cheeks and lips. Bloodless lips. Ashen skin. Closed eyes. Lashes two charcoal crescents.

Lina ran her hand over Eva's mouth, over her nose, feeling below her chin. No heartbeat. No breath.

"I'll get help. I'll go get…" Finley was already racing back up the stairs, through the arch where the door had been, his calls for Yara echoing.

"It's awfully hard to kill a witch"—wasn't that what the witchlings had said? Hadn't Eva bled herself into the sea and survived? Hadn't she faced down this very sea serpent and survived?

But hadn't Natalia drowned? Hadn't Lina watched her?

That was different, she told herself—that was magic spent, magic sacrificed. Magic didn't die, it was just used up. Eva was still here. She hadn't faded away. Didn't witches fade away like dreams at sunrise when they died?

So she mustn't be dead. Couldn't be.

She didn't have a *heart*—that's what the islanders said. What Marcin had said. She'd sealed it inside a bottle and cast it out to sea. She was like the sea giant in that old, old story, the one who'd hidden his heart outside his body so he couldn't be killed.

Lina stared at the gray, almost-translucent sheen of Eva's skin.

"Don't you dare go. Don't you dare." A ragged sob tore from her throat.

She dug her nails into Eva's shoulders. Into cold, clammy skin. She pressed her mouth against Eva's unresponsive one, blowing in breath, pounding on Eva's chest, trying to remember what Ma had taught her to do when a sailor went overboard.

She looked up when footsteps sounded. "Finley?"

But it was a slim, silver-haired figure in black standing at the top of the stairs. Jun. The witch whose humming and singing had taken away her pain in the ship's cabin after the regatta. He stared at her and Eva in obvious horror, stared beyond them both to the sea serpent swimming through the flooded ballroom in fretful, anxious circles, churning up waves that broke with a splatter against Lina's side.

"Help!" Lina croaked. "Please help!" She was ripping strands of hair from Eva's head now, knotting them desperately, wishing, pleading once more with magic. The strands started to glow.

Jun's shadow spilled over her.

"Marcin, he wore my face and..." Lina swore she felt Eva shudder.

Jun dropped to his knees. A wiry arm snaked around Lina's waist from behind, pulling her back and flush against his firm chest, away from Eva.

Lina squirmed as a hand clamped over her mouth, sweat-sticky skin smushed against her lips. "Shush. Shush, now. Oh hell, Marcin, really? It's one thing to say we're leaving Eva behind because she's stubborn, quite another to..." Hot breath tickled Lina's ear as Jun spoke his thoughts out loud. "I'm sorry, I really am, but I can't have you telling anybody."

Lina writhed furiously, a muffled shriek making it through the sweaty hand covering her mouth.

The arm around her tightened.

The sea serpent lifted its head from the water and keened.

The lights guttered.

The ballroom went dark. Utterly dark. The darkness of a night with no moon, when storms and smoke blocked out the stars.

The arm around Lina loosened. Let go. The palm covering her mouth peeled away.

She gulped in a great shuddering breath. The air was so heavy and gritty with magic that she could taste it, ash on the back of her tongue. She couldn't see an inch in front of her, couldn't see her own hands.

But she could feel it—something waking. For it was not an *empty* darkness.

There were staggering steps behind Lina, then a scream, but it cut off. A horrible, wrenching tearing, like cloth ripped in half.

But she did not think what was ripping was cloth. It was something thicker, juicier, meatier. Lina's heart raced faster, faster. Something brushed her side. She flinched but didn't dare move.

Someone moaned.

The light came back slowly, softly at first, as the haze cleared, as the black smoke coalesced into a queen and the world faded back into focus.

Eva stood over Jun. Scorched steel crown clenched in one hand, lurid crimson dripping from its spikes onto the pale staircase.

Lina didn't want to think what she'd done with that crown, did not look closely at Jun's crumpled, cowering form. She kept her gaze locked on Eva, whose eyes were open. Open and empty, like a hollow doll's. Lina had seen Eva look smug, had seen her look shocked, furious, mischievous, cold, and uncaring.

She had never seen her look lost, look naked, look *haunted*.

Something in Lina told her to turn away, turn away quickly. They weren't anything at all to each other, really. And yet it broke something inside of her to see Eva looking like that, and she was suddenly terribly frightened by the thought of never again seeing that familiar knife-sharp smile, that mischievous, smug version of the other girl. The thought was somehow unbearable.

Lina stood, weight on her strong leg. The words were out before she could think better of them, an echo of Eva's first words to her, back in the sea cave. "Did you enjoy drowning?"

Eva didn't move, didn't blink.

But there was a flicker of something in the depths of those dark eyes. A spark. Like fire. Like the gleam of starlight on the sea at night. Lina watched the color seep back into Eva's cheeks with a relief that made her weak, and something else that she wasn't yet willing to put a name to that made her chest grow tight.

Eva stalked closer, the *drip-drip-drip* of blood from the unforgiving spikes of her crown. Her free hand lashed out, wrapped around Lina's throat before she had time to breathe, and squeezed. "Are you sorry that you didn't stay to watch?"

30

EVA

FEET POUNDED DOWN THE STAIRS. Rough hands tore Eva from Lina, jerking her around to face a second set of merciless, storm-gray eyes. "What in hell are you doing, you ghoul? She came to *help* you."

A voice hoarse and low and trembling with fury, yet liltingly familiar. As the rest of the boy's features were painfully familiar. Those eyes, those cheekbones, those strangely square brows.

Lina's brother shook Eva so hard it felt like her teeth would rattle.

"Finley! Wait, Finley!" Lina had fallen back, a hand to her throat, coughing. Her other hand stretched out in anxious appeal.

Lina Kirk, always putting other people before herself.

"Finley!" Another voice. Yara was flying down the stairs after him. "E, thank God, I thought—"

"Finley." Lina pleaded with her brother. Her brother, who had come for her, to save her, like Natalia had once saved Eva.

The emptiness inside Eva's chest expanded. Her left hand clenched around steel, around the sharp spikes of her bloodstained crown. When the water from the sea cave had flooded in and the magic had wound around her like chains, dragging her deep into the dark, she'd wondered: Would she see Natalia before the end? Would she dream of her sister?

How badly she had wanted to. People said it happened, that they spoke to the dead as their own deaths drew near. That their loved ones came to offer them peace, forgiveness. That they urged them to live, to love, to follow their dreams.

Funny how what the dead wished for was always what the living most desired.

Natalia had not visited Eva, had not come for her as Lina's brother had. There had been nothing but the icy bite of the water and darkness. And she'd decided then that if *she* came back, she would offer no one forgiveness. She would wish for no one to live or love. She would haunt them all. Every last one.

Thomas Lin, whom she had trusted with her sister. Lina Kirk, who had left her to drown.

To be eaten by her own pet sea serpent. Only it hadn't eaten her.

Her loyal monster, the only creature she could trust.

Eva's gaze slid away from Finley, a tiny crease forming between her brows as she soaked in details her mind had not registered earlier. A tight, deathly stillness stole over her, constricting her chest and making her voice a hiss, a whisper.

"Who did that to you?"

This was not the Lina she remembered lowering her to the floor, welcoming in the tide. The deep bruises blooming below those eyes, across the bridge of her nose; the blood crusting above her lip, down her chin; the bedraggled, sodden sun-gold hair—Eva would murder whoever had done this.

"Marcin," Yara said quietly, tugging on Finley's sleeve, trying to make him release his grip on Eva's arms.

"He wore my face." Lina's eyes were red-rimmed and glassy. "I—" Guilt pinched her features. She forced out the words. "Thomas came for me. Marcin stopped us from escaping. He forced me to jump from one of the balconies. He said you wouldn't have to know I was gone. I don't know what happened afterward. Finley brought me back so I could warn you. I don't know what—I don't know if Thomas—" Her voice cracked, gaze darting past Eva as if she thought she might find Thomas Lin lurking in the curves of the ballroom's staircase. As if it might not be too late. "Were you going to give him to Marcin? Were you going to let Marcin feed him to your serpent as soon as I was gone? Even though I…I thought we…"

Eva stared. A bolt of lightning-hot irritation shot through her, head to toe. Did that really matter right now? Was that *really* the question to ask right now?

Marcin.

The name slid between her ribs like a blade, sinking through tender flesh to puncture something vital.

Marcin, who had spat into his silver hip flask and offered it to her. Marcin, who had spoken those nonsensical words.

I can't watch this island destroy you. Can't you see what it has done to you?

You made me do this.

Marcin, who had brought her to the island as a witchling, who still tugged her braids even though she was all grown up, even though she was queen. Marcin, who had raised her alongside Natalia, who was more truly her family than anyone she had left.

Betrayal cut so much *deeper* when you loved the hand that held the knife.

A part of her refused to believe it. Couldn't.

And Lina kept staring at her with those eyes, waiting, searching for an answer to her question. An answer Eva did not want to give.

An apology she did not want to give.

A thousand words balanced on the tip of Eva's tongue, but she didn't know how to say any of them. She had never been good at apologizing or explaining herself; a queen never had to.

And a part of her did not think she had anything to apologize for.

Eva's face was a mask as she withdrew into herself. Chill air and shadows wrapped around her like a cloak, nipping at anyone who dared come close.

Finley finally released her. Yara darted in to sweep a supportive arm around Eva's waist. Finley stepped back with one final warning. "You hurt my sister again, and, witch or not, I will kill you."

"I don't want to hurt her." A lie. Eva wanted to hurt her. She wanted to hurt him. Right now she wanted to hurt the whole world. She wanted to find Marcin and tear him apart. She wanted to rip him into tiny pieces and shred those pieces into tinier pieces. She wanted him at her feet bruised and bleeding. Begging.

Lina's face shuttered.

Behind Eva, someone moaned. Jun, cracking open his eyes. Still cowering, still curled in on himself.

More witches were arriving, exclaiming, surging through the empty archway at the top of the staircase, spilling down it in a living black tide. Echoes bounced strangely off the water and the walls. The scene unfolding with a slow, surreal, almost dreamlike feel. So many voices ringing and melding into one.

"Eva! Thank all the gods. Yara said Marcin attacked you?"

"The doors were sealed. We couldn't find you. Marcin said—"

"Where is he?" cut in Lina.

They ignored her. "Are we really leaving the island? Cyla says we're heading to St. Casimir's Square, that we're performing the sacrifice now."

At the mention of St. Casimir's Square, Finley surged forward. "It's not a full moon. You can't do the magic without the full moon. And Yara told me how you tried to find another way to calm the tide."

The words cut like a second betrayal. A betrayal from Yara this time, giving away Eva's past, her secrets, her failure. Yara, who wouldn't meet her eyes. Yara, who'd maybe been walking the same path with Finley that Eva had with Lina.

Another way. Eva slowly replaced the crown on her head as Finley babbled on, as the rest of her witches stared at him blankly. "Where did he come from?" someone muttered.

Another way with no blood price.

"What if we all gave something?" said Finley. "Each of us folk from Caldella. A tithe taken from every person, young and old. One of our treasures. Something it hurts to lose. The dark tide has a taste for suffering. So we each give it a small bite to sate it. We just need to gather offerings. We just need time to convince people."

There was no time.

A shock of icy black water splattered the backs of Eva's legs. Her serpent stirring, churning white water from black. A strange hunger seeped into her bones along with the wet and the cold, a craving she didn't think was her own.

She could hear it again, that drumming, that ravenous heartbeat. And she knew that if she left the ballroom, stepped out onto one of the palace's countless balconies and looked toward the city, she would hear flood sirens threading through the storm.

There was no time.

She could not afford to fail.

There was no guarantee the tide could be satiated with

anything but the life of the queen herself or the person she cared about.

Another way.

When had she stopped fighting for that? When had she bowed her head to the tide? A queen should answer to no one. When had she decided to give the sea anything more than what she wished to give it?

"Then where did you see Marcin *last*?"

Eva turned. Lina had a hand fisted in the fabric of Omar's coat. The sight might have surprised her once; Omar was well over six feet tall with muscles to rival a pirate's. But this was Lina, the girl who had stormed her palace, who had faced down a sea serpent and offered up her own life to save the boy she loved.

The girl who had danced magic on the bloodstained deck of Eva's ship, who had made her feel things she hadn't thought possible for someone without a heart. The girl who had come back to warn her, save her, even knowing Eva had deceived her, instead of seizing on her one chance to escape being sacrificed.

Foolish, infuriating Lina Kirk.

"St. Casimir's," Omar huffed. "Okay, lass? Marcin heard our talk and said he'd go ahead to check that everything was all right."

Of course he had.

It had probably amused him: Eva out of commission and Thomas in his hands, everyone talking about performing the sacrifice.

The bells in Cyla's silver locks jingled as she came to stand with Eva and Yara, something like understanding passing between all three in a glance. Because they too knew where Marcin would go. He wouldn't be able to resist the urge to perform a little sacrifice of his own in Eva's place, to drown Thomas Lin as she had promised they would at the start.

Lina's head swiveled toward Eva.

Cyla draped a heavy coat—black, as always, with a fur collar and cuffs—around Eva's shoulders, then handed her several braided lengths of hair: brown and blond and black, rich red and palest silver. Eva could see the magic in the strands. A blink and you'd miss it glimmer. A thread of cobweb catching a slant of winter sunlight. A ghostly gleam.

Tithes from her sisters to help with the magic, to bolster Eva's own as she offered the sacrifice, to help cast the spell that would calm the dark tide without the full moon's sway over the sea.

"It can't wait any longer," said Cyla. "Take Lina with you. Save the island first. Deal with Marcin when it's done."

Yara cut a glance to where Finley was arguing with Omar now, lips parting, looking anxious. "E, what Finley said—"

Cyla shoved a small, poison-green bottle into Eva's palm. A chill raced through her, a hint of frost blossoming on her skin, a sense of what magic lurked inside. "To hold her still if she makes trouble."

To hold Lina still while Eva chained her to the pillar.

The chill carried through to her marrow.

Perhaps, in the end, she was more like Natalia than any of them had thought.

"You're all to wait here. I'm going ahead to deal with Marcin." Eva's voice held an order that carried through the flooded ballroom, then dipped too low for anyone but Yara to hear.

Yara's lips formed an O as Eva whispered in her ear. Cyla's eyes narrowed.

"I'm coming, too!" said Lina, pushing closer.

Finley burst into protests. But Eva took Lina's hand, unable to resist lacing their fingers together for the first and final time.

LINA

FINLEY WAS SHOUTING AND LUNGING for her, but Eva pulled Lina close. No time for second thoughts, no time for hesitation, no time for fear. If there was even the slightest chance it was not too late...

Lina's stomach performed a tiny flip, and then she was coming undone, being unmade, folding into wisps of pitch-black smoke with only the feel of Eva's fingers laced tight through her own as an anchor.

They ghosted through the bones of the Water Palace, seeping through stone and wood and mortar, spiriting through abandoned salons and flooded hallways, snaking under the gaps beneath shimmering, glyph-engraved doors. Moving as air and darkness, as shadow and smoke, as one.

Lina didn't dare breathe or speak or swallow, lest she break apart the magic and forever be trapped as something neither solid nor spectral. As form and nothing, both and neither and something in between.

It was terrifying, intoxicating. The darkest kind of thrill.

Pure magic.

Her heart—if she even had a heart right now—pounded hard enough to burst.

And then all of sudden they were outside, spinning amongst the Water Palace's wicked spires, the night breeze chilling them, blowing them higher, silver cobwebs of low cloud left torn and twisting in their wake. The rising moon peaked through the fissures, so luminous, so close to full now, it set diamonds in the inky surface of the sea.

The waves looked so flat from up here. The dark tide was nothing but a darkly sparkling stage to dance upon. The rain had turned to pearly mist. Lights winked in the storm-ravaged city as the wind pushed them closer and closer.

The Witch Queen comes on wings of night...

Never had the lyrics felt so true. They descended on St. Casimir's Square in a great cloud of whirling black smoke. No bonfires here now, no dancers. No wild drums or wail of pipes, only the distant, desperate shriek of flood sirens.

Magic gathered Lina back into being, air and darkness pouring into the contours of a girl with bobbed blond hair, gray eyes, and a stubborn chin.

Eva let go of her hand, and the sudden absence of that touch left Lina strangely bereft.

But she immediately started running, limping, crying out. Deserted shops flashing by, her steps slipping on slick stone cobbles. She flew past the column-lined arcades that enclosed the square on every side but one, falling into the long shadow cast by the pillar in the center, racing for the prone figure chained at its foot.

Thomas.

She made it halfway.

Black water lashed out, a liquid whip snaking around her ankles and yanking her off her feet. Her chin cracked against the cobbles, but the hot stinging in her palms and knees hit first. Agony flared on impact as Marcin materialized from the shadows.

Wind gusted, slamming him back, away from her. Eva swept past, coalescing from sea and sky in a wild whirl of ash and wind, black hair streaming, a single glowing strand of red string floating free from her fingers, silver dancing shoes landing with a lethal click.

Marcin staggered to a knee, spat and smeared a hand across the cobbles in a single fluid gesture. The stone beneath Eva softened, crumbled to sand. She sank in up to her ankle, stumbling off balance. More cobbles ripped free of the earth. Solid. Glistening. Sharp. Firing like bullets.

Lina threw up her arms, covered her head with her hands.

Eva dissolved into smoke, parting around the projectiles, freeing herself from the sand. For a breath, the raging smoky air held the vague shape of a body. A featureless form and face. Then it whirled into a towering, shrieking black cyclone, bearing down on Marcin.

Sand and stone rose to form a wall around him. But air and darkness needled through the cracks, sending tendrils spearing at his arms, his throat.

Lina seized the chance, pushing to her feet, crossing the last distance to Thomas. His chains rattled as she yanked on them. They were wrapped around his chest, his waist, his ankles, iron rubbing tanned skin raw where it shackled his wrists.

Rust flaked and stuck to her palms and fingers, a sharp metallic taste burning the back of her throat. A sickening suspicion knotted her insides. Were these the chains Natalia had worn? The chains that had held her to the pillar as the dark tide came crashing down, as the black waves swept in to take what they were owed?

The sea roared, pounding and smashing against the edge of the square that led straight onto the waves, sending up sweeping crests of crystal spray, spilling and spitting sea foam over the cobbles.

Too far away to feel.

But Thomas was drowning anyway.

Coughing and choking and retching brackish water down his front as magic filled his lungs with saltwater. His body jerked against the chains, one eye bulging, the other swollen shut.

"Eva!" The cry wrenched from Lina. She fell to her knees, fingers scrabbling over the ground, searching for a loose cobble, for something to use to break the chains. Knowing with a piercing, heartrending certainty that Eva wasn't going to help.

Because she didn't care. Because she had always been planning to give Thomas to Marcin.

She felt it again, that same awful splintering in her chest when she'd searched Eva's face in the flooded ballroom, waiting and hoping desperately for a denial. Because some foolish part of her had started to trust the other girl, because some foolish part of her had started to *care*.

Lina caught up a loose end of chain, bringing it down on the cuffs linking Thomas's ankles. Rusted iron shrieked and clanged like a bell again and again, sparks firing off the metal.

All while Thomas was still drowning, still choking, briny water spewing down his front, flecking the base of her neck, the crown of her bowed head.

Still drowning, until he wasn't.

The first great shuddery gasp of air split the night.

Lina looked up, looked behind her. That wild tempest of dark smoke had poured itself back into a body. The whole world stopped as she met Eva's eyes.

And then Marcin was striding past Eva, toward her, hair as wild as flame. Anger rippling off him like heat. Elegant ash-black clothes askew and skin so pale he looked more ghost than living creature.

Was he starting to fade away? Did he have so little magic left?

"You would take even this away from me." He spat into his hand.

And again Eva moved between them like a shield, a pace in front of Lina, a pace away from Marcin. Wisps of black smoke coiling off her olive skin like steam. "Oh, I am going to take much more from you than this," she said.

And yet she did not move.

Eva's fingers were frozen mid-spell; strands of hair and red strings stretched taut, but she did not tie a knot. It was as if some invisible force were holding her back.

Lina wanted to scream at her. *He tried to kill you. He tried to kill me. He wants to let the island drown.*

Sweat glistened at Marcin's temples. The bump in his throat bobbed up and down. "Eva, please. Do you think this is what Natalia would have wanted? For us to fight like this? For us to waste ourselves, our magic, on some silly quarrel?"

"Silly quarrel?" said Eva. "You left me to *drown*."

"You didn't give me a choice! I did it because you would have let us all drown. Because I didn't want you to have to suffer anymore. I did it because I care about you. Because I couldn't bear to watch you hurt. Give me Thomas Lin, Eva. And then we'll go back to the palace. He's the reason we lost Natalia. And this island is what destroyed her. This cursed city ate away at her piece by piece, just as it has eaten away at you. Do you think she wanted this for you? Do you think she wished to chain you here, always at the mercy of the tide? For you to suffer year after year, as she did? You were never meant to be this island's queen. You should never have *been* queen."

Marcin took a single step forward. "You helped kill her, Eva. You and Yara. All that talk about finding another way, giving her hope and then *failing* so spectacularly and snatching that hope away from her."

Eva's face was stricken. Marcin drove the knife home.

"She would never have done what she did if you had not encouraged her first."

Eva's lip trembled, the sight making something pinch inside of Lina.

"If Natalia had left me in charge," finished Marcin, "we could have escaped all this."

Lina wobbled to her feet, hands on Thomas's shoulders for support. He slumped against the chains, against her, eyelids fluttering. Her name a soft exhale.

Marcin's gaze snapped to her, and her heart lurched. "Is that why you won't let me kill him?" he said. "Because of her? You've truly managed to make yourself care for one of the sacrifices, haven't you? For someone other than yourself." His tone was half-incredulous, almost disbelieving.

Lina stared at Eva, her pulse falling in and out of rhythm.

"And yet she loves someone else." Marcin wiped a bloody cheek with his thumb, spat into his hand. "But does she love him enough?"

Eva's head jerked toward the stone pillar, toward Lina. She yanked a glass bottle from the pocket of her coat, hurling it at Marcin. Glass exploded at his feet, plumes of fog twisting free of the shards. Where liquid had splattered, frost formed, a pale glaze staining his boots, stealing up his legs, his torso, hardening like ice.

But not before he painted the air with blood and spit and will, not before a savage smile stretched his lips and magic thrummed through the air like fire.

Lina braced herself, blinding light illuminating the shock on her face, but the magic was not aimed at her.

32

LINA

ALL SHE WOULD REMEMBER AFTERWARD was a flash of light and the sudden absence of sound. An all-encompassing silence, a deafening ringing in her ears, the hush and stillness that followed the final note of a performance. That anxious heartbeat before applause. Black waves struck the stone edge of St. Casimir's Square, salt spray holding a pose in midair, a million glass shards frozen.

Then the world rushed back, and Lina knew what was happening even before it happened. She had sung this song. She had danced this story. She knew it as well as she knew her name. Chains clanged and shattered. Muscle and bone shifted beneath her hands. Agonized screams ripped from Thomas's throat as his joints popped and ligaments snapped. His back arched, skin stretching and shredding, fading to a horrible gray. Hardening into crusted, sea-slick scales.

He was a giant adder writhing in her embrace. A sea serpent stranded on land. A soaring, sinuous monster with dripping venomous fangs. Hissing and twisting.

Lina held on, held tight. She had sworn she would all those nights ago. But her arms could no longer fit around his body, and her nails scrabbled frantically, fruitlessly to find a grip on his scales. She slid and slipped, clinging to the monster's neck as it uncoiled, as it and she rose high into the air.

She dug her nails in. She would not lose him now, not when she'd come so far, not after everything. She would not lose *here*.

The serpent dashed its head against the ground, the impact jolting through her bones, rattling her teeth. Something in her rib cage screamed. Lina clenched her jaw.

It was an illusion. It was magic, a spell cast to make her let go. She *knew* what she was holding. Knew the true shape of the boy she held in her arms.

"Thomas." His name was a ragged gasp.

The monster shuddered and melted in her arms. A pulsating mass of hot sinew and skin. It grew hair. Matted fur reeking of rot and musk, pricking and scratching her palms and cheeks. Her eyes watered at the stench. He was a rabid brown bear. Eyes rolling, jaw snapping, claws raking scars across the cobbles.

A voice shouted at her to remember what she was holding. And she did, she did, she was holding Thomas Lin. The boy who had won his freedom from a witch. The boy she'd admired for two long years. A boy with sun-kissed hair and sea-tanned skin, with dark brown eyes that held a hundred untold secrets.

Lina bit through her bottom lip. Hot blood dribbled down her chin.

The bear tossed its head. Her arms felt like they were about to break.

Hold on.

The bear sniffed the air. Its spine contorted. Twisted. Disappeared.

She was standing, holding fire. A white-hot coal burning bright between her cupped palms.

Flames engulfed Lina. Scorched through the layers of her skin as if it were paper, curling it, blackening it, flaking it into glowing ash. Wave upon wave of furious heat. Her cheeks blistered.

She spun, flailing in terror, trying to beat the flames away.

Where—

The flames snarled. A sea of roiling red and orange stretched in every direction, endless. A fire that would never burn out. The illusion was made real because she'd started to believe in it. Lina's eyes stung with smoke. She stumbled and fell, squinted at her grazed palms and found them empty.

Her fingers spasmed, opening and closing on air and flame. On emptiness.

Gone.

Thomas was...

When the queen turned the lad into fire, the girl's heart failed her. She lost herself to fear and forgot what she was holding. She and the lad burned alive. Burned until there was nothing left.

Lina's throat seized with anguish, with heartrending panic. She tried to recapture the feel of him in her arms, his weight, his shape. But it was like trying to embrace the reflection of the moon on the sea, to clasp smoke or hold hands with a shadow.

Who was Thomas Lin? How well did she really know him?

She pictured herself holding him, kissing him, as she had imagined so many times before, her favorite daydream. How many times had she spun in her head how it would happen, how it would all unfold? The details and scenery changed, but the ending was always the same…save for this time.

Because now she could only remember kissing Eva. The swoop of heat in her stomach, the dark thrill of lips and teeth and tongue. Of a sky set ablaze and eyes that gleamed like starlight on the sea at night. The silky feeling of black hair tangled between her fingers.

Thomas Lin had always been a daydream. A dream that paled in comparison to a memory that was so much more real.

She'd lost him. She would burn here forever. Because her heart and courage had failed her. Because she had not held on. Because she had let go, and the fire was all around her, burning her to ash. She did not love him enough to keep him. She did not even know if she loved him at all.

Lina let out a sob. Heat boiled the tears off her cheeks.

Arms snaked around her waist from behind. Hands cupped hers, cold and steady and unwavering. "You *know* what you are holding. Did you cause me so much trouble over him for nothing? Do you dare think you can disappear from me without finishing what you started? Keep fighting."

Lina felt like she was coming apart, and coming back together.

She shut her eyes and remembered the sunburst of warmth in her chest when Thomas had carried her home, remembered him following her into the revel despite his fears, remembered him coming to rescue her with Finley. She clung tight to those memories, clung tight to him.

Thomas. I'm holding Thomas Lin.

Maybe she didn't feel the same way about him that she once had. But those feelings had still been real, even if they'd shifted, even if they'd changed. Love or not, naive or not, foolish or not, what she had felt for him was still real. And she had come all this way to save him, so she would. She'd made him a promise. She'd dragged him back into all this, and she would drag him back out.

Darkness smothered the flames. Black smoke ruffled her hair.

She held on to the shape of him while Eva held on to her. The Witch Queen burning with her, the tight embrace keeping her safe and whole. The blistering heat faded. The smoke started to lift.

The air tasted of salt and sea, of rain, and of that first fresh inhale after the rain, after the storm had washed the world clean.

Lina knelt at the foot of the stone pillar with Thomas in her arms. His eyes were shut, but he was breathing.

Eva relaxed her grip on Lina.

Everything had gone quiet save for the waves lapping hungrily against the fourth side of St. Casimir's square. The shadows grew deeper, darker, and more velvet, clouds chasing across the surface of the nearly full moon.

But a faint glow still leaked through, limning the words carved deep into the pillar's stone with silver. Marcin, standing watching them, read aloud: "'Our love keeps us from drowning.' Or should it be 'Our love keeps us from burning'? Seeing as you would jump through fire for her." He looked past Lina. "So, Eva, what will you do now?"

33

EVA

"I WOULD HAVE SPARED YOU the choice." Marcin's hair twisted in the salt breeze. The rest of his body was unmoving, legs pinned firmly to the ground with frost, with ice that looked black in the moonlight. "I didn't want you to get attached. I didn't want you to have to hurt."

Then why didn't you help when Natalia was still alive? When I tried to find a way to break the tide's hold over the island and almost died?

"If you had let me take care of things, if Natalia had left me in charge, I would have set you free from this, but you wouldn't let me. You know what it costs to calm the dark tide. You know what the magic requires."

Of course she did. The spell was burned into Eva, listed like the ingredients in a cookbook or an old grimoire.

Take the life of the one you love and mix with the tears you shed for them. Add three drops of blood, three strands of hair, and feed it all to the sea by the light of May's first full moon.

And so they came to the moment, from which there was no escape. Eva stood, looked down, gaze locking with Lina's. Lina's breathing hitched.

Was it love, this searing ache in the hollow inside her chest? This awful twisting in her gut? This absolute refusal to allow that life to extinguish itself for the sake of Thomas Lin? There was certainly something she wanted here—Lina's fierce devotion to Thomas that she envied and craved for herself.

Eva suspected she had ruined any chance of *that* merely by being herself.

Black water bubbled through the cracks between cobbles. Ribbons of liquid darkness unfurling like hungry smoke. Spreading and swallowing up the ground. Swallowing up St. Casimir's Square. Soon to swallow up the rest of the island.

She could not afford to fail again.

She *would* not fail again.

But she would also no longer give the tide anything more than she was willing to give it.

"Will you do as Natalia did and chain yourself to the pillar in her place?" said Marcin. "Or will you let the city sink to save the two of you?"

Eva looked away from Lina, gaze returning to that flame of red hair, to those fiery hazel eyes. To Marcin, who had raised her, who had betrayed her, who would drown her, punish her, because she would not make the choices he wanted her to make.

Marcin, who had taken a piece of her heart long before she had sealed it inside a bottle and cast it out to sea.

"You forget." Eva yanked one of her red string bracelets off and tied a knot, and then another, and another, and another, fingers fumbling with the loops. Chains slithered through the shallow water, iron grinding, grating over stone. "You forget that I love you, too. That out of everyone save Natalia, I have loved you *most.*"

If she hadn't, she would have taken his magic the second they returned from the spring regatta; she would have thrown him into the sea cave and fed him to her serpent. If she didn't love him, she wouldn't have hesitated, and her hands wouldn't be shaking now.

And if she hadn't hesitated, things would never have gone this far. The Water Palace wouldn't have flooded. Her sisters wouldn't be panicked, divided. Lina would not have been hurt. *She* would not have been hurt.

Because that's what caring did, in the end. It lowered your guard and got you hurt, got you killed.

Safer never to care at all.

Chains wound around Marcin's legs, chipping off shards of night-black ice, snaking around his torso.

"You forget that I will suffer to lose you the way you did not suffer to lose me."

Take the life of one you love and mix with the tears you shed for them.

If there was one person Eva was beyond certain she loved…

It should have felt like a victory. Like relief. A month ago, it would not even have been a possibility. Black waves roared, wrecking themselves against the edge of St. Casimir's Square. Crashing, clamoring, rising higher. Spilling over.

The dark tide had come to take what it was owed.

Natalia's life had calmed it. A witch's life would work.

She would do as Caldella's queens had done for centuries. She would let the sea eat her sorrow, taste the salt of her tears. One last time.

Marcin's eyes were wide as saucers as she moved closer, cold fingers reaching to dust a lock of hair from his pale brow. A single tear raced down her cheek, but when Eva spoke her voice was steady. "My city will not sink. Natalia's city will not sink. Because I am going to use your life—yours, Marcin—to save it."

34

LINA

WHEN THE FULL MOON FINALLY rose above Caldella four days later, there were no dark waves to greet it.

Only a glittering emerald sea, a city sighing with relief, and music. Low and somber. Songs that were more ache than sound. Requiems, buoyed by the salt breeze, twining through the tightly stacked rainbow of town houses, played on a solitary violin. Played for all the boys who had lost their lives to the tide on moonlit nights like this one, boys both brave and frightened, and for all the witches who had sacrificed their hearts and selves to keep the island safe.

Lina tapped the blue window shutters in her cousin Ivy's room as the final note of Finley's playing wrung out, a tiny charm to banish bad thoughts, to stifle that creeping fear inside of her. Once. Twice. Three times, because three was the right number. She slid a headband that glittered like stars into her hair and smoothed down her spangled silver dress. Draped a pale feather boa over her shoulders and tied her blood-coral beads in a fancy double knot around her neck.

She hummed along as a new song started. A rowdier tune this time, a melody like freedom and fire, a melody of hope. Her oldest cousin, Julie, on pipes, upstairs in Uncle's rooftop garden, seated amidst the orange blossom trees beneath the sailcloth awning where Laolao liked to smoke.

Downstairs, the aunties were keeping time; Lina could make out the steady, feverish *click-clack* of mah-jongg tiles even with the bedroom door closed. She went to open it.

Found it locked.

"Finley!"

No answer. Just the distant, familiar sound of Uncle clearing his throat.

"Finley!" Lina rattled the door handle. "Ivy! David?"

Another pause, longer, and finally a shuffle of footsteps. "Not so fun when you're on the other side of the door now, is it?"

Lina cursed and smacked her palm against the wood. She could see her brother's shadow moving through the crack at the bottom of the door. "I'll climb out the window," she threatened.

"Aye, and fall and die?" The lock snicked, and Finley eased the door open a smidgen, an impish sliver of handsome face peeking through.

Lina grabbed the door handle and pulled, leaning back on one heel, throwing all her weight into it. Finley did the same on his side, grinning.

"I swear to God!" Lina attempted to wedge a shoulder between the door and the frame.

Finley let go of the handle, and Lina was flung backward with a shriek as the door flew open, landing on her butt with a thump. A small white puff of a dog scampered into the room, yapping and eagerly trying to lick her face. "Tam! Leave off!"

Finley helped her stand.

Lina scowled. "You drew your eyebrow on crooked."

"Naw, it's my real brow. It's grown back."

Lina squinted at her brother's face and was sadly forced to admit that the eyebrow in question was indeed the real thing. "Well, it's grown back crooked."

"I think you'll find it gives me a roguish charm."

"Gross." Lina elbowed past, whistling for Auntie Van's dog to follow.

"And who are you all dolled up for? Uncle says you're grounded."

Which was why they were staying with him and Laolao and the rest of Uncle's immediate family. So Auntie Van could enforce Lina's prison sentence, as well as pop into the room Lina was sharing with Ivy every ten minutes to fuss and scold and pat her, as if to reassure them all that Lina wasn't a ghost.

Lina paused at the top of the third-floor landing and batted heavily mascaraed lashes. "Would you like to carry me down?"

Finley leaned his hip into the banister and crossed his arms. "Not particularly, no."

"Even though my ankle's a little sore today and it's your fault I broke it?"

Her brother stiffened. Lina's heart beat off rhythm. The pipes wailing from the rooftop were suddenly extremely loud. But—

The bump in Finley's throat bobbed. "You're going to use that excuse for everything now, aren't you? I'll never be able to make it up to you."

"Damn right," said Lina. "I'm going to hold it over you for the rest of our lives. We'll be ancient and wrinkled and shrunken to the size of peas, both of us walking with sticks, and I'll still be whining, 'Finley, you knob, buy me that necklace there—you owe me. Remember that time you broke my leg?'"

Finley's mouth twitched.

They were going to be all right. It would always be there, the memory of her fall from the top of the steps of St. Dominic's sticking like scar tissue. And maybe it was weird to try to make a joke out of it, but it helped ease the stiffness. They would be all right. They would keep working on it, like Finley would work on mastering his temper and Lina would work on her exercises, until they found a new way to move.

Finley swatted down his cowlick. "Hurry up, then."

"What?" She didn't actually need to be carried down.

He knelt, hands behind his back, ready to piggyback her. "You getting on or not?"

Lina climbed on.

Finley fake staggered and heaved an exaggerated groan. Lina smacked him. He took the stairs carefully, one at a time, passing by the living room and then the first-floor foyer, passing aunties laughing and ranting and gossiping, their voices so loud they likely carried all the way back to the Witch Queen's palace. They dodged uncles hiding in armchairs with their fat fingers laced atop their rounded bellies; cousins and random kids, yawning and looking bored, playing cards or taking the piss, gnawing on gingerbread cookies and the flaky remains of egg tarts.

Of them, only Jana looked up and narrowed her eyes. Their cousin pushed what Finley teasingly called her doctor's glasses up her nose.

Lina ducked her head. She'd already gotten the biggest scolding upon their return about taking better care of herself. Jana had given her strict orders to rest *and* a whole new set of strength-building exercises for her ankle.

Finley passed right out of the house and into the street with a promise that they were only popping out to check on the tide. Lina was unreasonably annoyed that they believed him, that they let *him* out. Because of course her brother had managed to weasel his way out of being punished for anything that had happened. He'd come back with her from the Water Palace like some kind of hero.

Auntie Van's dog, Tam, scampered after them.

"Where are you—"

"Where were *you* planning on slipping off to?" Finley cut in.

"Josef tells me Thomas Lin's leaving the island tonight on a fishing trawler bound for Skani with no plans to return. He also said he heard Lin ask a certain someone to go with him."

The wooden walkways leading down to the quay creaked, groaned. The fall of Finley's steps and the click of Tam's claws were washed away by the soft shushing of saltwater lapping at the boards.

Water no longer black as deepest midnight, as dark as a starless, moonless sky, but calm and shallow and shimmering. A brilliant emerald green set alight by the amber lanterns laced between the town house rooftops like bunting. Water a color Lina had only ever seen in the months after a successful sacrifice.

The first successful sacrifice in two long years.

And the last, if the rumors were true. Caldella's Witch Queen had sent word: She would bow to the tide no longer. She would feed it no more lives. They would find another way to break this yearly curse that plagued their island.

No more boys given to the sea. No more glorifying death and striking bloody bargains with the tide. No more trading innocent lives for safety.

Lina drew in a breath. "And what, you think I'm going with him? Like this? With just the clothes on my back? Like Mama stowing away on Ma's ship?"

"You've always liked a good story." Finley set her down by the red-and-white-striped post where his broom boat was moored.

Lina hesitated, but when her brother did nothing, she started to unmoor it, rope landing in the bottom of the boat with a thud before she paused a second time, tugging at a strand of freshly dyed hair. She was still unsure about its new bright, silver color. Maybe she should go natural, or grow it, or chop it all off. She could never decide. For a second, she faced the gray spires of the Witch Queen's palace, which you could see no matter where you stood on the island. Then her eyes flicked back to her brother.

Finley had crouched down to cup a handful of water, letting it trickle through his fingers as if he still half expected the darkness to start creeping back. As if he expected the water around the broom boat to all of a sudden bruise black, tendrils of shadow snaking across the surface, spreading like an oil spill.

"You're not going to stop me? What if I said I *was* going with him?"

Finley looked up as Lina clambered into the boat. There was something solemn in the set of his shoulders, an out-of-character sternness in his storm-gray eyes. And then he grinned, a flash of perfect teeth, reaching out to put a hand on her head and muss her hair, eliciting an outraged squeak. He kicked the broom boat away from the quay. Tam barked.

"You're not going anywhere."

Lina's reaction was immediate. "You don't know that!"

"'Course I do. I'm your brother." Finley cracked his neck. "An hour, and then I'm whistling for the boat to come back. You know Uncle's going to skin you alive."

Lina shrugged as the broom boat swung out into the current. "I've faced worse things."

"For now," Finley called after her. "Ma and Mama dock at dawn. You're going to have to face them."

At dawn. A thrill of longing, relief, and nerves shot through Lina. Her mothers home tomorrow, home and safe. She made a face at Finley and rapped the side of the boat with her knuckles, sending it surging through the water. There were so many things she had to tell them, so many things she was never *ever* going to tell them unless she wanted to be grounded for a million more years.

She could imagine what the rest of the family would tell them. One day, Lina vowed, she would stop being the cousin everyone gossiped about, the cautionary tale the aunties whispered about to their own children.

There were things she needed to ask Ma and Mama, too, but she didn't know if she could. Lina admired her parents plenty, and she wouldn't mind being like them, but at the same time, she didn't want to *be* them. She wanted to be herself. She wanted her own story. She wanted to be different.

And a part of her was pretty sure she was, different from them, because she'd liked Thomas, too. She didn't think she was going to stop liking boys even if she wanted to kiss girls now as well. And she wasn't sure if that made her, well, *enough* to fit into her mothers' world.

Lina shook her head quickly. She didn't want to think about

it. Liking boys or kissing girls. Kissing witches. Kissing Eva. She didn't want to think about Eva at all.

Because it wasn't as if Eva was thinking of her.

The Witch Queen hadn't looked at Lina once while she performed the sacrifice. Not when she'd chained Marcin to the pillar. Not when she'd stood stiff and silent as she fed him to the sea.

Lina had been busy herself, dragging a half-conscious Thomas into the shelter of St. Casimir's column-lined arcades as the black waves came crashing down.

But even afterward, when she had left him, splashing through the water toward that bowed figure with its streaming hair and crown of scorched steel and spikes, Eva hadn't turned. And by the time Lina managed to reach the place where she'd stood, there'd been nothing but curls of vanishing smoke.

There'd been nothing the day after, either. No sign of any of the witches. None of the usual festive celebrations that followed a successful sacrifice.

Lina had been left with a strange, hollow kind of emptiness, and she'd wondered whether she would catch a glimpse of Eva if she joined the revel a year from then. A glimpse of the wicked Witch Queen as she danced in and out of the revelers in disguise, appearing one second as the person you loved, transforming the next into the person the boy beside you loved, tricking you into taking her hand, tricking you into kissing her.

Lina bit her lips and tasted salt.

She wondered now if it was really true that there would be no more sacrifices. If there really would be no more revels and bonfires and dances on St. Walpurga's Eve. She wondered if she would ever see Eva again.

She shouldn't want to, but she did. Her heart beat faster when she imagined it, and her mind kept drifting, conjuring up images of a girl with a smile so sharp it left teeth marks in her daydreams. She didn't know what this thing was between them. She didn't know if there *was* anything between them, what Eva really felt for her.

But she wanted to find out. And she had a feeling that whatever did happen, no matter if it was the most complete and spectacular disaster, it would be a story worth telling afterward.

A cloud passed over the moon as Lina drew nearer her destination, Caldella's longest pier. Icy spray caressed her cheeks, set crystals in her lashes.

The broom boat bobbed alongside the wooden planks, slowing as it drew even with a figure walking along the pier's edge. A boy with sun-kissed hair and sea-tanned skin. A boy with a guitar case slung across his back.

Thomas Lin's steps slowed, too. "Did you do something with your hair?"

Lina's hand went automatically to her head. "Sort of. I'm still not sure about it."

"It looks good."

"Thank you."

The pier creaked. The breeze whispered, rustling Lina's dress. A quiet stole over them. Thomas took smaller and smaller steps. You couldn't freeze a moment or stop the world from turning, but you could hold on for as long as possible, absorbing every last breath before things changed.

A lump formed in Lina's throat, and she was filled with the same overflowing sadness she felt when she reached the end of a story, when she realized something *was* ending.

"I hear it's cold in Skani," she tried.

Obviously. It's the land of frost and ice. Stop talking. Just stop talking.

"I meant it," said Thomas, "when I asked if you would come with me."

"I know, but I—I know, but I can't." Lina couldn't bring herself to say aloud that she didn't want to, that she wasn't willing to give up her family, her friends, that she wouldn't leave the island she loved for him, the island where she'd learned to dance. Her sinking city with its ravenous sea, its witches and enchantments.

And she didn't think she could tell him that she wasn't sure she still wanted *him*. And that maybe she wanted to figure out more about who she did want and who she was first, before she made that kind of decision.

Thomas stopped and sat suddenly on the edge of the pier,

guitar case scraping the wood, long legs dangling out over the water. Lina wobbled to her feet in the boat.

The tide was high, and their heads were almost level. Thomas leaned forward, reaching out. For a wild second, Lina thought he was going to kiss her. And for a second, it seemed he thought so, too.

Her heart skipped a beat. But Thomas hesitated, and the moment broke.

He held out his hand instead.

Lina took it, his fingers twining together with hers. Palm rough, warm, and a little clammy.

"I asked too late, didn't I? If I'd said something about how I felt before all of this…" He looked up at the sky, at the full moon, letting a breath out, letting go. "I can never repay you."

"It wasn't meant to be a trade."

"Still." Thomas squeezed her hand. "I won't forget it. Any of it. I won't forget how we danced at the revel. I won't forget how you came after me. I won't forget you, Lina Kirk. Never. For as long as I live."

Lina swallowed.

Thomas untangled his hand from hers. Hitched the strap of his guitar case higher on his shoulder and, turning on unsteady feet, walked fast this time, without looking back.

Lina waited until he reached the shadow of the fishing trawler, then rapped the broom boat with her knuckles and sailed away.

35

E V A

IT WAS THE WITCHING HOUR. The murk and midnight hour. An hour when dark things came out to play, and Caldella's Witch Queen liked to think she was the darkest of them all.

Eva's steps echoed as she followed the narrow, sloping passage down to the lowermost levels of the Water Palace until the musty air mixed with the scent of salt and sea. Wind teased wispy black strands free from her crown of braids, and she paused when the passage ended abruptly, the tide nibbling gently at crumbling stone.

She stepped out onto the surface of the emerald water, out into the full moon's light. Charmed shoes left a chain of silver-edged ripples behind her as she crossed the night-dark waves and walked on, into, and over the sunken ruins of the old city.

The living city loomed ahead, rising shadows and warm golden light winking in hundreds of windows like handfuls of scattered stars dropped by a careless god. Life and laughter drifted through those windows, too, from rooftop gardens and open doors, palpable relief catching on the breeze.

Eva listened carefully as she walked to those carried sounds, to the islanders' hopes and fears, to their dreams and secret desires. Voices tangled in her head, and she separated them out, following each thread to the end, spending a little magic to search for one voice in particular.

It wasn't currently speaking, but singing, a tune that grated on Eva's ears.

The Witch Queen comes on wings of night,
The Witch Queen has your heart's delight.
Hold her, hold her, hold on—

Heat flooded her cheeks. Yara had fallen into peals of helpless laughter when she'd heard the newest rendition of the famous song, the witchlings into fits of near-hysterical giggles. The first bright sounds in the palace since...

Eva's steps faltered and then kept going. She couldn't decide if she wanted to forbid the islanders from singing the song, use magic to steal all their voices, wipe the words from their memories, or just turn them all into seagulls.

"But if you do that," Yara had pointed out, "who will you have left to rule?"

And what was a queen without her subjects? A fallen queen. A queen of nothing and no one.

Still, she didn't have to *like* it, and she didn't have to *agree* with what the song was implying. Eva preferred to see her leaping into the fire after Lina Kirk as a moment of fleeting insanity, a delayed side effect of Marcin's sleeping draught, an unfortunate by-product of nearly drowning in the flooded ballroom. As for sparing Lina and sacrificing Marcin…

Well, Lina wasn't the one who had tried to kill her.

"They fear you now, you know," Cyla had whispered, referring to all the other witches. "They worry what you'll do if they step out of line."

Good.

The knowledge did not trouble Eva as much as it maybe should have, as much as it might once have done. If she was to rule through fear instead of love, then so be it.

Let them fear her. She was never going to be her sister.

She followed the singing, which eventually melted into humming as she approached the old bell tower. She ran a fingertip along the crumbling bricks. The tower's spire cast a shadow over the broom boat bobbing below its rusted cupola, over a girl in a silver dress and fluttering feather boa, her storm-gray eyes fixed on the full moon. A girl with hair the pale diamond sheen of starlight on the sea.

Lina jumped, almost spilling off the broom boat's bench seat when Eva stole up silently beside the boat and lit a cigarette, orange light flaring suddenly.

"God damn it! You—Couldn't you *say* something first?" Lina leaned out of the boat and splashed a great wave of water at Eva.

Eva stepped nimbly out of the way, then stepped into the boat as if she owned it. "I could have you executed for that."

"Seems a waste after everything you went through to save me."

"Maybe I regret saving you." She regretted the words the second they left her mouth.

Lina seemed to shrink. She tossed the end of her feather boa over one shoulder in a carefree fashion, but her spine was stiff.

Eva flicked ash off the end of the cigarette. If she'd still had a heart, it might have beaten a tiny bit faster. But she didn't. So *it* didn't. She sank down onto the bench seat beside Lina. "I don't regret saving you. I would do it again. Every time."

An anxious beat passed in which she debated whether or not to leap back out of the boat or turn herself into smoke.

She took a quick drag instead, held the cigarette out.

"I prefer cigars," said Lina softly, but she took the cigarette anyway, placing the lipstick-stained filter between her lips.

Eva blew out a breath and watched it spiral up into the sky. A strange tingling feeling, like pins and needles but all over, was crawling under her skin, and she was alarmed to realize it was panic.

She crossed her ankles, long trouser-clad legs in line with Lina's bare ones, their thighs almost touching because the bench seat was too small.

She should leave. She should turn back the way she'd come. Return to the Water Palace. This was a stupid, foolish idea. Yara should have stopped her. Cyla should have stopped her. What kind of family were they if they didn't stop her from looking like a fool?

Safer not to care.

Safer never to care, because caring hurt, and caring got you killed.

But Eva had always been a little reckless with magic and with her heart. She'd bled her veins into the sea for love of her sister, had cut out her own heart in grief, and even now, when she had no heart to speak of, she still couldn't quite resist the risk.

"Have they banned smoking inside the palace now?" said Lina, "and that's why you have to lurk out here like some lowly criminal?"

"Actually, we could hear your singing, and the sound was so terrible that everyone begged me to come out here and make it stop."

Lina scowled.

A sharp smile tugged at Eva's lips, then died. "I heard Thomas Lin was leaving the island, setting sail on the midnight tide."

And I thought you might be going with him.

"Please tell me you didn't come out here to sink his ship," said Lina.

"The idea hadn't occurred to me. However, now that you mention it..."

Lina cut Eva a look that was half exasperation, half... something else.

"I thought you might be going with him." She dropped her gaze as she said it, tried not to make it into too much of a desperate question.

"No. I'm not."

A knot inside Eva's chest unraveled and then retied itself a thousand times tighter.

"No more sacrifices?" said Lina, breaking the silence. A tiny orange spark, the lit end of the cigarette passed between them.

Eva nodded. No more sacrifices. "Yara said—" She didn't know why she was telling Lina. It wasn't as if she would even understand. "She said perhaps that was why Natalia made me queen." Not because she'd trusted Eva to do what she had for the island, but because... "Because I tried to find another way to calm the tide, and she thought I would continue to fight for that." Natalia had not expected Eva to give up. "It still might not be possible," she added. "There might be no other way."

"We'll keep trying to find one," said Lina. "Together. However long it takes."

"That wasn't a request for your help."

"Too bad." Lina shifted, body leaning into Eva's side, letting her head fall to rest on Eva's shoulder.

Eva nearly swallowed the cigarette.

"Come and watch me dance when I'm allowed to again, when my ankle's stronger."

Eva took a long and shaky drag, tipped her head back, and

took her time blowing out the smoke, enjoying the way Lina started to fidget with impatience. "Only if you come dance for the sea serpent."

Lina let go of her necklace. She might have been smiling—you could hear it in her voice. "Because it likes me?"

"Because I like you," said Eva, before adding quickly, "I can't think why."

Lina was definitely smiling now, head still resting on Eva's shoulder but face lifted to the night sky. She drummed her knuckles on the broom boat's side, sending it bobbing forward, sailing them through shadowed and moonlit ruins. They shared the remaining smoke between them, with no other sound to disturb them but the soft *shusha-shusha* of the tide.

ACKNOWLEDGMENTS

There honestly aren't enough words to convey my gratitude to all the people who helped make *The Dark Tide* into a real book.

First and foremost, a giant thank-you to Aully Qian, who read this story first and all its many, many iterations thereafter. I'm blessed to call you my friend. I would not have gotten here without you and I cannot wait to see *your* work published and out in the world one day!

To my truly magical agent, Rena Rossner—you made my dream come true! I can't thank you enough for believing in me and my story.

To my fabulous editor, Annie Berger, for taking a chance on the queer witchy book of my heart. And to Cassie Gutman, Sarah Kasman, and everyone else at Sourcebooks Fire who helped make this story shine. I'm so grateful my book found such a wonderful home!

To my Aussie editor, Amy Thomas—your enthusiasm for this story means the world to me.

To Naomi Hughes, for your amazing feedback early on, for all your advice, and for your general awesomeness.

To all my amazing friends for your never-ending, enthusiastic support, and for understanding when I had to drop off the face of the earth to get things done. I'm so lucky to know each and every one of you!

To my grandmother—please forgive me for mentioning your leather slipper. I love you always and forever.

And, of course, to my mum, dad, and sister—thank you for putting up with all my weirdness and always loving and supporting me.

And finally, to all the readers who followed Lina and Eva's story to the very last page, thank you from the bottom of my heart.

ABOUT THE AUTHOR

Alicia Jasinska is a fantasy writer hailing from Sydney, Australia. A library technician by day, she spends her nights writing and hanging upside down from the trapeze and aerial hoop. *The Dark Tide* is her debut novel. Visit her online at aliciajasinska.com.

FIREreads

#getbooklit

Your hub for the hottest young adult books!

Visit us online and sign up for our
newsletter at FIREreads.com

 @sourcebooksfire

 sourcebooksfire

 firereads.tumblr.com